EYES THAT DO NOT SEE

A Novel Inspired by Actual Events

EYES THAT DO NOT SEE

A Novel Inspired by Actual Events

KENT B. KEARNEY

ISBN Paperback: 979-8-9876090-0-2
ISBN Ebook: 979-8-9876090-1-9

Design and publishing assistance by The Happy Self-Publisher.

INTRODUCTION

Ireland, the Irish. What comes to mind when you hear those words? For many it is thoughts of beautiful green countryside or if you have visited, maybe the very friendly people. Perhaps you envision a land with pristine lakes and rivers, verdant green valleys, rocky craigs and ancient castles. Or maybe you are reminded of the country's many famous poets, playwrights, and novelists. Men like James Joyce, Oscar Wilde, William Butler Yeats, or George Bernard Shaw, to name but a very few from many more. Or famous Irish singers or actors. And then there are the famous Irish dancers performing their jigs and reels. If you are into history or politics, maybe names like O'Neill, O'Connell, Parnell or Collins and Pearse come to mind. Or if you are a college student in the middle of March, perhaps it's just St. Paddy's Day and green beer. Oh, and let's not forget beautiful red hair with emerald-green eyes and a lively Irish accent.

However, there is another story of Ireland of which you have probably heard very little. Oh, you may have heard of the potato famine and the great Irish diaspora. Historians have written volumes about the famine and its effects on the Irish, the British and the United States. But there is one segment of this equation we have heard very little from and for a very good reason. The Irish peasant immigrants themselves. Nearly all of them were ignorant. Unable to read or write not by choice but because for generations the ruling British forbid it. Consequently, when faced with the famine, for millions of Irish their only choices were starvation or immigration, if they could scrape together the money. If you have seen pictures of the U.S. withdrawal from Saigon with people grasping for any possible means of escape. picture that multiplied by thousands all starving and trying desperately to survive. Even if they could manage to immigrate to America, most arrived here in rags, ignorant, broke, and unwanted. Then, just when some of them were starting to make it in America, America decides to have a civil war where thousands more Irish are to die a horrifying death.

The following story is about one of those immigrants, my great grandfather Henry Charles Kearney. He too was unable to read or write, at least very well. It is likely a story similar to the stories of the millions of Irish who managed to survive and even come to prosper in America.

I have included at the end of the novel some very brief histories that apply to the life and times of my great grandfather. I do encourage you to read them to add more context and understanding of what was occurring and what Henry Kearney endured during those times.

1

It was early in the first year of the twenty-first century. I remember it well because it was not only a new century, but like a time of the changing of the guard. One generation had passed and now it was time for the next generation to take their turn. Like the old saying: "Time is like a river. Once it flows by, it will never flow this way again."

We (my wife Gale, our daughters, and I) pulled into the gravel driveway of my parent's home. It was a cold January day, but no snow lay on the ground in the small central Nebraska farming community of Sumner where I had grown up. My parents had lived in this 1920s bungalow for nearly thirty years. They had moved to town in the seventies when my brother moved into their former home on the homestead north of town.

We had laid my father to rest some three years before in the Jewell Cemetery west of town. Yesterday, we had laid my mother to rest beside him and today we were gathering to decide what was to become of my parents' lifetime accumulation of personal property. What to do with all the things in this old home that had been host to so many Sunday dinners, family reunions, Thanksgiving, Christmas, and 4th of July gatherings? What to do with the pictures on the walls or the buffet drawer full of old photographs? Photos where your children ask, "Who are these people?" and you just smile behind invisible tears, lost in memories of days long gone by.

When I say we were gathering, I am including my sisters, brothers, their spouses, and some of their children. By mutual consent we decided the town bungalow with its wide front porch, large garden area but no garage would be put up for sale as soon as we got it cleaned out. We all kind of entered the house together. Each of us, I'm sure, experiencing a range of emotions from resignation to the task before us to longing for the times of laughter and enjoyment of yesteryear. As we were Kearneys, the first thing on the agenda was to make a good big pot of coffee. Once the thirty-cup percolator was going, we gathered in the living room to decide how to proceed. Everyone was amicable so by unanimous consent it was agreed if anyone wanted a certain item, they could have it, but selection would begin with the oldest sibling then continue to the youngest. After a few rounds of this process, we moved on to the grandchildren and used the same system. I couldn't help but notice that one of my daughters selected my parents' dining room set with its mismatched chairs that would work well in the dining room of her new home. The other selected the piano that my mother had loved to play in her own self-taught style. She had never had a lesson. After their selections, it was obvious I would need to make another trip to haul their new belongings. The problem for the family then became what do we do with all that remained? We knew we could take some of the large items to an auction house, clothing and knick-knacks to Goodwill, and most foodstuff to the dump.

My brother Stan and I started hauling out the clothing and other things from our parents' closet and laying it on the bed. It was in that closet, after hauling out a bunch of shoe boxes, that we found a black metal box about a foot long by ten inches wide and maybe six inches deep. Neither of us could remember ever seeing it before. The box was locked but attached to the handle on the lid with a piece of string was a key. We tried the key, and it opened the box with ease. Inside were some old greeting cards, a gold-chain necklace with a heart shaped locket attached, a few old coins, and what looked like books underneath, wrapped in an old dish towel. When we got them out, though, we discovered a bunch of school tablets and journals all bound together with string. When we untied the string, we saw that each one was numbered, and had the name Mary Ann Kearney written in neat script on the cover. I opened tablet number one and though the ink had dulled some, you could clearly read what she had written.

My name is Mary Ann Jones Kearney. I married Henry Charles Kearney on February 28, 1867. Since then and even before our marriage, I listened to my husband's stories and have found them to be so fascinating and heart rending that I thought someone should write them down, and at this time no one seemed more suitable for the task than me. Henry can neither read nor write to any great extent and since at this point in our marriage it is just the two of us, I shall fill my spare time by putting his stories on paper, to the best of my ability. There is no way for me to determine the absolute truthfulness of what Henry has told me and the Irish are well known for their ability to tell a story with a little added embellishment. However, I have decided to simply write the story in the same way my dear Henry related it to me. It will be up to future historians, if any should read these lines, to determine whether the facts are accurately stated.

I looked at Stan and said, "Wow, these were written by our great-grandmother! I want to read every one of them to learn more about her and about our great grandfather, Henry. He was our family's first immigrant to America."

Stan answered, "I would like to read them too, but you can go ahead and read them first as I have enough on my plate at work for a while. I wonder why Mom or Dad never mentioned having these before?"

"It doesn't look like anyone has ever unwrapped the tablets or journals, and I think if Mom knew about them, she would have read them. Maybe Dad, if he had any idea they existed, just told her, 'That's some stuff my mother saved from my grandmother, just stick it in the closet and we'll look at it someday.' But that day never came and they probably just kind of forgot about it."

I put the tablets back in the box along with the other items and relocked it with the key dangling from the lid. I put the box with the other items I had selected and then went back to the emptying of the house. Stan and I did tell our siblings about our discovery, and all were okay with me reading the tablets first as they either had to get back to their jobs or had a long drive home in an already overpacked vehicle to places like Chicago or Missouri the next day.

By days end we had boxed up, bagged up and loaded up all that we could. My brother Rob and I agreed we would return the following day with pickups to haul the furnishings and saleable items to the auction house or Goodwill and along with our wives do any remaining clean-up. I'm sure our wives were thrilled with our volunteering their services for another day.

When we arrived back to our home that night, I took the black metal box and placed it in the middle of the desk in my home office. I really wanted to sit down and start reading that very night but knew I would have another long day of work the next day, so opted for a good night of sleep instead.

It turned out to be a couple of days before I could find the time to get back to the black metal box on my desk. In the evening of the second day, I sat down and again opened the box and removed the items. I examined the coins first and determined they must be nineteenth century British coins. Next, I examined the necklace with the heart shaped locket. It didn't appear to be of much value and though the locket opened and had a place for a photo in each half of the heart, it was empty. I removed what I thought were just old greeting cards but among them was a funeral card for a George Orr. I would have to research him further. All the cards were signed, though on some, the ink had faded to such a degree that I could no longer read the signature. Others, I could read but wasn't sure who the people were. A name of Nimrod Slack, another of Adamson. I was going to have to research those two. Other names like Wood, Hothem, and Freeze, I recognized as names of people in the area when I was growing up. They were family names of people whose ancestors had also homesteaded in the area. That left only the tablets and journals to be examined and I looked over each of them in turn to see if there were any hints other than the writing inside before again opening tablet number one and beginning to read.

2

My name is Mary Ann Jones Kearney. I married Henry Charles Kearney on February 28, 1867. Since then and even before our marriage, I listened to my husband's stories and have found them to be so fascinating and heart rending that I thought someone should write them down and at this time no one seemed more suitable for the task than me. Henry can neither read nor write to any great extent and since at this point in our marriage it is just the two of us, I shall fill my spare time by putting his stories on paper, to the best of my ability. There is no way for me to determine the absolute truthfulness of what Henry has told me and the Irish are well known for their ability to tell a story with a little added embellishment. However, I have decided to simply write the story in the same way my dear Henry related it to me. It will be up to future historians, if any should read these lines, to determine whether the facts are accurately stated.

To begin, all Henry and I can do is relate the story of his birth as to what he remembers being told by his father and other relatives. He was told by his father, Thomas, that he was born on the Irish Sea. A body of water separating Ireland from England. His mother was returning to Ireland from Liverpool, England on one of the ferries that ran between the two islands. The sea was buffeted by winds and the rough waters caused Henry to arrive early. Henry has no idea on what date he was born but believes it was the year 1836. He later decided to choose February 29, 1836, as his birthday because that was the date of the very first running of the Grand National at Aintree. I am sure if 1867 had been a leap year, February 29th would also have been our wedding date.

His earliest memories are from when he was about three or four years old. He remembers living in a small, one-room house with a thatched roof, a fireplace on one end and minimal furnishings. Maybe a table and a couple chairs, and a sort of homemade cupboard. There was a bed of sorts. Just a raised platform with straw filled ticking for a mattress. They had a single window with no glass but a wooden shutter that could be closed in the winter months. Beside the entrance door were a few wooden pegs to hang hats and coats. Outside there was a shed where they kept a couple nanny goats and occasionally a pig. A small meadow area was beyond that for pasture close to a little creek where the goats could be staked out. Lazy beds for raising potatoes were fenced off beside the shed. Up the lane, there were several more houses much like theirs where other tenant farmers existed, all living on land now owned and controlled by a mostly absentee English landlord.

Henry can remember some happy times in the evenings when tenant families would gather and listen to stories related by a seanchaí that was passing through the area or dancing a jig when someone brought out a fiddle or squeezebox. The men would enjoy a couple taoscans of poteen after a hard day's work. Henry remembers that his father, Thomas, also tended and trained horses for the manor to earn a little extra money.

There was never a whole lot of food for anyone among the tenants. Mostly potato dishes and chowders were the mainstay with some turnips and always goat's milk for the youngsters. Meat was rare, usually one of the tenants raised a few pigs and kept a boar and two or three sows. He would sell or trade young pigs to other tenants who would feed them with weeds pulled from the lazy beds. The pigs were then butchered to provide salt pork for meat during the winter months. Often though, the tenants could not afford to buy the pigs, so they survived without it and their only meat was the occasional small wild game they managed to trap or kill and baby goats.

Henry recalled playing between the houses one day when he heard his mother yell for the neighbor lady. He has no memory of the lady's name, but she and another neighbor came hurriedly over and entered their house. Henry, being curious, ran home and was about to enter when the neighbor lady met him at the door and said, "Do not come in. Go find your father and tell him to come home. The baby is coming."

Henry and his little friend then ran to find his father and all three hurried back to the house, but Henry and his friend were still not allowed to come in. After what seemed like hours to Henry and after his friend had long gone home, his father came to him from the house. He leaned down to little Henry and grasped his shoulders. Henry remembers looking into his father's eyes. They were very red and swollen like he had been crying. Through falling tears and a cracking voice he said, "Henry, the baby didn't live." Then through sobs as he hugged Henry, "Your mother is gone. She didn't make it either."

Henry, at his young age, could not fully understand what his father was telling him. He remembers holding on to his father and hugging him. Trying to comfort him in his small way because he just wanted his father to be better. Henry felt, at that time, he never realized what he was being told and still didn't days later when he asked his father, "When is mom going to come back?"

His father replied, "I'm afraid it's just you and me now son. Mom won't be coming back."

3

After I had read this, the first chapter in young Henry's life, two things were painfully obvious, One, in my great-grandfather's first four of five years of life, he had a very meager existence and had already experienced the loss of his mother. Secondly, I realized I had a serious lack of knowledge about the history of Ireland. In school I had always just considered Ireland as a part of the British Isles because that is what we had been taught. I, like most Americans, had heard of St. Patrick and the story of him driving all the snakes out of Ireland. Likewise, I had heard about the potato famine and the mass migration of the Irish to America. I was aware of Ireland's Gaelic heritage and the "Troubles" between Ireland and Northern Ireland, though I knew little of the details of either.

I decided I needed to do some dedicated reading of the history of Ireland before proceeding to read any more of my great grandmother's writing in the tablets. I also needed to be able to translate or understand what she was referring to when she used words like "seanchaí," "poteen," or terms like "lazy beds." To that end, I bought a tourist book which included a section on common Gaelic/Irish words and their meaning. I also checked out from the library or bought a few books on Irish history, plus a couple historical novels. I include here a very brief version of a history of Ireland and its rocky relationship with England. I should probably note that history is usually written by the victors, but in this case, I was reading books written by Irish historians and writers.

Ireland was conquered by England in the twelfth century, but they had little interest except along the coastal area around Dublin known as the Pale. That all changed when Henry VIII broke with the Catholic church and formed his own Church. The Catholic monasteries in Ireland were destroyed, their land confiscated and given to Henry VIII's English supporters. This taking of land and giving it to English patrons was continued by Henry's daughter Elizabeth I. Then to add insult to injury, in the mid sixteen hundreds Oliver Cromwell, who hated Catholics and cared little if he extinguished all the Irish, arrived with 20,000 troops intent on turning Ireland into another England. His Act of Settlement confiscated another eleven million acres and again parceled it out to "Anglo" supporters.

Some of these Anglo-Irish estates were huge and supported hundreds of poor Irish peasant families, who often subsisted on a couple of acres or less This was followed by the horrible "Penal Laws," separating Irish Catholics from all political and economic power on the island. Catholics could not own land, could not vote, could not even educate their own children. In 1800, the Act of Union dissolved the then mostly Anglo-Irish Parliament and Ireland became a part of Great Britain much like Scotland and Wales.

Now that I knew the Irish were basically slaves living on English landholder estates and deprived of any education, I had a better understanding of Irish life in the nineteenth century. I was again ready to read my great grandmother's journals.

4

After the death of his mother, young Henry spent all day, every day with his father. Henry said, "My father probably grew very tired of my constant questioning of, 'Why this, why that? or How come this? or How come that?' but he never showed it. He was always very patient and would go into great detail to explain things to me. If I was asking why we had to stake out the goats?"

He would explain, "We don't want the nannies to just wander anywhere. We need them to provide milk for us as well as their babies, called kids. To do that, the goats eat grass, and we move them from place to place in the meadow, so they have plenty of grass to eat; but also, then the grass in the area we just moved them from has a chance to grow back."

Henry said, "I absorbed what he told me like a wet sponge. It also helped me to understand why, a year or so later, it was my job to not only move the goats around but to also fetch a pail of water so they could have a drink. He also showed me how to milk the goats, which became an added chore if he was held up working with the landlord's horses."

"Another of his lessons was to store the goat's milk in a cool place and let the cream rise to the top. Then you could skim off the cream to make butter."

"My father also told me more about potatoes than I ever wanted to know. I can remember him saying: 'Son, this is a seed potato. See its eyes?'"

My response was, "Potatoes have eyes?"

"Well!" As he knelt and pulled out and opened his pocketknife. "Not like our eyes where we can see things. But "using the knife blade to point,

he said, "see that spot right there; that's a potato eye. When we put this seed potato in the ground, a new potato plant will begin to grow right out of that eye."

He also explained, "When you're planting potatoes, you want the ground to be nice and loose and you want it to be of a certain temperature." With that said, he would pick up a handful of dirt and squeeze it in his hand. "You don't want the earth to be too cool or the plant won't start growing. You can look around and see other things are starting to grow, so the time is close. But with practice, you can pick up a handful of dirt and know the time is right."

He would go on to explain, "There's also a certain time to start digging the potatoes in the fall. You want the warm days to be past so you can safely store the potatoes and they won't rot. And, when you're digging them, you start wide and push the plant upwards and make sure you don't cut potatoes with your spade. And another thing, during the summer months you walk among the plants pinching off any potato bugs and killing them, because we need the potatoes a lot worse than them damn bugs do."

Above all else though, as Henry explained, he was giddy with excitement when he could go with his father to work with the landlord's horses. Henry loved the horses, and it seemed like the horses loved him too. Whether it was draft horses, riding horses, or thoroughbred racehorses, Henry could walk among them patting and petting them and they would nuzzle him like he was their long-lost friend. Thomas noticed it too. Whenever Henry was there the horses seemed calmer, more at ease.

As the years passed, Thomas taught Henry all he knew about horses and when the opportunity presented itself, he taught Henry how to ride. Henry enjoyed every minute of it even though they had to be careful none of the landlord's English friends caught him riding the horses. It wasn't a great life, but they got by, father and son working together side by side on their little five- acre farm. It was larger than some of the other tenants who were surviving on as little as two acres or less.

Then, in the early fall of 1845 they heard about something strange affecting the potato crop. The plant may look healthy but underground all the potatoes were just a black smelly mush. Thomas began their harvest and thankfully his potatoes looked fine. Then on the second day of digging some of them didn't. Some plants definitely had the disease, whatever it was. He and Henry managed to salvage enough so they would have potatoes for the winter and seed potatoes for next year, but not enough to enable them to pay all the landlord's rent.

In July of 1846, the potato blight was everywhere in Ireland and destroyed three quarters of the potato crop. The Prime Minister in London, Sir Robert Peel, knew something needed to be done because the Irish peasantry was beginning to starve and were congregating in the towns and crossing into England searching for work and food. This was especially true in port cities like Waterford, Wexford, Dublin, and even Liverpool where they may be able to book passage and immigrate to America or elsewhere. Under the Poor Laws Act, he had workhouses built where the Irish could get food and shelter in exchange for work details. Also, public works projects to build roads and bridges commenced. Unfortunately, the roads in Ireland consisted mostly of old trails that crossed the property of English landlords who insisted the roads not be built through their property, so many of the roads ended up leading to nowhere.

5

The winter of 1846-47 was particularly harsh. Thomas had heard of some tenant farmers being evicted under horrible circumstances. Forced out into the night cold without food or water and their homes destroyed. The farmer, his wife, their children, and maybe even aged and crippled grandparents, all forced out into a winter night with nothing but the clothes on their backs. The peasants carved out homes in road banks and lived on whatever they could scavenge from the land.

Thomas and eleven-year-old Henry still had a few seed potatoes which they planted in the spring of 1847. However, by the arrival of summer, Thomas knew the blight was back. To make matters worse, the landlord and his horses were gone, so there was no way to earn extra income. Thomas had seen the auction bills and knew the estate was to be sold under the Encumbered Property Act come fall.

Unlike his son, Thomas had received some education and could read and write. He had managed to teach Henry to count and to do elementary arithmetic by scratching in the dirt with a stick. He insisted Henry learn to speak well, but reading and writing were a different matter. They had no books to learn to read and they had no pen, ink, or paper to learn to write. Henry had learned a few words by seeing them next to drawings. He knew words like horse, oxen, and faire because he had seen them associated with pictures.

The estate auction was held in early September and before the first frost of October, Thomas, Henry and all the other tenants had been told to vacate the premises. All their livestock had been confiscated for unpaid back rent. They were being evicted. Henry remembered his father rushing in breathless and telling him, "Put your shoes on. Grab your coat, hat, and mittens. Gather up any solid food stuff you can, put it in a burlap sack and let's go."

Henry wasn't exactly sure what was happening but knew it was no time to ask questions, so he did as he was told. Thomas also grabbed his things and out the door they went. They ran to a grove of trees next to the little creek then stopped and looked back. A group of men (Thomas told him it was the sheriff and a bunch of ruffians) had reached their home and were tearing off the thatched roof. Others were using battering rams to knock down the walls of the tenant houses next door. There was now no doubt, the new English landlord was not going to have any tenant farmers.

Thomas turned to Henry and said, "We will make our way to Skibbereen southwest of Cork. I heard there is a workhouse there where we might find some work and food to eat." He then pulled an old envelope from his pocket and handed it to Henry, telling him, "Stick this letter in your pocket and don't ever lose it. If anything should happen to me, it has names of people who may help you."

Henry put the letter into his coat pocket along with the tin whistle he had won at the fair a couple of years before. He took one look back as the ruffians were knocking down a wall of their home, and turned and ran to catch up with his father, already walking with the burlap sack over his shoulder and carrying a jug of water he had filled from the creek.

That night they stopped by a stream where they could have water to drink and refill the jug. Thomas gave Henry a soda bread biscuit to eat but ate nothing himself, saying he wasn't hungry. In their rush, Henry hadn't gotten much in the sack. Three biscuits, a few crackers, a small sack of salt and a sack with some flour and a hunk of hard goat cheese. He had put in a small jar of honey, but the lid had come off and it had leaked onto the cheese and into the flour. All together it was probably less than one good meal. He had put in a crockery cup, but it had broken somewhere along the line. Henry couldn't remember his father eating anything for the two prior days either when the tenant's animals had all been taken. Before they lay down to sleep, he asked, "How long will it take us to walk to—what was that town?"

Thomas answered, "Skibbereen, it's down on the Atlantic coast. It's probably four or five days to Cork then another couple days to Skibbereen, so a good week or so."

With that, they gathered some loose leaves to lay on and tried to sleep. During the night, Thomas had awoken to see Henry shivering from the cold, so he covered him with his coat.

They arose the next morning to a cloudy dreary day. They started walking, but when it began to rain with some sleet mixed in, they took refuge in a grove of trees. They ate nothing for breakfast or lunch and when the rain stopped, they set off again. Now the road was slick with mud, making it hard to walk, so they moved to the wet grass along the side where walking was easier. Henry was thinking about his shoes and how thankful he was that he had them. It was the only pair of shoes he had ever owned. A child at the manor had outgrown them and Thomas had gotten them for his son. When Henry got them, they were way too big, and he had seldom worn them except in the winter. Now they were still a little big and one sole had a small hole worn in it, but it sure beat being barefooted. He never really had any socks. He just wrapped rags around his feet then stuck them in the shoes. When they were way too big, more rags. Now that his feet were bigger, fewer rags.

They hadn't traveled very far that day, but Thomas stopped at some abandoned and mostly destroyed tenant houses. He found a protected corner in one of the homes where some of the thatched roof was still intact. They gathered more of the thatch to sleep on and to cover up with to keep out the cold. Thomas gave Henry another biscuit to eat and took one small bite of the cheese for himself. Both went to sleep hungry.

The next day the sun was shining but it was not what you would call a warm day. Thomas and Henry did make good progress because walking kept them warm. It was also the first day they got to see the effects of the famine. It was toward evening and Thomas had begun to look for a good place to spend the night. He spotted a bunch of peasants spread all over what looked to have been a turnip patch. The men were scratching for anything that might be a turnip while the mothers, half naked and shivering in the cold, eyes dark and sunken, were holding their children close as the babies screamed from hunger. Thomas and Henry kept walking until Thomas thought he had found another good place for the night. It was another group of destroyed tenant houses, so they attempted to repeat the previous night's arrangement. Again, Henry was given the last biscuit and Thomas took a bite of cheese. Henry noticed that his father wasn't looking so well. Even though Henry's own stomach was screaming from hunger, he offered the biscuit to Thomas, but his father refused it and told Henry to eat it. When they awoke the next morning, the burlap sack was gone. Thomas theorized that one of the men from the group of peasants had followed them and stolen the bag while they slept. Although by this time, there was little food worth eating left in it.

They once again headed south toward Cork, but Henry noticed his father was walking a little slower. He told Henry, "I'm powerfully thirsty! I can't seem to get enough water to satisfy my thirst."

Henry handed him the water jug although they had just drunk from a spring at the side of the road where they had filled the jug. Throughout the day, Henry had to hand his father the water jug several times even after finding a livestock tank where they had filled it again. Henry also noticed his father was giving off a rank odor. It wasn't like sweat; this was different. Also, Henry noticed his father's skin was starting to look like those peasants they had seen in the field with his eyes dark and sunken. He knew they both needed to find some food, and the sooner the better.

The next afternoon they came over a rise and could see Cork in the distance. Henry noticed they were no longer walking alone. Groups of other displaced peasants were beside, behind, and in front of them. All walking toward Cork and all looking emaciated and starving. Some of the men and women were carrying young children, while others carried small bags holding all their life possessions.

When they had reached the town, Thomas grabbed Henry's arm and motioned toward a tree. He indicated he needed to sit and rest for a spell. It was a walnut tree so Henry searched around for any fallen walnuts, but he was obviously not the first to search, because not even a discarded walnut shell could be found. He had just settled in beside his father when he heard someone from a passing group of peasants say, "I heard The Quakers have set up a soup kitchen in town. We need to go there and get in line for something to eat."

Henry perked right up and said, Come on Dad! Let's go get in line."

Thomas tried to rise but couldn't seem to get his balance and sat back down as he motioned to Henry. He kind of mumbled.: "You ga ga go get s..s..some s..soo..soup and br.. bring m..m me some."

Henry didn't want to leave him, but Thomas kept motioning for him to go. Henry followed the crowd to where the Quakers had their soup kitchen and got at the end of a lengthy line that seemed to be moving way too slowly. Finally, someone handed him a bowl and motioned him to move ahead but Henry halted and asked, "Can I have another bowl for my father?"

"No! Your father has to get in line just like everyone else."

"But my father is having trouble walking. Please, can I have another bowl?"

"My instructions were one bowl per person, Now move along."

Henry was beside himself as he moved forward, where a man took his arm and marked the back of his hand with a piece of charcoal. Henry asked: "What's that for?"

The answer: "To keep people from getting in line again and trying to get a second bowl of soup."

That had been the only thing Henry thought he could do. He was desperately trying to think of some other plan. He sat down and ate a few bites to stop his own screaming hunger. He thought of saving some from his own bowl but had nothing to carry it in. He had been instructed to put his empty bowl on the table at the end where it could be rinsed and used for another person in the line. He thought of just walking out with the bowl, but people were watching. Not able to think of any other choice, he finished his bowl, holding the last big bite in his mouth and breathing through his nose as he tried to hurry back to his father.

He was too late. As he went up the road toward the walnut tree, he could see his father was lying or had fallen over on his side. He knelt beside him and swallowed the soup. His father was dead. Henry didn't know what to do. He laid down beside his father and just sobbed for he didn't know how long. In the cold of the night, he had snuggled closer and used the back of his father's coat to keep warm. Toward dawn he reached into his father's pocket and removed his pocketknife and his few coins. For what purpose, he did not know. In fact, he didn't have any idea what to do next. He knew he was now an orphan with no home, no food, and nowhere to go. He lay beside his dead father wondering if and how he should bury him, and then began sobbing again.

Henry awoke to the sound of a team of horses pulling a two-wheeled hay cart. He sat up as the team approached and he saw a man seated on the cart. The man pulled the cart to a stop and looked down at Henry and said, "Is that man dead?"

Choking back tears again, Henry replied, "Yes, he is my father and he died yesterday."

The man asked, "What you gonna do with im?"

"I don't know. We were trying to get to Skibbereen to the workhouse for food and work," said Henry in a plaintive voice.

"Well, my name is Al and I'd say your t'day is gonna be a mite better than yer yesterday. I'm headin to Skibbereen and you can ride along and give me a hand when I need ya. Ya sees, I gots this job wheres I travel 'tween Cork and Skibbereen picking up all the dead bodies. One days I goes from Cork ta Skibbereen an da next I goes from Skibbereen to Cork."

As Al was climbing down from the cart, Henry noticed there were already two bodies in the back, a man and a woman. He grimaced, but then Al picked him up and set him down on the seat of the cart. Without giving Henry a chance to say yes or no, Al picked up his father's body and put it in the cart. Al then climbed back into his seat, gave the reins a whip and they were off toward Skibbereen. Al told Henry they had to move at a fast clip because it was a fair distance to Skibbereen to make it in one day.

They had traveled a mile or so when Al said, "Ders a couple more right ahead."

He pulled the team to a stop beside the bodies and climbed down from the cart. Henry climbed down too though he wasn't sure why. The bodies were a woman and her toddler son. Al reached down and with his thumb and forefinger gently closed the woman's eyes. He then did the same for the toddler saying, "I'se always close der eyes cuz dey has no more seein ta do in dis world. Dey be like da damn English. People starvin all round dem and they look with eyes dat do not see." With that, he reached down and picked up the woman and started toward the cart.

Over his shoulder, he said to Henry, "You bring along da boy over here to da cart."

Henry wasn't sure he could do it but stooped down uneasily and did as he had been told. The body was stiff with rigor mortis and much lighter than Henry expected. Once the bodies were in the cart and they were back atop the seat, they were off again. The sun was rising further in the sky and Henry thought Al must have decided it was time to tell him his story.

Al said, "Ise weren't too sure bout taken dis job but twern't any uders to be had. A man's gotta feed his family any way he can. Course dat sum-a-bitchen Trevelyan in England wouldn't pay me by da day. Hadda be piece work. So much per body delivered fer buryin. Some days Ise makes da whole trip fer nothin. No dead bodies to be found. Course bisness picked up a bunch lately. Some days over dozen but now deys talkin bout limitin me ta such-an-such 'mount. Dey do dat and maybe I'll just start leavin some bodies lay."

They had come across another body so the story telling stopped while Al got down and loaded another body in the cart. As he climbed back up, he said: "Lookin like tis gonna be a decent day. Yous getting hungry?"

With that he pulled up his lunch sack hanging on the side of the cart. Reached in an grabbed a soda biscuit, broke off about half and handed it to Henry saying, "That'll be all yous getting 'til we get to Skibbereen. Figgered yous maybe earned dat much. Res is mine cuz Ise a lot bigger en yous and Ise hungry.

They ate their lunch on the move and in silence except for Henry's stomach screaming from hunger. Mid-afternoon they had picked up one more body and Al turned to Henry and asked, "You ain't tol' me yer story. Gots yer dad in back what happen to yous ma, an wheres yous come from?

Henry thought a bit then answered. "My mom died when I was just little. I don't know the name of the place where we lived. It had a big house where the owner, from a place called London or something like that, lived sometimes. Then a bunch of us tenant farmers down the hill by the stream. The landlord guy, Dad called him, had a bunch of horses including racehorses and dad taught me to ride them."

Al said, "Sounds like mos of Ireland dese days. Don't reckin I can fig'er wheres 'xactly yer from then. Maybe Skibbereen is da best place ta drop ya off."

As they came over a rise in the road, Henry asked, "What do you do with the bodies?"

Al Pointed in the distance and said, " ya see dat big long building out dere. Dats da workhouse and in behind dat is a big field where we bury da dead. Some days ders a preacher man or somebody to say a few words over 'em, some days not. I'll drop you off by da office, den I'll go on round back to da field."

The sun was setting when Henry climbed down from the cart and Al pointed at a door where he was to go in. As Al and the cart pulled away, Henry glanced at the dead bodies, including his father, kind of bouncing up and down in the back of the rough riding cart, shuddered, and gave Al a weak wave good-bye. He went toward the indicated door but saw there was a short line of other starving peasants ahead of him, so took his place at the end. It was dark outside when a soldier motioned Henry inside and indicated he should sit in a chair in front of a desk. An official looking guy came in, sat down at the desk and removed a form from a drawer and said, "Name?"

Henry answered. "Henry Charles Kearney."

"Age?"

"Eleven I think."

"Home address?"

Silence followed, so the official looked up and asked, "You don't know your home address?"

Henry answered, "Our home was knocked down, so we didn't have one."

"Where are your parents?"

"Both dead," Henry said.

"How did you get here?"

"Walked most the way. Al brought me from Cork."

"Is Al a relative of yours?"

"Nope."

"Do you have any other relatives?"

At this inquiry, Henry suddenly remembered his father's envelope and pulled it from his coat pocket. He handed it to the man and said, "My father gave me this and said to keep it, so I'll want it back. But I don't know what it says because I can't read."

The official took the envelope and read the postmark of Moneygall, County Offaly, Ireland, then removed the letter from inside and read it to himself. Turning back to Henry, he asked, "What was your father's name?"

Henry responded with, "Thomas."

"Do you have a grandmother named Esther?"

"I don't know."

"Your father never mentioned his mother to you, or you never met her or saw her?"

"No, not that I can remember. He gave me the letter and said if we ever got separated maybe someone in the letter would help me is all I know."

The official wrote some information on a notepad, refolded the letter, put it back in the envelope and handed it to Henry. He said, "I'm going to write a letter to this Esther Kearney in Moneygall that appears to be your grandmother and ask her, or someone, to come and get you. Until then, I'm assigning you to one of our bunks for children that came open today because we had a couple kids die. The soldier outside will take you to it and you remember the way, because that is where you will sleep until you are told otherwise. You are too late for supper but follow the others in the morning to the dining hall for breakfast. That is where you will get all your meals. We do have a school, such as it is, where you will receive lessons during the day. Empty your pockets before you go, but you can keep the letter. Any questions?"

Henry couldn't think of any, so just shook his head, then put his father's knife, the few coins, and his tin whistle from his pockets on the desk. The official said anything of value would go toward his upkeep then wrote a number on a ticket and took Henry to the door where he handed the ticket to a soldier and told him to deliver Henry to his bunk. The soldier took Henry up about three flights of stairs then down a hallway and into a large room with bunkbeds everywhere. The soldier pointed to a door to a small room and said, "Chamber pots in there." Then he led Henry to his bunk and said, "you're in the bottom one." He turned and left.

Henry looked at the bottom bunk and saw there were already two body forms in it. He looked up to the top bunk and counted three forms up there. Not sure what to do, he sat on the edge, then lay down. He then heard in a loud whisper, "What the hell you think you're doing?"

Henry sat back up and whispered, somewhat tentatively, "Laying down to sleep. The soldier said I was . . ."

"Christ man! He didn't tell you to sleep on top of me." And with that exclamation, one of the boys in bed also sat up and said, "My name's Pat O'Conner, what's yours?"

"Henry Kearney."

"Well Kearney, this is how it is. The bound for hell English, besides starving us to death, decided us kids could sleep three to a bunk. Well, we tried with all three looking at the foot of the bed and it didn't work. We were too wide, and somebody got shoved out. So now we sleep one head up, one head down, then another head up. Our feet may get tangled occasionally but at least we all have room to turn over once in a while and, Kearney, your head goes that way." He pointed to the opposite end and laid back down.

Henry got the message and lay down the other way.

Then from Pat O'Conner came an even louder whisper, "Holy shit, Kearney, you have shoes on! You rich or something? Quit kicking me in the balls! None of us kids have shoes. Quit kicking and put your clodhoppers on the floor."

A voice came from the next bunk over. "Would you two quit your damn yapping and go to sleep!"

Henry, afraid his shoes might be missing in the morning if he took them off, was unsure what to do; so, he put one foot on the floor, the other at the edge of the bunk and tried to get some sleep even though his stomach was aching for him to eat something.

6

In the morning light, both Henry and Pat O'Conner sat up on the edge of the bunk and looked each other up and down. When the third bunk mate sat up on the opposite side, Pat, thumbing over his shoulder, said, "That's McKinney. He don't talk much, maybe because he's kinda sickly. What's your story Kearney?"

"What do you mean?"

Well, you got shoes on, and you have a coat and a cap and most of us don't. Why you in the workhouse?"

Henry answered, "My dad and I started walking to Skibbereen when we got evicted and they knocked down our house. Then my father died from starvation outside Cork and this guy, Al, brought me here on his cart because I'm an orphan and had no place else to go."

Pat answered, "Wow, that's tough. Kinda like McKinney's story. His parents are dead, but he has a couple older sisters downstairs."

Henry, now warming to this Pat O'Conner kid even if he did refer to everyone by their last name, said, "So what's your story and can you explain this place to me?"

Pat answered, "Let's go get something to eat and I'll tell you on the way."

The starving Henry was all for that, so they headed for the hallway with McKinney tagging behind. In the hallway, Pat said, "My parents are here along with my six brothers and sisters. I'm kind of in the middle with three brothers and three sisters. My two older sisters are married and as a dowery my dad gave them and their husbands a piece of our farm, about two acres to each. It was tough to make it, but then we all got evicted and here we are in this place."

Henry asked, "Speaking of the workhouse, how does this place work?"

Pat explained, "It's a big place. The ground floor has the kitchen, dining hall, offices and the different work areas for guys, plus the school off the dining hall. The second floor is for girls over three, the third floor for the rest of the women, the fourth floor for boys like us and the top floor for men sixteen and up. The second and third floors also have work areas for women and off the second floor above the dining hall is where you go if you're sick and the dead people are carried there too, before they're slid down a ramp into the burial carts. The carts haul the bodies to the burial pit and dump them in. As the pit fills up, they keep us digging it longer and longer and just keep filling it up with bodies. Must be hundreds and hundreds of people buried out there by now."

When Al had told Henry his dad would be buried in the field behind the workhouse, Henry had envisioned neat rows of individual graves like he had seen in cemeteries; not hundreds of bodies dumped in a pit and covered with dirt. It upset him to think about it and he teared up for a bit, but they had reached the dining hall and were receiving their allotment of breakfast. Pat said, "They only give us kids half of what the men get to eat because we're littler and some days get schoolin instead of working." Then he added, "But today's Sunday so instead of school we'll get preached at by one of them Protestant preachers. My mom said we're Catholic, so pay them no attention cuz they don't know what they're talking about."

Henry didn't understand what Pat was talking about when he said he was Catholic, and the preacher was a Protestant. He had spent all his time with his father since his mother died and had never gone to church. He knew what a church building was, he had seen them, and he had heard people say they went there to pray, get married, and get buried, but that was about the extent of his religious up-bringing. Apparently, Henry's father was not a religious man so neither was Henry.

When they had finished eating, they took their dishes to a table next to the kitchen where Irish women were washing them. Pat said, Come on I'll show you where the school is located."

Henry was starting to think he liked this Pat O'Conner kid. Pat was friendly and seemed to have lots of knowledge about the how, when, and where of the workhouse, but it was a new experience for Henry. He had never had friends before. He had always been with his father. He had known some of the other tenant farmer's children and had done things with them but only occasionally. Consequently, he had never developed any close friendships before.

Suddenly, McKinney following behind Pat and Henry said, "Wait! I can't make it. I don't feel well, and I have to go to the toilet then I'm going back to bed."

Pat started to ask, "Do we need to take you to . . ." but McKinney had already turned and was heading back. Pat shrugged, turned and motioned to Henry as they went ahead to the school.

When they entered the room, Henry saw the man at the front talking and gesturing with his hands but none of the boys seemed to be listening to him at all. The preacher man stood on a small, raised platform and had a bible open on the pulpit in front of him. Henry had never attended school, but he had been in one once when his father had taken him to a fair and they had gone inside to a food booth. That school had had benches for the students arranged in rows and shelves on the side full of books. A large map was mounted on the wall at the front showing oceans and land areas. His father had shown him Ireland and then told the names of other areas like Asia, Europe, Africa, and America. This room had none of that. The boys sat haphazardly on the floor, some in little groups talking to each other, and there was not a book to be seen except the one on the pulpit. Henry could hardly hear anything the preacher was saying, but after a while he said in a louder voice, "Let's bow our heads in prayer." Some boys did and some didn't, but when the preacher was done, he closed his bible, put it under his arm and left the room.

Pat said, "Come on I'll show you something." Pat led Henry back to the dining hall and snuck through the kitchen where Irish women were preparing the noon meal, then through a pantry to a back stairway where he whispered to Henry, "This is the backway to the second and third floors where the women are. They use them to come down to fix meals. Come on!" Pat dashed up the stairs and through the door to the second floor. Henry quickly followed, though he was feeling uneasy about this adventure. Pat went at once to the second bunk where a girl about their age was lying on the bed, seemingly asleep. Pat took her hand, looked into her eyes and said, "Hi, how are you feeling? I brought a friend for you to meet. Come over here, Kearney."

"Sarah, this is my friend Henry Kearney. He arrived yesterday."

Henry, not knowing what else to do, walked over, looked down and nodded. Sarah had green eyes and red hair like Pat, but he knew as soon as he looked at her that Sarah was a very sick girl.

Pat said, "Kearney this is my sister, Sarah. She's a year younger than me. How old are you, Kearney?"

"I'm eleven, maybe twelve."

"Jeez, you and Sarah are the same age. I'm twelve, be thirteen in January."

Sarah managed to say, "Hi Kearney, thanks for coming." Then she turned to Pat and said, I feel terrible and need to sleep now, okay?"

There were several other girls looking at them, but no one said anything. Pat motioned to Henry with tear-filled eyes, and they snuck back down the stairs and out into the dining hall. There they went to the end of the line for the noon meal, Henry thankful they hadn't been caught.

Pat said, "I know she's not going to make it. My little brother didn't make it either. No one was there to be with him when he died. My older sister, Kate, told me Sarah was sick one day when she was working in the kitchen, and I came through the line. I had to go see her. I didn't want her to die without seeing and knowing someone loved her, so I figured out a way to get there. I know she has the fever and doesn't have long."

Henry and Pat continued their workhouse routine for another week before Pat's sister was able to tell him Sarah had died a couple of days before. Pat put up a brave front for Henry, but Henry knew it hurt him deeply. It was a week after that when Henry was awakened by Pat kicking him as he quickly swung his legs over the side of the bunk. With eyebrows raised in horror he stared at Henry and said, "McKinney's dead. My leg touched his and it was cold."

Henry looked over and there was McKinney staring straight at him, eyes wide open. He was not breathing. Henry reached over and with thumb and forefinger gently closed his eyelids and held them for a second. When he removed his hand, McKinney's eyes stayed closed.

Pat said, "Where in the hell did you learn that?"

Henry replied, "A friend showed me on the way here. Told me those eyes would see no more, so he always closed them."

Pat asked, "What do we do now?"

Henry responded, "I suppose we tell the soldiers and they'll come and get the body. Then we'll probably get a new bunk mate."

"I like you, Kearney, but I don't want any more bunk mates. Especially if they're just going to die in bed while I'm sleeping next to them."

Pat and Henry reported the death to the soldier outside the office, then went ahead through their work routine, today emptying all the chamber pots on their floor. When they returned to their bunk that evening McKinney's body was still there in their bunk. They went and told the soldier again but were told to forget about anything being done about it until the next day. They returned to their bunk and Henry asked Pat, "What do you think we should do now?"

Pat said, "I don't know about you, but I'm not sleeping in that bed!"

Henry nodded in agreement and they both spent the night sleeping on the floor next to the bunk. The next morning, they again reported that McKinney was dead, gave them their exact bunk number and were assured it would be handled. However, when they returned in the evening the body was still there. Pat was suggesting maybe they could move McKinney to the floor and then they could have the bunk, when two Irish peasants arrived with a soldier and loaded McKinney's body onto a stretcher and were leaving when Pat asked, "What took you so long?"

"Too many dead and you guys aren't digging the pit fast enough," the English soldier replied.

"Damned English." Was Pat's reply under his breath.

Then Henry and Pat looked at the bed and then at each other and in a simultaneous motion flipped the straw filled ticking over so neither would have to sleep where McKinney had died. They still slept facing opposite directions, expecting a third bunkmate to arrive at any time.

A couple of weeks later Pat and Henry were on their way to breakfast when they were stopped by a soldier who asked, "Are you Henry Kearney?"

Pat pointed at Henry, while Henry nodded that yes, he was.

"Report to the office after you've eaten."

"Oh God!" said Pat. "What now?"

Even though they were always hungry, that morning Pat and Henry had a little trouble eating while worrying about the office summons. When Henry headed to the office, Pat wished him luck and headed for his work detail.

Henry entered the office with trepidation and said, "I'm Henry Kearney and was told to report to the office."

The soldier/clerk reported to the officer inside and motioned Henry inside and indicated for him to sit in the chair, which Henry did. The official, the same one who had checked Henry in, looked up from the letter he was reading and said, "Good news! Your grandmother has sent someone to pick you up and they will be here tomorrow. You'll be out of here by tomorrow night and we'll have another bunk for one of those poor devils out there." He pointed out the window.

Henry's mind was spinning. Who, what, tomorrow but, but who? He didn't know what to say so he just sat there for a moment trying to make sense of it all. The official told him he was released to his work detail and that someone would come and get him when his ride arrived. Henry stumbled to his work and through most of the day. He didn't see Pat O'Conner until they lined up for supper and Pat came up wondering what happened at the office. Henry told him. "Apparently, I have a grandmother and she sent someone to get me, and they're arriving tomorrow. I'm getting out of this filthy hell hole."

Pat was crestfallen, saying, "I have one bunkmate die, now you're leaving. You are the only friend I had in this God forsaken place. What am I supposed to do now?" Catching himself, he said, "But, I'm happy for you, Kearney. You get out of here and hopefully get to a much better place."

Henry felt sorry for the only friend he had ever had. They had the bunk to themselves again that night (probably a clerical error or maybe McKinney was watching over them). For the first time they both lay in bed facing the same direction. They talked of their dreams and aspirations. Henry to work with horses again and Pat to have a place where he could farm free from the English yoke and the rest of his family was all around. They both eventually drifted off to sleep, Henry still with his shoes on.

The next morning, Pat and Henry hadn't even gotten through the breakfast line when a soldier came for Henry. Pat and Henry kind of boy hugged, and Pat said, "See ya, Kearney."

Henry said, "Yeah, see you." He turned and left with the soldier. Pat and Henry never saw each other again.

In the office, the same official with another seated man told Henry, "This is your dad's brother, Kyle. Your uncle, and apparently, one of the people Thomas said may help you when he gave you that old letter." Handing back Henry's now empty coin purse and his father's old pocketknife, he said, "I know I'm one of the hated English. Our Parliament looks at the starving Irish but with eyes that do not see. It does cheer me when one of you Irish can perhaps get a chance for a better life. Good-bye and good luck Henry Kearney."

7

Kyle took Henry with him, and they climbed aboard a cabriolet coach with the top down, pulled by a team of horses. Neither Kyle nor Henry talked much that first day. They were mostly just trying to feel each other out and Henry slept a lot and ate whatever Kyle handed him. On day two of the trip home, Kyle turned to Henry and said, "How old are you now?"

Henry, still feeling unsure about what was happening said, "I think I might be twelve now. I kind of lost track of days in that place."

"I can certainly see why. Twelve, huh. I have a son Mike, a little more than four years older than you. He went out on his own this year. Going to make his mark in the world. We didn't have any idea about you and Thomas. We all thought you probably died years ago.

Henry answered, "My mother did. When I was just little. Can you tell me where we're going and maybe what I should expect when I get there?"

"Well, you're going to live with your grandparents. William and Esther Kearney in Moneygall, a small village on the border between County Offaly and County Tipperary. Your grandmother said no grandchild of hers was going to rot in one of those filthy workhouses." Your grandfather is a shoemaker, and the family has been shoemakers for generations. Even shoemaker for an Irish king a few generations back. It kinda looks like you could use a new pair of shoes, and some clothes and a bath. You don't smell so good. Some of Mike's old clothes will probably fit you. I brought along some jerky, dried fruit, and some bread. Are you hungry again? I don't need to keep handing it to you, just help yourself.

"Yes!" said Henry as Kyle handed him the sack. Henry couldn't even remember the last time his stomach felt full. Kyle urged him to take it a little easy, but Henry just kept right on eating until he felt stuffed. Kyle said, "I thought I brought enough food to get us a little further up the road. Now we'll need to make it all the way to Limerick tonight before we can eat. We can get up and have some breakfast in the morning because you just finished eating both yours and mine for the rest of today."

Henry felt a little embarrassed but thought to himself that Kyle sure reminded him of his dad and definitely resembled him too, though a little taller. Kyle could see, that after his feast, Henry's eyelids were getting a little heavy, so he reached in back and grabbed a blanket and told Henry, "Cover up a little, scoot down in the seat, put your head against the seat back and take yourself a nap." Henry didn't argue, and a few minutes later was sound asleep with a full stomach for the first time in a long while.

It was completely dark when Henry awoke as they were entering Limerick. Kyle pulled to a stop in front of an inn and went to secure them a room for the night. When he appeared again, he told Henry, "You can hop down and go to our room. I'll be back as soon as I take the rig to the livery."

Henry replied, "I would rather go with you to take care of the horses, if that's okay."

"Sure, come on along," he said as he stepped up and directed the team to the livery.

After entering the barn, they both got down and as Kyle went to talk with the liveryman, Henry, as his father had shown him, disconnected the team's harness from the coach, led them forward, began talking to them, and brushing them with a horse brush he saw to the side. It had been a long time since he had such an enjoyable experience. He really missed his horse buddies from his days at the manor. Kyle arrived with the liveryman and said, "Good job! Here let me help to remove their harness so you can give them a good brush down."

Henry grinned and nodded as the liveryman went to get a few oats and hay for the manger in the stall where the team would spend the night. Kyle and Henry then walked back toward the inn, with Kyle thanking Henry for his help.

They had a good night of sleep, but upon awakening Henry felt an all too familiar grumbling from his stomach. He was hungry again and told Kyle. Kyle said, "Well, I had a little different plan, but I guess we can go have breakfast first."

While they were eating their morning meal in the café at the inn, Henry asked, "What was your plan for this morning?"

Kyle replied, "As soon as you're done stuffing your face (Henry needed to learn a few table manners that Kyle was sure grandma would instill); I'm taking you over to the bathhouse and barber. While you're getting a good bath--with soap, by the way, and getting your girlie curls clipped. I'll go get you some new duds. You can keep your shoes and your cap and coat, but we're going to have you looking halfway decent when you meet your grandparents."

Henry wasn't too sure about this whole bath thing, but the thought of new clothes was kind of exciting. They went over and entered the bath house where a gentleman escorted Henry to a back room where a tub was waiting. It already had water in it and the bath attendant added hot water from a kettle on the stove. He showed Henry the bar of soap on the side of the tub where a clean terry washcloth also hung. He showed Henry the clean towel by the basin and the hooks on the wall to hang his clothes, then stepped from the room, closing the door behind him.

Henry stripped down and stepped into the tub. The water was hot but not too hot. The experienced attendant had judged it about right. Henry sat down and began scrubbing with the washcloth and soap. He was amazed by two things—How quickly the water cooled off and how filthy it became from his scrubbing. After he had washed his hair and was exiting the tub he guessed; yeah, he really hadn't had a bath since before they'd been evicted several weeks ago. He was drying with the towel when Kyle and the attendant reentered the room, Kyle carrying new clothes over his arm saying, "Here you go kid, new drawers, pants, shirt, socks and a new belt." Turning to the attendant, he said, "Take those old things hanging on the hook out back and burn 'em. Oh, but leave the cap and coat."

Henry rushed over wrapped in the towel and yelled, "Wait! " He went to his pants pocket and pulled out his father's old pocketknife and empty coin purse and put them in the pocket of his new pants. Kyle kind of watched in amusement because as Henry was transferring the items, his towel dropped to the floor leaving him standing there stark naked. At the same time as Henry started to reach down for the towel, Kyle was holding out his new drawers for him. Henry started to slip on the wet floor, but Kyle managed to grab his other arm just in time before he went down, saying, "Get these new duds on before you fall and break your damn neck."

After Henry was dressed, they proceeded to the haircut, a first for Henry by a barber. He looked in the mirror with his new clothes and haircut and thought he looked rather good, until he glanced down at his shoes. They looked a little beyond worn out. But then he thought back to Pat O'Conner's comment, and he was thankful just to have shoes. He and Kyle then went to the livery, hitched up the horses and got back on the road. Kyle had gone to the café and gotten them some food provisions while Henry was getting his haircut. With only twenty or so miles to go, Kyle had told Henry they should reach Moneygall by evening. Like the previous day, they occasionally met groups of displaced peasants heading to who knows where, and all looking emaciated.

Just before arriving at Moneygall, Kyle pointed out to Henry the farm to the left that was owned by his grandfather and that he, Kyle, was running and would someday probably inherit. To your right, Kyle told him, is a part of the Summerfield plantation. Your Aunt Katheen married Richard Summerfield, so she lives down that road a ways in a beautiful home.

This got Henry thinking, so he asked Kyle, "If I'm Irish and you're Irish, how come grandfather's farm wasn't destroyed by the English like my father's?"

Kyle thought for a minute then said, "Good question! A couple hundred years ago when maybe your great great great grandfather was making shoes.

He was sitting in his shop one day looking through his sales records. He noticed that there weren't very many Irishmen buying his handmade shoes. On the contrary, almost all his sales were going to the English aristocracy and their families. Being an intelligent man, he decided his best course of action was to get religion--Protestant religion. So, when Cromwell came over to rid the island of Catholics, he was spared because he belonged to the correct church. The English aristocracy in Ireland was happy because they could continue to have their custom fit shoes made by the best shoemaker they could find, and he was happy because he wasn't beheaded and could keep his shoe shop."

Henry wasn't sure he understood all the Catholic or Protestant religious stuff. Same stuff Pat O'Conner had talked about, but he did understand it was the Irish who were Protestants that were a lot better off than the ones who were Catholic. So, he thought maybe he would choose to be a Protestant. But, thinking further, he decided he still kind of hated the English.

Kyle pulled the coach to a stop in front of a nice looking home with a picket fence in front and shade trees along the side. He told Henry, "Hop down, this is it. The home of William and Esther Kearney, your grandparents. When we get inside, remove your hat and coat and hang them on the hall tree, then I'll introduce you to the assembled family."

With that said, Kyle took Henry's hand and led him to the front door, knocked once, then went ahead and entered. Henry did as he had been told and hung up his hat and coat just as an elderly woman and what must have been a maid met them in the entrance hallway. The older lady gently touched Kyle's shoulder while looking him in the eye. She then turned to Henry, smiled and said, "Why don't we go into the parlor, there's some people there anxious to meet you. Kyle, you can do the introductions."

Kyle and Henry followed the lady and the maid into the parlor where the maid excused herself. Kyle leaned down and whispered to Henry, "That was Millie and she's great. You're really going to like her."

The older lady, Henry assumed was his grandmother, continued to the end of the room where she sat down next to an older seated man who was holding a cane in front of him with both hands. Kyle put his hand to Henry's back, and they followed the lady to the other end of the parlor where Kyle said, "Henry, I would like to introduce you to William Kearney, your grandfather, and Esther Kearney, your grandmother."

Henry gave a little bow, as his father had told him to do when being introduced. There was no response from William, but Esther reached out and clasped Henry's hand in hers and smiled saying, "Glad to finally meet you, young man."

Moving to the next person, a man, Henry followed Kyle who said, "Henry, this is my older brother and your uncle, William Henry Kearney and seated next to him is his wife, Margaret. They have three daughters, all younger than you. My brother is also a shoemaker after apprenticing under our father and now runs the shoe shop in the village."

Henry again gave a little bow with William Henry and Margaret acknowledging it with a nod. Moving in unison to the right where a woman was seated, Kyle said, "Henry, this is my sister, she's younger than me but a year older than your father. Your aunt Kathleen Summerfield. She is married to Richard Summerfield, and they have two little boys at home. Was Richard unable to make it this evening?"

Kathleen nodded to Henry's bow then said, "No, he had some kind of meeting with an agent to help some of the displaced tenants to immigrate to America. Sorry for his absence."

Moving again, Kyle said, "And Henry, this is my wife Molly, the queen of my heart, and we have the one son Michael, who I told you about."

Molly laughed at Kyle's introduction, clasped Henry's hand and said, "So glad to meet you, Henry. I think I can bring over some of Mike's old clothes for you to wear for work or play. Wouldn't want to mess up them new ones you have on. Maybe Henry down there can fix you up with a new pair of shoes, too."

William Henry agreed that he could handle that. Then grandfather William spoke for the first time, "Won't be much time for any playing. What are you now 12 or 13? That's old enough to start earning your keep. We'll find plenty to keep you busy."

His grandfather said it with such earnestness that Henry was sure he was serious about putting him to work. He hoped it would be with the horses.

Having made the introductions of those present, Kyle went on to say, "Henry you also have three more uncles who have all immigrated to America. They are all younger, Francis, a year younger than your dad, then Joseph, and Fredrick. Francis immigrated in 1836 and with his glowing accolades of life in America, Joe and Fred followed a couple of years later."

Esther then spoke up saying, "Henry, you may have noticed your grandfather is named William and our oldest son is named William Henry. To avoid confusion, everyone has always referred to your grandfather as William and our son as Henry. Now you have presented us with another Henry, so I was wondering if it would be okay if we called you Hank? It is a sort of nickname for people named Henry.

Henry's head was spinning. He had always been Henry, although he could recall his dad calling him Hank a few times when teasing him or when he was perturbed with him as in 'Alright, Hank, what have you done now?' He did think Hank made him sound more grown up. He wasn't at all sure how to answer his grandmother but finally said, "I guess we can try it for a while, but I might fail to answer sometimes if I forget."

Esther and the others chuckled at his response and Esther said, "I think that is very understandable, Hank, welcome to our home. Now, should we get something to eat? I believe Millie has prepared us a wonderful supper."

Henry was more than ready to eat again but reminded himself he had to remember what Kyle had told him about table manners, (Don't just stuff the food in. Watch how others are eating and then do the same and don't forget your please and thank-yous.) He also noted that Millie must be more than just a maid. She apparently was also the cook.

At supper, several inquired about his life until now, but Hank limited his response to living with his father on the tenant farm until his father died, when a fellow named Al took him to the workhouse and that he really liked horses. He said, "Father took care of the horses at the manor and let me help him. He taught me how to ride, how to take care of horses, and how to recognize if they were sick or had other problems. And I think horses like me too."

Kyle laughed and chipped in, "I think that's true. When we stopped in Limerick last night, he unhitched the team and was already brushing them when I got there. The horses were looking at him like where have you been all my life."

After some small talk after supper, his new aunt and uncles prepared to go to their own homes and Esther, putting her arm around his shoulders, said, "Hank, let's go have a look at the room where you will be sleeping."

She took him down a short hallway and entered a room on the right, saying, "This is it. You'll have the bed to yourself with plenty of blankets and pillows. I've laid out one of the boys' old night shirts for you to wear to bed and there is a chamber pot under the edge of the bed if you should need it during the night. Over here is a washstand with a wash bowl and a pitcher of water that Millie will refresh every day. There is a washcloth and towel hanging here on the side. On this adjacent wall here, we have your wardrobe where you can keep you clean clothes. Dirty clothes go in the wash sack Millie will bring you. I know Molly is bringing you some old clothes of Michael's, but I think you and I will go downtown tomorrow and buy you a few things. Oh, and here at the window is a shade you can put up or down but should always pull down when readying for bed. Do you know how to turn down the wick in the lamp and blow it out before retiring? Would you like to go to bed now?"

Hank was amazed at the splendor, having never seen anything like it, but did manage to inquire, "Is there a privy out back somewhere or do I use the pot?"

Esther replied, "Oh yes, let me show you the way."

Back in the hallway, she showed him an exit door on the left just before the door to the bedroom where she indicated William and she slept. Opening the exit door, she stepped out to the back porch and told Hank, "Just follow the walk to the back and you'll see it. It's right next to the carriage house.

The next morning, they let Hank sleep in but when he did arise, Millie fixed him an eggs and bacon breakfast. Something he couldn't remember having for years and years. Millie seemed to enjoy the enthusiasm of Hank eating his food almost as much as Hank enjoyed eating it. After he finished eating, Esther instructed him on the proper way he should have eaten and taken advantage of the napkin that should have been in his lap. Hank was committing that information to memory when Esther said, "We'll head to town when you're ready, buy a few things for you; then visit Henry at the shoe shop. He can show you how shoes are made and perhaps have a pair to fit you."

Hank replied, "I'll be ready in a minute. Just let me grab my jacket."

It was the jacket Esther had found for him among some old clothes of her sons. The first hints of spring were in the air. It was going to be a pleasant, sunny day. It was just a short walk uptown to where most of the village businesses were found. They had just passed a couple of them when Esther directed him to enter a general merchandise store. She went straight to a small section of clothing for boys where she gathered some more underdrawers and socks she was sure would fit Henry/Hank. They then met a man Hank took to be the store proprietor. The man said, "Who do we have here, Mrs. Kearney?

Esther replied, "Mr. McCall, I would like you to meet my Grandson Henry, called Hank, Kearney."

"Pleased to make your acquaintance," said Mr. McCall to Hank and held out his hand.

Hank shook the man's hand and said, "Pleased to know you as well." They moved to the front of the store, where Esther paid for the merchandise.

Mr. McCall wrapped their purchase in craft paper, tied it with a string and thanked them for their purchase as they exited his store.

As Esther and Hank walked along, Esther pointed out some of the other stores though there weren't many in the small town. They crossed the street and entered a storefront with a sign across the front above the entrance. It was a large white sign with black lettering and trim with a picture of a shoe to one side and a boot on the other. The lettering read: Shoemaker – Bootery, and a second smaller line read, William Kearney Proprietor.

Immediately Hank caught the aroma of new leather. A pleasant smell he associated with the smell of harnesses for the horses his father used to get from the tack room at the manor. Upon hearing the little bell ring from the door opening, William Henry appeared from behind a curtain at the back of the store. Behind a sales counter and to either side of the door from which William Henry had appeared were row after row of little drawers with what appeared to be code numbers on the drawer fronts. After exchanging greetings, Henry asked, "What are all the drawers for?"

William Henry explained, "As the English aristocracy desired that each shoe be custom made to fit each of their feet, the Kearney shoemakers had devised a system of measuring and making a pattern of each customer's feet and assigning it a code. The patterns and measurements as well as color and style were then put in one of the small drawers and the code inserted on the drawer front and into an index book cross referenced with the patron's name. In that manner the patrons did not have to return in order to get new shoes. They could order them by mail unless they felt their shoe size had changed. As the Kearneys had been shoemakers for generations, they required a lot of drawers, though some were reassigned upon learning of a patron dying."

Hank just said, "Wow, that's a lot of customers."

William Henry went on to explain, "We do have down time when we've received no orders, so then we make boots and shoes in the most common sizes to sell to the public. Come over here, Hank, I think we may have a pair of work boots that will fit you."

Hank sat down in the chair provided and removed his old worn-out shoes. William Henry measured his feet then went over to the adjacent wall and brought back a pair of brown work boots for Hank to try on and said, "Walk around a little bit, then let me check how they are fitting you."

Hank walked around and said, "They feel really different, but pretty good I think."

William Henry pinched the toes and the bridge and said, "Yes, I think those will do nicely, so they're yours. Now, follow me to the back and I can show you how shoes are constructed."

In the back, Hank saw an old work bench covered with leather scraps, nails and an old tack hammer, glue, and a worn-down knife. William Henry seated himself on a stool at the bench and explained to Hank, "First we select the fine leather for the uppers and trace the patron's pattern onto it. Then we trim it to the pattern, then stitch the two halves together. Then for shoes, we punch holes for the laces and put in placeholder laces of leather scraps. Then the uppers are stretched over a wooden last or mold. The leather is worked with pliers and the hammer until it perfectly fits, then the laces are properly aligned and tacked into place. Then a heavy leather welt is sewn in place on the bottom of the upper. This supplies the connection between the uppers and the outsole bottom where the sole is sewn on, and the heel is attached. After the welt is sewn on, the tacks are pulled and the shoe last removed, which William Henry demonstrated. He then spread glue, glue they made at the tannery he informed Henry, between the welt and a first strip of leather for the outsole. Then he attached a small metal strip applied with glue to keep the shoe from breaking down between the sole and the higher heel. Then he added another strip of leather applied with glue. Then a final, thicker but shorter strip is sewn on which can be replaced or enables the shoe to be resoled. Then several smaller strips that have been glued one atop another are attached for the heel. The sole and heel are then trimmed with a sharp knife and finally edge sanded for a clean edge. The uppers are then polished to a high shine and as final steps an innersole is installed and new laces added." Holding up a newly finished pair of shoes, he added, "And that is that."

Hank was most certainly impressed. He had no idea of all the steps necessary to produce a single pair of shoes. He asked, "Are you going to try to teach me to make shoes?"

William Henry responded. "Well, your grandfather and I talked about that. I said if I have a son someday, I will wish him to follow in my footsteps to become the next Kearney shoemaker. For now, though, I think it might be wise to begin teaching you the trade. However, we did agree to have you start at the beginning and learn the leather tanning process first. Your grandmother thinks you need to learn to read and write before trying to pursue a trade. As a compromise, we decided to have you work at the tannery from 6 am until 4 pm. Go home and further your education from then until supper time around 7 pm. The tannery is just at the edge of town next to the farm, so an easy walk. Do you have any questions?"

Hank was thinking these people have given me more than I've ever had. I have clothes, food, and my own room to sleep in. I guess it isn't too much to ask me to do some work. His only question then was, "Are you or is somebody going to take me to this tannery place in the morning?"

William Henry answered, "I will take you and introduce you to Max, our foreman at the tannery, and he will show you what you will be doing and how to do it."

With that decided, Esther and Hank left the shoe shop. As they were walking home, Esther asked, "Hank have you ever been to school or had any formal education?"

Hank answered, "I'm not sure what you mean by formal education, but I've never gone to school. I always went with my dad, and he taught me how to add and subtract numbers and taught me to always talk correctly, kind of. Sometimes I don't understand what people are saying to me. We never had any books or writing stuff, so I didn't learn any of that."

"Would you like to learn to read and write?"

"Yeah, it would be nice but I'm getting kind of old to be learning in school."

"No, I was thinking of teaching you at home as best I can. At least give it a try if you are willing."

"Okay."

They had reached the front door and had just opened it when they saw Millie reaching over to pick up a sack. Millie said, "You just missed Molly. She came by and dropped off some of Mike's old clothes she thought Hank might be able to wear and I was about to take them to his room."

Esther answered, "That was nice of Molly! Hank, why don't you take the things we bought plus the sack of clothes down to your room and try on Mike's to see if they fit okay? If they don't, Millie may be able to hem them up or whatever is needed."

"Okay," said Hank as he gathered them up and headed to his room.

A while later he came back to the kitchen where Esther was talking with Millie as she prepared lunch. Hank said, "The shirts and jacket fit well. The sleeves may be a little long, though. Esther turned and looked at him as he exclaimed, "The pants are all too long, though."

Esther laughed a little as Hank was standing there in his stocking feet with a pair of Mike's pants on that nearly completely covered his feet.

"Maybe a little," she said. "Millie, can you hem the pants up so they will fit a little better?"

Millie said, "Yep, I can handle it. Can't have him walking around with his pants over the end of his shoes."

8

The next morning at 5:00 am, Hank was awakened by Millie tapping at his door and announcing, "Breakfast will be ready in 10 minutes and Henry will be here to take you to the tannery shortly. Rise and shine!"

Hank dragged himself out of bed, thinking 5:00 am comes awfully early, but he managed to get dressed and to the table in time for breakfast. He had just finished eating when William Henry arrived to pick him up. Together they walked to the tannery, arriving several minutes before the 6:00 am starting time. Once inside, William Henry introduced Hank to a large balding red-headed man with a full beard. "Max, this is Hank, and Hank, this is Max. He'll be showing you what to do."

Max shook Hank's hand and said, "Pleased ta meet ya Hank, ma names Maximillian O'Toole but everybody jus calls me Max. Henry here told me to teach ya everything I know. Should take all of a couple a minutes." This was followed by hearty laugh from Max. "Follow me and we'll get you started."

As they walked through the building Max explained, "We're jus a small tannery. We only tan hides for Mr. William Kearney's boot and shoe making and he's particular about his leather. In cities like Dublin and Belfast there are large tanneries that tan pig skin, sheep skin, and horse hide besides beef hides, and they sell it to whoever wants to buy. Those cities also have factory booteries that make boots and shoes for whoever can afford them. Often middlemen who then sell 'em to stores to resell to the public. Here we buy hides from whoever is butchering in the area, but we check them over fairly good to make sure there are no scars and such damaging the hide."

They arrived at the far end of the tannery and exited to a dock area where Max said, "This is where we get the hides in and after inspection, put them in barrels of salt water which keeps them from drying out, and the salt draws out some of the oils and such from the hide."

Hank heard this but also noticed the dock was right next to the William Kearney farm's horse pasture and there were horses frolicking just across the fence. Max noticed Hank's attention had been diverted and said, "A beautiful animal, aren't they?" Then let out a whistle which caused one horse to raise its head and come trotting toward the fence. Max and Hank walked over to the fence where each scratched the horse's chin and patted her neck. Max reached into his jacket pocket and pulled out a handful of oats and let the mare eat them from his hand saying, "I've always liked horses, so some days I bring a few oats in my pocket. Give a whistle and this mare has learned the whistle means I have some oats for her. Sometimes the others will all follow her over to see if they get some oats too."

Hank said, "Good thing to remember. Sounds more fun than lugging fresh cowhides into saltwater barrels. You'll have to teach me how to whistle through my teeth like that."

Max laughed and said, "Sure thing, but better get back to showing you the rest of the tanning process."

They reentered the building and Max took Hank through all the different steps necessary to tan leather including the scraping of both sides of the hide. One to remove all the hair from the outside and the other to remove a thin layer of fat and any flesh on the inside. Max told Hank the scraping is what he would be doing for a while until he mastered the technique.

So, the next few days, Hank went to the tannery for the day then arrived back at the house a little after 4:00 pm where Esther had set up a table in the parlor for his reading and writing lessons. She had made up cards with all the letters of the alphabet and had Hank memorize them. She also went over the vowels and vowel sounds and how to sound out words.

However, Hank didn't go directly into the house from work at the tannery. Working in the tannery stunk to high heaven and Hank would arrive at the house smelling the same. Esther had a sort of shower made up in the carriage house where Hank was to remove his clothes, wash up and put on clean clothes before entering the house. Millie would then gather his soiled clothes and wash them and hang them on the line.

Hank also noticed something else. His grandfather took no interest in him at all. He never spoke to him even if Hank greeted him. William either went to the farm or to the shoe shop during the day, arrived home for supper and maybe talked with Esther a bit or to Millie, but never to Hank.

When Sunday arrived, Esther told Hank to put on his best clothes that Kyle had bought for him because it was Easter Sunday, and they would all be attending church as a family as they would every Sunday from then on. Hank wasn't sure what Easter Sunday meant, but knew people went to church on Sunday to listen to the preacher. Pat O'Conner had taught him that at the workhouse.

William, Esther, and Hank could walk to church on this beautiful spring day, but Hank couldn't help but notice the carriages either passing by them or at the church. The Anglo-Irish aristocracy was arriving in all their finery. Some arrived in their enclosed Clarence carriages, others in Barouche or Phaeton carriages with their tops folded down. The ladies all dressed in beautiful and undoubtedly new dresses and the men in suits complete with silk waistcoats, ties, and the finest top hats. When they entered the church, each family was ushered to their assigned pew to be seated. Hank noted the Anglo-Irish landlords were seated toward the front, including Richard and Kathleen Summerfield and their children. The Kearney's pew was toward the back of the rows of pews and besides Hank, Esther, and William, held the William Henry Kearney family and Kyle and Molly Kearney.

Once everyone was seated, the organist began playing and all rose as the minister (Esther had informed Hank the gentleman was to be referred to as the minister or as Pastor Jones, never as the preacher) walked down the center aisle and up to the pulpit. He raised his hands and asked everyone to bow their head in prayer just like at the workhouse only now everyone did bow their head as the minister gave prayer. The minister then read from the Bible, followed by his sermon where Hank heard for the first time that Jesus, the son of God, had died on the cross for all our sins and that whosoever believes in him shall not perish but will have everlasting life in heaven. Hank had never heard anything like this before and wondered to himself if he could maybe see his father again in heaven if he believed? He would have to ask Esther about that and thought he would have to learn more about this religion stuff.

There was another prayer at the conclusion and then the congregation was ushered outside, where several gathered in conversation. Hank was introduced to Henry and Margaret's three daughters and Hank noticed Margaret was again with child. He had not noticed that when they were first introduced. Hank also met Richard Summerfield for the first time and his two young sons tended by Kathleen. Richard looked different than what Hank had expected. He was rather large with a potbelly, a handlebar mustache, and not a handsome man. Hank thought to himself that the rather attractive aunt Kathleen must have seen something besides good looks in Richard. However, he was friendlier than Hank thought he might be since he was English.

Kyle and Molly gave them a ride back to the house and stayed for Easter dinner. Hank assumed dinner had been prearranged. After dinner, Kyle and William retired to the parlor and talked about things on the farm without asking Hank to join them. He was definitely under the impression that his grandfather wanted nothing to do with him.

For the rest of the year and into the next, Hank spent his days in the tannery and the evenings with Esther, trying to learn to read and write but now with the addition of Bible readings and stories. Hank enjoyed hearing the Bible stories even if he was struggling with the reading and writing. Attendance at church every Sunday became a normal part of his routine. Max would occasionally send Hank over to the farm with Kyle when work was slow. Hank enjoyed that because he and Kyle got along well, and he would allow Hank to tend to the horses. It was on one of those visits with Kyle that Hank asked, "Uncle Kyle, there is something I don't understand, and I thought maybe you could explain it to me. How come my dad didn't stay here and work? How come he went off and worked somewhere else?"

Kyle answered, "How come I get all the tough questions?" He thought for a moment then said, "I guess you're old enough to hear the whole story as your Uncle Francis related it to me. There used to be a family on the other side of town named McGhee that had two daughters. The oldest, Jeanne, had found a position as a maid in Liverpool and was working there. Unfortunately, Mrs. McGhee got sick, and Jeanne was called home to help care for her with permission from her employer. When Jeanne arrived, Thomas saw her, and it was love at first sight for both of them. Every chance Jeanne could get away from tending her mother and Thomas could hitch up a team, they were together. Going on picnics down by the river, or up in the hills to overlook the valley. But when Mrs. McGhee got better, Jeanne had to go back to Liverpool to work as a maid.

Now go forward a few months and Jeanne discovered she is pregnant. She hid it as long as she could but eventually her English lord found out and she was fired. He had no use for an unwed pregnant Irish maid so sent her out. He was good enough to buy her passage back to her folks in Ireland. That's where you come in. You were born on the trip back across the Irish sea. Jeanne went to her parents and through her sister and Francis got word to Thomas. Well, they were still in love, so Thomas and Francis went over to the McGhee's. Don't know if you knew this, but Francis and Thomas, being only a year apart, were like two peas in a pod. They were not only brothers but best friends. Between Jeanne, Thomas, and Francis it was decided Jeanne and Thomas should get married so, somehow, they arranged a marriage by a Catholic priest as the McGhees were Catholics.

The three of them then picked you up and went ahead to your grandparents' house where Thomas announced that he and Jeanne were married and were here to present their new grandchild. Thomas kind of expected that the news would not be received well by his father but did not expect William's tirade to follow. William said, 'No bastard child of a Catholic whore was going to live under his roof.'

This caused Thomas to get mad and he grabbed his father and threw him up against the wall, ready to slug him. But he thought better of it and let him back down. William straightened himself, turned to Thomas and said, 'Get out of my house and take your trash with you. I never want to see your face darken my door again.'

So that was it. William just could not see or accept what had happened. Thomas, Jeanne, and you were banished. Esther, through Francis, managed to get Thomas some money and related to him to write to Francis when they got settled. Thomas did manage to write that one time and Esther answered. That was the old letter your father gave to you to keep. That is also why a few months later Francis immigrated to America."

Hank was dumbfounded. He had a lot to absorb but was glad Kyle had told him the story because now a lot of things started to make some sense. When he went back to the house, he couldn't concentrate on any of Esther's lessons and when William arrived for supper, Hank had a bitter taste in his mouth and a sudden rush of hatred for the man before him. He couldn't care less if the man ever spoke to him again.

Hank had little choice but to continue with his routine at the tannery and Esther's lessons, but when William Henry and Margaret had a baby boy in August, he knew he was never going to be a shoemaker. One afternoon when Max had sent him to the farm, Kyle approached and said, "We just got a letter from Michael. He'll be coming home for the holidays and he's looking forward to meeting you. I told him you were a horse lover like him."

"Glad to hear it," said Hank. Kyle had talked about Michael working with racehorses. He'd told Hank that Richard Summerfield had written a letter of recommendation for him to an English lord and how Michael had been hired as a stable hand but was now an assistant trainer. That got Hank to thinking about his own future. He knew he was becoming a man.

Puberty had mostly passed, and he now had a few whiskers growing on his upper lip and chin. He had never gotten the growth spurt lots of boys have. He was a little over five feet tall and would probably grow no taller. Esther had told him it may have been because of poor nutrition in prior years. He also knew the tannery held little interest for him and now that Henry and Margaret had a son, William Henry would groom their son to be the next Kearney family shoemaker. Hank would really like to work with horses but had no idea how to achieve that goal.

As he walked to the house that late afternoon for another of Esther's lessons, he was dreading it. He had learned the alphabet but learning to read or write had been a real struggle, and now he felt he was getting too old to still be receiving those lessons. He saw a commotion at the house, so he ran to see what was going on. Molly intercepted him and took him to the side of the house where she said, "Millie sent a neighbor to get me because William collapsed on the floor and Esther had been unable to help him get up again. Kyle is on the way here as is William Henry. It looks like he may have had a stroke and may be paralyzed on his left side. Esther and the doctor are with him now so why don't you wait in the kitchen with Millie until Kyle and Henry arrive."

"Alright," Hank said and went to the kitchen where he found Millie pacing and wringing her hands with worry. She seemed relieved to see Hank and had him sit down saying, "I'll fix you a bite to eat. It gives me something to do besides worrying."

Hank was sitting at the table eating when Kyle entered and motioned for him to stay seated. Kyle headed to the bedroom where William had been taken. This whole scenario revived long forgotten memories for Hank. Memories of when his mother had died, which made him think of how William had banished his parents. That raised mixed emotions about Hank's concern for William's health. Finally, Kyle returned and said, "It appears your grandfather is indeed paralyzed on his left side and will be confined to bed for quite a while. Esther and Millie will be his caretakers and Esther will not be able to continue your lessons. Why don't you go gather up a few of your clothes, enough to last several days, and you can come and stay with Molly and me for a while at the farm."

Hank did as he was told, gathered some clothes and placed them in a pillowcase, not knowing what else to do. He got in the buggy, seated between Molly and Kyle, with no one speaking all the way to the farm. Each was lost in their own thoughts. While Kyle handled the team, Molly led Hank to Michael's bedroom, telling him, "We'll put you in here for now and see how things go. Michael will be home in a couple of weeks, so we may have to figure out something different."

The next morning Kyle awoke Hank, told him to get dressed and meet him in the kitchen. Once Hank came stumbling out still half asleep and half dressed, Kyle said, "Sit down; we have some decisions to make. You've been working at the tannery with Max for well over a year now, do you want to continue working there or would you rather be working here at the farm?"

Hank didn't have to think too long before saying, "I do like Max, but I think I would rather work at the farm where I can be around horses instead of stinking cowhides."

Kyle replied, "I was kind of expecting that answer. I'll tell Max right after I take you out to get started milking cows. When that's done, we'll feed the calves, then take the hayrack out to start hauling in hay to store for winter feed for the horses. The fall harvest is pretty much wrapped up, so you got out of doing that work."

Hank was thinking, doesn't sound like I'll have much time to spend with horses, but said, "Okay sir, I'm ready to go to work."

"Why don't we have some breakfast first. How do you like your eggs?" Kyle and Molly didn't have a Millie for help, so Molly had arrived in the kitchen to begin the breakfast preparation. As soon as Kyle had slurped down the last of his hot tea he and Hank headed for the barn while Molly cleaned away the dishes.

As they walked toward the milk barn, Hank asked, "How big is this farm, Kyle?"

"That's Uncle Kyle to you! Okay? Well, we are nowhere near as large as the plantations around here including the Summerfields. Your grandfather managed to acquire around 300 acres in his name, and I've added about another 100 of my own, so nearly 400 acres. We raise wheat, oats, and hay plus pastureland to support a sizable cattle herd and enough left for a small dairy herd and horse pasture. There's you and me plus three or four hired hands to keep it all going. A couple of the hired hands and their families live right here and raise garden vegetables for all of us. They also gather berries down by the river and make jams and jellies for us all and pick the fruit from the fruit trees around here. A couple more hands walk out from town and only work part time. We try to keep them working enough so they can support their families and we share some of our bounty with them."

Hank was thinking that it was quite a bit different than the plantation where his father had been a tenant farmer, but said nothing about that. He said, "That sounds awfully big to me. How big is Aunt Kathleen and Uncle Richard's place?"

"Well, I'm not exactly privy to that information but I've heard several thousand acres. Some of it is pretty rough ground, so most of it is devoted to cattle raising now. There were some tenant farmers but, with the new laws, Richard paid their passage to America, and I heard he gave them a little extra money to get settled there. From what I hear he is one of the few landlords treating his tenants halfway decent. Not sure they all wanted to leave Ireland, but at least they will have a shot at making a new life in America."

"Yeah, that sounds a lot better than the way Dad and I were treated."

Kyle had handed Hank a milk bucket as they had been milking while they were talking. Kyle had milked three cows to Hank's one but at least he had milked one and knew it because his wrists were aching from the chore. Cows were a little different than goats, but the process was the same. They carried their pails to the icehouse, where they were stored until the cream could be scooped from the top and a portion of the milk saved for them.

The rest of the milk was poured into buckets and fed to the dairy calves in a pen outside. Kyle explained that the hired men often did this chore but, because of William's condition, he had sent them out to start loading hay as he wanted to stay close to home in case his mother needed him.

While Kyle went to tell Max that Hank was now working for him, he sent Hank to the house to see if Molly had heard any word about William. Having heard nothing, Kyle and Hank then went to the horse barn and harnessed up a team to attach to the hayrack. Hank was already petting the horses when he asked, "Have you given these horses names?"

Facetiously Kyle answered, "Yes, we have. I would like you to meet Hank and Kyle, two of the finest work horses in the land."

Hank laughed out loud and said, "I can think of no other names that suit them better."

The next two weeks passed with some improvement in William, but he was constantly hollering for Esther out of the right side of his mouth. He seemed confused and very irritated, furious with his inability to care for himself at all. Esther looked drained, and Kyle was now concerned about her health. Kyle and Molly or Kyle and Hank checked on Esther and William every evening. Henry or Margaret checked on them every morning. Millie did her best to take care of things at the house as well as all the comings and goings. She always tried to have a tea kettle going so tea could be served if anyone wanted it. Millie too, was looking a bit stressed.

Everyone's spirits seemed to lift when Michael arrived for his long-awaited trip home from Liverpool. He came to his grandparents' house first; Molly having written to him about his grandfather's stroke. He entered by giving Millie a hug while spinning her around, placing her back on her feet and moving to his grandmother. He clasped Esther's hands in his and then gave her a hug while asking where William was. Esther pointed to the bedroom and Michael went down the hall and into the room and said, "Hello grandfather! How we doing today?"

William kind of squinted and raised his right hand as if to wave hello but instead yelled, "Esther, Esther you out there? I need you!"

Esther rushed in, but William couldn't remember why he wanted her. She helped him scoot down in the bed, covered him and said, "Why don't you take a nap, dear. I'll be back in a little while."

Michael wasn't sure if his grandfather knew him or had even really seen him, but with that, Esther and Michael partially closed the door and went into the parlor to catch up on Michael's exploits. Millie entered and served them tea and crumpets. It was about an hour later when Kyle, Molly, and Hank arrived to check on Esther and William. Michael had seen them arriving and kind of hid next to the wall in the parlor until Millie escorted them in, when Michael exclaimed, "Surprise! I'm home."

Molly gave a jump and then emitted a little scream of excitement before grasping Michael to give him a hug. Kyle just had a big grin and Hank looked down and shuffled his feet until Kyle said: "Michael, I would like you to meet your cousin, Hank."

Hank and Michael shook hands and Hank said, "Pleased to meet you, Michael."

"Just call me Mike, nearly everybody does these days. Man, I've been hearing about you for over a year now. Every time I got a letter from Mom, she was telling me something about you. I guess Dad says you like horses about as much or more than I do. You work on the farm now, or are you still over at the tannery?"

"I've just started working at the farm and I think I'm going to like that better. The smells at the tannery were almost too much for me some days. Uncle Kyle has told me about you too, and I want to hear everything about the horse races, especially those steeplechase races."

After checking on Esther and William and seeing if Millie needed anything, they moved to the carriage, and all headed home to the farm together. Mike was still telling Hank about a specific steeplechase race called the Grand National when they arrived home. Mike told his mother, "Don't worry about the bedroom. It's a double bed and Hank isn't that big. So, I don't think he can kick me out of bed for the couple of weeks I'm here."

Hank said, "Yeah, that is okay. I don't think he can kick me out either and maybe I can get even more information about Aintree and the races there."

Kyle couldn't help but notice the instant camaraderie between Mike and Hank and their joint love of horses. However, with Christmas rapidly approaching, there were lots of things to get done, though it would be nice to have Mike home for the holiday. For several years, Richard and Kathleen had hosted a large Christmas dinner for the whole family on Christmas day. However, Kyle and Molly hosted a Christmas Eve meal for the families of their hired hands. Their home wasn't all that large, but by utilizing the kitchen, dining room, and parlor they could seat everyone.

The Christmas Eve supper went off without a hitch with everyone enjoying a traditional Irish Christmas meal. However, the Christmas day dinner was pretty subdued as Esther didn't think William should attend, so neither would she. That necessitated Millie staying with them, so she could not visit her family either. Richard and Kathleen's boys and Henry and Margaret's girls had a great time though, and the whole family enjoyed spoiling the new baby.

It was a few days later when Mike and Hank were sitting on a rail of the corral fence with Mike explaining how steeplechase racing began in Ireland with races from church steeple to church steeple, hence the name. He also told Hank he would be leaving the next day to return to Aintree and go to work. They saw Richard approaching in a Tilsbury coach with a riding horse attached at the back. He pulled the one-horse rig to a stop in front of them and said, "Glad I caught you Mike before you headed back. See the mare back there, she was my favorite riding horse until the last week or two. Every time I try to mount up, she rears up and I thought maybe you could tell me what's bothering her."

"I can give it a try," said Mike as he untied her from the back of the coach and led her into the corral.

He walked around her, put the reins over her neck, put his left foot to the stirrup and started to mount up. He had no more than sat in the saddle when the mare reared up. Failing to unseat Mike, she then pitched forward, then reared backwards again. This time Mike slid off her back and to the ground, worried she might come clear over and land on him.

Hank, seeing this, jumped from the rail and secured the reins. He led the mare along the fence, loosened the cinch and put the saddle on the ground. After climbing the fence rails, he gently climbed on the back of the mare. He reached the reins and again gently turned her away from the fence. The mare went forward with no problem. He was seated well back on her back and leaned forward as he took the mare in a circle to the right and then to the left, and finally in a series of figure eights with the mare never bucking once.

Mike exclaimed, "Wow, you look just like a jockey riding her."

At that, Hank rode her over to the fence and hopped down. He went over and turned the saddle upside down and placed his knees against the lambswool of the underside on each side by the stirrups. This spread the saddle tree, exposing a split on the left side. A needle-sharp piece of wood was projecting through the lambskin. Hank called Mike and Richard over to have a look and said, "The saddle tree is broken and every time you put a foot in the stirrup or swung into the saddle with your full weight the poor horse was getting stabbed with that piece of wood. I imagine she has a pretty sore bruise, and you can see a little swelling there on her left side, so let her heal up for a few days, and get a new saddle and she'll be fine. Though she might be nervous at first."

Mike was impressed and said, "How did you know?"

Hank replied, "I noticed when you took the reins and walked around her that her eyes looked scared. Then when you had your quick dismount, I could see the pain in her eyes and knew something was wrong with the way she was cinched or something with the saddle. So, I thought I would give it a try bareback.

Richard was also impressed and said so. "I've been around horses my whole life and never have seen anyone able to read a horse's eyes like that. I know when they lay their ears back watch out, but reading their eyes is a new one. If you ever want a job working with horses, come on over to my place."

Mike said, "I think I could get you a job with my boss in Liverpool too, if that would interest you."

Hank was beside himself with excitement. He said, "You mean I could go with you and work with the racehorses?"

"Well, they may start you as a stable boy mucking out the horse manure, but you sure seem to have a natural talent with horses."

Richard responded, "If that is really what you want to do, I could write you a letter of recommendation to give Lord Sefton in Aintree. Like the one I wrote for Mike."

Both Richard and Mike could see Hank's excitement at the prospect so Richard said, "Maybe we should run this by Kyle first. He may have different plans."

This tempered Hank's enthusiasm some but as they turned to go visit Kyle, he was walking toward them to see what was going on. They explained to Kyle what Hank had done and how he was now kind of excited at the prospect of going with Mike to work with racehorses.

Kyle thought for a moment, then said, "I think that might be the boy's calling. I've seen him work his magic with horses before. Horses and him just seem to get along. Another thing is having him and Mike both at Aintree, they can kind of keep an eye on each other. That'd be one less thing for Molly to worry about if they were together. Course you two boys are going to have to tell Esther. She might not be too thrilled, to see you both go."

Hank thought Kyle was correct about Esther. Even though she was now tied down with William's care, she still had found time to pass on a small leather-bound New Testament book for Hank to try to read. She had bought it new for him in town. She had also told Hank she was proud of the way he had studied an old atlas, so he now had knowledge of where certain countries and cities were in the world. She had even been amused when he questioned her about the world being round because all he had seen was a lot of up and down.

After Richard had left and the other three returned to the house, Kyle told Molly of the plan then climbed to the attic to retrieve a suitcase for Hank to pack his clothes in. Kyle, Mike, and Hank harnessed up a team to the carriage and headed for Moneygall so they could gather the rest of Hank's clothes and the boys could say good-bye to Esther and William.

When they arrived at the house, Hank went in to pack his things while Mike and Kyle went to see William. Kyle understood Hank's reluctance to have anything to do with William so said nothing. They met again in the parlor, where both Mike and Hank gave Esther a big hug. Esther smiled through tears welling up in her eyes and said, "Goodbyes are so hard but inevitable. You boys take care and I do want to receive an occasional letter from each of you. You hear that Hank, an occasional letter?"

Hank wasn't sure he was able to write a whole letter, but he would ask Mike if he could perhaps add a sentence or two at the end of one of his letters. With that, they turned and gave Millie a hug at the door and headed back toward the farm. They were still in the driveway outside when the sweet smell of fresh baked goods wafted from the kitchen. They knew Molly had been baking some goodies to send with them on their trip. Fresh baked soda bread, some barmbrack and some boxty on the pan. Boxty is better eaten hot, but she had sugared the top to sweeten the offering. Molly handed Hank the letter of recommendation Richard had written and delivered that afternoon. After trying a few samples of Molly's baked goods after supper, they retired for the evening to be well rested for tomorrow's journey.

9

Before sunrise Kyle had the carriage ready as Mike and Hank finished a quick breakfast. They had to make it to the post road early in order to catch the mail coach on its trip to Dublin. Fortunately, they made it in time and there were but two other passengers so they could sit inside the coach. Mike, knowing it was a two-day trip to Dublin, struck up a conversation with the other passengers, a man and his daughter who was about the same age as Hank. Mike introduced himself and Hank and asked, "Are you heading to Dublin, as we are? We need to catch the ferry to Liverpool so we can return to our work after the holidays."

The man answered, "My name is Lawrence O'Meara, and this is my daughter April. We visited my parents in Ennis for the holidays and are now returning to Dublin, where I have a haberdashery.

Mike turned to the lovely April and asked, "Did you have a pleasant visit with your grandparents? Do you enjoy traveling through the countryside by coach? Have you made the trip before?

With a look into Hank's eyes and then a glance at her father, April answered. "I have made the trip a few times and do enjoy the countryside. Although I do wish the ride was not quite so rough. Seeing my grandparents is always a pleasure, but father says they spoil me too much."

With that, she again looked into Hank's eyes perhaps expecting a response from him. Hank, however, sat there red-faced and petrified. He had never in his whole life been around any girls near his own age and had never seen such beauty as the one sitting before him now, with her raven hair, deep brown eyes, perfect complexion, and sparkling white teeth. He didn't understand the warm feeling he was enduring or why his throat was suddenly so dry. He managed to give a weak toothy grin before Mike spoke again. "He's kind of shy. He's an orphan and has never really been around girls such as yourself before."

April said, "Oh, I see." While again looking into Hank's eyes and smiling a demure smile.

Her father then struck up a conversation with Mike to divert his attention from his daughter, feeling safe that Hank would be no problem. They stopped at an inn for a ten-minute break around noon where a new team of horses were harnessed to the coach. They would not stop again until the inn for the night was reached as darkness was falling. Mr. O'Meara and Mike managed to keep conversation between them going with an occasional contribution from April, but Hank was struck dumb the entire trip. He spent the trip staring out the window with just a glance or three at April to take in her beauty. They had supper that night with April and her father and after returning to their room, Mike teased Hank about his inability to talk to a girl. Hank pleaded with him for a little help in how one is to go about conversing with the fairer sex. Mike said, "Well, just pretend like you're talking with Millie or Esther."

"Neither Millie nor Esther looks anything like the vision of beauty we were with today. Can't you give me a little more help?"

"Well, ask her things like where do you go to school? Do you have brothers or sisters? Do you have a pet dog? You know you would make a rather good pet dog! You heel well, sit well, and never beg. Maybe she could just take you for a pet."

Hank hit him in the side of the head with a pillow, saying, "Thanks for all the help, asshole!"

The next morning while boarding the coach, Hank did manage to say good morning to April. She in turn said, "Good morning to you, Hank. Perhaps today you can tell me a little more about yourself."

There it was again, the dry throat, the flushed skin and the inability to utter a single word. Hank only said, "Uh er ahh. Mike, we didn't forget anything in the room, did we?"

"Nope, don't think so. After you, April," Mike said as they stepped into the coach with Hank following.

Once again Mr. O'Meara and Mike dominated the conversation, but Hank did manage to say he had never been to Dublin or Liverpool and was going with Mike to train horses for Lord Sefton. This brightened April's eyes and she stated, "Oh how exciting! What kind of horses?

To which Mike answered, "Racehorses mainly. Both flat races and steeplechase. Hank here has a gift with horses. I wouldn't be surprised to see him have horses dancing on their back legs one of these days."

That brought a laugh from both April and her father and another red face for Hank, but he did manage to say he really liked horses and then asked, "April, do you ever go riding?"

"Well, I tried a couple times at my grandparents but must admit I prefer to ride by coach."

To which her father replied, "We live above the shop in Dublin and rarely go much beyond the neighborhood. Nearly all that we need is close by so if we need to go further, we take a hackney cab or, on occasion, rent a carriage."

As they arrived in Dublin, Hank was amazed by the size of the city and the hub bub of people, carriages, omnibuses, and all other means of conveyance heading every which way. Their coach stopped in front of the general post office building where they all disembarked with Hank following Mike's lead and April following her father in the opposite direction but with a wave of her hand when she saw Hank looking back. Hank returned the wave then smiled to himself thinking it had been the most pleasant ride he ever had.

Mike led him through the Temple Bar area then along the river Liffey to their hotel, close to the Ha'penny bridge. They checked in without incident but had been confronted by a constant stream of displaced and emaciated peasants begging for whatever you could spare to help them get passage to America or Liverpool, or even something to eat. The begging peasants brought back images to Hank of his time at the workhouse and the trip with his father to Cork. He hadn't seen such things in his time at Moneygall. Most tenants had already been displaced by the time he arrived, and it was a small rural area far from any cities where the starving Irish congregated in hope of finding food.

The following morning, he and Mike boarded a ferry to cross the Irish Sea for Liverpool. It was a bright sunny day with a tailwind so the crossing would be smooth and quick. Having never been on the open sea before, Hank was both mesmerized by all the water and the view of Ireland and a little seasick. Fortunately, it passed by the time they docked where the river Mersey meets the Irish Sea. They had reached Liverpool and as they disembarked, Hank was surprised to again see hundreds and hundreds of poor Irish either begging or waiting to board one of the ships bound for Canada or America. The peasants, having spent the last of their money to secure passage, had nothing left to buy food and sometimes boarding could be days away.

10

Mike and Hank arrived in Aintree at the estate of Lord Sefton in the afternoon and proceeded directly to the stables where Mike introduced Hank as his cousin to Tom Murphy, the head trainer. Tom read Hank's letter of introduction and handed it back to him saying, "Looks like you come highly recommended. I know Mike's a good worker, so we'll probably take you on, but we'll show your letter to Lord Sefton in the morning when he's coming to check on the progress of a couple of geldings. Helps to make sure it's okay with him."

Hank said, "Thank-you and pleased to meet you. How do I approach Lord Sefton in the morning?"

"Mike, you know the stalls where we have those two geldings, you and Hank meet me there about eight in the morning. That's when Lord Sefton usually arrives, and I'll handle the introduction and show him your letter of recommendation. Now Mike, he can bunk with you for the time being anyway, so take your stuff over there and I'll see you in the morning."

With that done, Mike and Hank left for the bunkhouse where Mike introduced Hank to the other stable hands. They found Hank an empty bunk with a storage locker next to it for his clothes, then went with the others to the kitchen for supper. That evening, Mike explained to Hank Lord Sefton was instrumental in the building of the racetrack at Aintree, but stabled his horses here at the estate and had built a track for exercising and training his horses. He said, "In the morning I'll give you a quick tour of the stables and show you the grandstand and racetracks for the Grand

National before we meet Lord Sefton at eight. You got any questions before we hit the sack for tonight?"

Hank said, "I probably should have a whole bunch but I'm so excited about everything, I can't think of a single one."

The next morning, Mike and Hank took their tour, then met with Lord Sefton and Tom Murphy. It went well and Hank was ready to begin his new job as a stable hand with Tom Murphy as his boss. Tom told Mike to show Hank where to begin and then returned to his own job of exercising the horses. Mike said, "Follow me, I'll show you where your tools are and where to begin."

Hank followed Mike to just outside the stable where Mike showed him a large wheelbarrow and a manure fork. Hank took both and followed Mike back into the stable where Mike said, "Start with the first empty stall and work your way to the other end. Load out the straw and manure into the barrow and take it to the pile in back. Farm hands will spread it on the fields later. Then come back sweep and put down fresh straw. Check that there is plenty of fresh hay in the manger and put a measure of oats in the feed box from the granary. We'll be taking the horses out for exercise and want to bring them back to clean stalls. They've already taken the first ones out so get to it. You'll have to work steady to keep ahead."

Hank nodded and went to work as Mike left to retrieve another horse for exercise. So the routine went for a couple of weeks. Then Mike told Hank he would be gone for a few days. He along with Tom Murphy and a contingent of jockeys, groomsmen, and trainers were taking a couple maiden horses and a couple novice horses to a steeplechase race in Haydock Park, north of Aintree.

When they returned, they had one less horse, put down with a broken leg, and one less jockey, killed when he fell from his horse and was kicked in the head by another horse. The next week it was to Hexham for another novice race with the loss of another jockey, injured in a fall. When they returned, Mike hurried to find Hank and said, "We lost another jockey with a broken leg today and I talked with Tom on the way back about training you as a jockey because of your size. He has his doubts but may give you a shot because we're short on jockeys now."

"Really? I've never even rode a jumper before! What am I supposed to do to learn that?"

"Talk to the jockeys every chance you can get. They know we're short-handed and will try to help you if you do get the shot. Plus, Tom would probably start you on the trainer horses over hurdles then move you up to the higher jumps on the steeplechase course."

That evening after supper, Hank was talking with every jockey he could corner and Mike was right, they were forthcoming with tips on riding the jumpers. However, Hank didn't stop there. The next day he was talking with trainers, grooms, and even the horses to learn all he could. Hank's interest didn't escape Tom Murphy's attention, so on the third day he called Hank over and said, "I'm a little skeptical about making this call because you're a little young, and riding jumpers is very dangerous. However, tomorrow I want you to start working with Mike and the horse he's training. We'll see how you progress before making any further decisions."

Mike was actively training a four-year-old gelding named Nordic Thunder. The horse had won a couple flat course races in 1849 but was now being groomed for hurdle races and then hopefully chases as steeplechase races were called. Suffice it to say that Nordic Thunder did not like the hurdles. His instinct was to go around them rather than over them. When forced by the jockey, he would jump them but usually at a severely slowed, out of step pace. That was the state of things when Hank arrived as a new amateur jockey. Mike had just completed lowering a few hurdles to as low as they could go. He helped Hank on to the saddle and said, "Let's start at a decent trot and see how many of the low hurdles he'll take in a row. Hopefully, all of them."

Hank rode to a starting area and turned and headed toward the hurdles at a gallop. Nordic Thunder took the first and second hurdles in stride but at the third bolted to the left sending Hank over the horse's head and crashing to the turf on the other side of the hurdle. Hank jumped to his feet unhurt as Mike exclaimed, "That went well. Let's try it again and this time try bringing the horse over the hurdle with you. Okay?"

Hank grabbed Nordic Thunder's reins and started back toward the start, stroking the horse's neck and talking to him all the way. The second attempt went better than the first simply because Hank managed to stay astride the horse, but Nordic Thunder again bolted at the third hurdle. However, this time Hank had noticed something and asked Mike, "Can we put another rail on the turf behind the hurdle to force the horse to slightly extend his landing but maintain his stride? I think he is out of step when he reaches the third hurdle, so he bolts instead of jumping."

Mike thought for a moment then answered, "Good thought but I'm thinking just the opposite. Let's put the rail in front of the hurdle so he starts his jump slightly sooner. As the hurdle gets higher, we'll want him to do that anyway. If he lands closer to the hurdle after the jump, the quicker he's back to full stride for the next hurdle. Let's give it a try."

They placed rails slightly in front of the hoof marks Nordic Thunder had left when starting his jump. Then Hank once again mounted up and headed toward the hurdles at a gallop. This time Nordic Thunder jumped all five hurdles they had assembled. Hank was quickly out of the saddle and heaping praise on Nordic Thunder as he stroked his neck. Mike approached grinning and said, "I think that's it. He has another full stride after the jump to adjust his step for the next hurdle and now he knows how to do it. Let's run through it a couple more times to make sure he's got it."

Two more runs and Nordic Thunder had no problems, and a third run without the front rail went well also, so Mike and Hank headed back toward the stable. Mike said, "The Grand National is coming up in a few days so we'll have a lot of other horses and their trainers and jockeys coming to town. We'll be moving some of our horses to the racecourse and out of the stable at the manor until it's over. This will be your first chance to watch the race not to mention all the hullabaloo that happens around it."

Hank asked, "What hullabaloo around it? What do you mean?"

"Well, the Grand National is a lot more than a horse race. People from all over come to Aintree and Liverpool for the race, but every sort of huckster and shark comes to town also to try and separate people from their money. There will be all kinds of hawkers of food and trinkets as well as illegal bookmakers, card sharks, cockfights, pickpockets, and ladies of the night. Then you have residents tending horses and all manner of carriages right in their yard, for a fee of course."

All Hank could say was, "Wow!"

Mike was right. A full week before the race was to be run on February 27, 1850, dust clouds rose from every road leading to Liverpool. The train that now ran between Manchester and Liverpool was chock full of race fans on every run. Mike had told Hank over thirty horses were scheduled to run in the Grand National and another twenty or so in the novice chase before the big event.

When the big day arrived, Hank rose early but Tom Murphy, Mike, and a host of others were already gone to the racetrack. Hank along with a few other amateur jockeys, grooms, and stable hands were left behind at the estate with instructions to exercise the horses remaining. Hank was severely disappointed that he didn't get to see the race or all the excitement around it, but understood he was the new kid at the stable.

When Mike returned in the evening, Hank immediately pestered him to tell him all about it. Mike said, "Well, we didn't win or even place, but we did manage to have horses finish the race. The exciting part for you and me was Little Ab or Abd-el-Kader, an Irish horse won. It's only the second time a horse from Ireland has ever won. He's probably owned by a member of the Irish gentry but he's still an Irish horse. As far as the sideshows go, they seemed more subdued this year. The government was not allowing any more blood sports like cockfighting, dog fighting, or badger baiting to be held. At least not out in the open. There might have been some illicit ones behind the pubs or at the edge of town. Some of the poorer punters can't bet on the race so they bet on those things instead."

Hank responded, "I don't care about any of those but would have loved to see the horses run."

The rest of the year 1850 Hank spent refining his hurdle racing abilities and some actual steeplechase practice at the end of the year. In 1851, Tom Murphy continued to bring Hank along as a stable jockey and took him to ride warm-ups at several chases all over England. The highlight for Hank, though, was finally getting to ride the course at Aintree and to watch the races there. Once again "Little Ab" was the winner of the Grand National.

Hank was also constantly talking with Mike and especially Tom Murphy about horses and how to treat various problems they may develop. To Hank, Tom Murphy was a veritable fountain of knowledge about the physiology of horses. Tom knew their muscles, their bone structure, and what to do to restore a thoroughbred to peak racing condition if he came up lame, got colic or whatever. However, Hank was not only learning from Tom Murphy, but Tom Murphy was also learning from Hank. Tom had noticed no matter what horse Hank was riding, horse and rider just kind of merged into one smooth as silk unit. When Tom would ask, "How do you think they'll be running today?"

Hank would answer with something like, "The number one horse is not feeling it today and number two would rather have more oats, but number three can't wait to get out there and run."

More often than not, that is exactly the way they would run. Once again, it was almost like the horses were talking with Hank and he to them. Tom thought it was a crying shame Hank wasn't just a little smaller so his size could qualify him to be a jockey in the flat races because he could be a great one. But the fact was, Hank was too big for flat races and had the wrong birthright to make it as a jockey in the jumps. Tom knew it was Hank's dream and was dreading the day he was going to have to tell him his dream was for naught.

When the 1852 racing season began, Tom started taking Hank to every steeplechase he could and used him not only as a warm-up stable jockey but as an actual jockey on the stables number two horse or as a pacer horse jockey. He hoped another stable might see how good he was and sponsor Hank into one of the riding or hunt clubs necessary to get a professional jockey license but to no avail. Hank even rode some winners at some of the smaller tracks and by the end of the year had ridden on nearly every major track in England except the Queen's course at Epsom.

1853 began much like the prior year with Hank still riding as a stable jockey and occasionally getting a real ride in a novice or maiden race. The Grand National that year was to be ran on March 2 and a couple of days prior to the race Tom called Hank over and said, "We've lost Tom our second jockey to a broken leg and Lord Sefton has managed to obtain a special dispensation for you to ride as our number two rider behind his nephew, Baron Goodman, as the official licensed jockey. We're going to use you to set the pace and keep up with the leaders and out of trouble. The Baron will follow directly behind you."

Hank knew that Tom thought they had a legitimate chance to win the Grand National this year with their thoroughbred, Asher, and now he would be riding Gwynne, their second horse. Hank also knew that Lord Sefton's nephew, the Baron, was an excellent jockey even if he was among the few licensed aristocratic jockeys still riding in races.

March 2nd broke with a rain shower and cloudy skies, so as Tom Murphy gathered them together to go over strategy, they all knew it would be a soft and heavy track. Tom stuck with his original strategy with Hank being a pacer on Gwynne and with Baron Goodman following close behind on Asher. The theory was to let Hank and his horse eat the wind so Asher could save energy for the second lap finish. Hank was also instructed to avoid trouble on the jumps, if at all possible, even if it meant going to the outside. There had been thirty horses scheduled but nine had been scratched at post time so twenty-one were at the start.

Hank managed to be in the middle of the line at the release with the Baron just to his right. It was a mad sprint over the first couple of fences but at the third, one horse took a spill and brought down two or three others with him, while a couple more had to pull up. Some managed to remount but were now far behind. At Becher's Brook, three more took a spill and Hank had to manage to jump over one of the struggling horses while the Baron swung to the outside. One more fell before completing the first circuit. Another pulled up at the start of the second circuit. Then at the canal turn, Hank's horse was bumped hard by another horse pulling up. Hank cleared the next fence but noticed his left stirrup strap was broken and coming loose. His mount had also spent all her stamina and was slowing in the plough. Rather than risk injury to himself or his mount, Hank pulled up as the Baron aboard Asher streaked on by. There were now less than half the starters still in the race and a couple more would fall or be pulled up before the finish. Peter Simple pulled away at the end run in, followed by Miss Mowbray two lengths behind. The Baron aboard Asher tried to stick with the leaders but came in third and was fading at the end. Little Ab, the winner in the two previous years, managed to come in fifth, weakened and well behind the leaders. Peter Simple was apparently good on a soft track and became the oldest horse at 15 years to ever win the Grand National.

Hank led his horse, Gwynne, to the paddock where he met Tom Murphy. Tom said, "You ran a good race and did the right thing by pulling up."

Hank thanked him and turned to see the Baron arrive with a different opinion, "Why in the hell did you pull up? If you'd taken two more fences, Asher would have had enough left for us to have won this thing!"

Hank answered, "I didn't think Gwynne had enough stamina to clear the next fence and even if she did, I wasn't sure I could stay upside with a broken saddle."

The Baron just glared at him before stomping off and said, "Sometimes you must make sacrifices for the good of the team, you bastard! You cost us the race."

Hank was crestfallen. Nothing Mike or Tom said to him could cheer him up. Mike suggested they go see some of the attractions outside the track, but Hank wasn't interested. In fact, Hank was worried whether he would even have a job after the Baron talked to Lord Sefton. Tom tried to assure him that cooler heads would prevail. Tom said, "You and Mike take the rest of the day off and go have some fun and we'll see you in the morning."

Mike failed to get Hank to cheer up or to go anywhere other than back to his bunk where he laid for the rest of the day. The next morning, he woke up with Mike and they both made their way to the Lord Sefton stables. Sure enough, all the horses had been returned from Aintree racetrack, so both Mike and Hank returned to their regular duties exercising horses. At about nine thirty Tom Murphy showed up and took them to the side, saying, "I've just had a talk with Lord Sefton. Hank, he instructed me to pull you from any more rides for a while. Maybe the rest of the year. He said I could keep you on as an assistant trainer, but he had to do something to placate the Baron."

11

Hank was disappointed but thankful he still had a job. He decided he had to look at it as an opportunity to learn more from Tom and a chance to work closer with the thoroughbreds. And indeed, that was Tom's first lesson for Hank as he explained, "In the eighteenth century three Arabian stallions were imported to England and these three and their progeny are the basis for our thoroughbred British and Irish racehorse today. The three stallions were the Byerley Turk, the Godolphin Arabian, and the Darley Arabian. Other Arabian horses were imported, but these three foundation stallions and their offspring contributed the most to the establishment of thoroughbred racing stock. They were the sires for succeeding great studs like Herod and Eclipse. Eclipse sired an astounding 862 winners and near 90% of today's thoroughbreds can trace their male line back to him."

Hank replied, "I wish I knew how to write better. I would have liked to have that all written down so I could refer to it."

"I'll write it down for you as best I know it, but the aristocracy has it all down in a book anyway. Probably at the Jockey Club," replied Tom.

Throughout the summer, Hank continued as an assistant trainer. Staying behind as Tom and Mike and the rest of the racing contingent went to race after race. Then, just before the arrival of autumn, Mike came running for Hank with a letter in hand saying, "Hank, Hank wait up. I must talk to you."

"What's the matter?"

"I received a letter from my mother, Molly, and I need to read it to you."

Dear Michael,

So much has happened in the last month I scarcely know where to begin but know we need you to come home as soon as possible. Your father hurt his back in an accident and is bedridden for a few months and it is nearly time for the fall harvest. We desperately need your help.

Alas, sadly, your grandfather had another stroke and has passed away. Esther is in terrible shape, and we could use your help there as well.

Lastly, and you should tell Hank this, we received a letter from your uncle Francis' wife in America. He caught consumption and he has also died. In his will he left a part of his farm in Pickaway County, Ohio to Hank. I suppose because he has no children and he and Thomas, Hank's father, were so close.

Awaiting your prompt reply or appearance.

Your loving Mother

Mike said, "I've already talked with Tom and explained the situation. I told him I was leaving today to catch the ferry from Liverpool to Dublin. He said he understood but wondered if I was planning to return and if you were leaving too. I told him I didn't know if I could come back but would have you talk with him. "

Hank's head was spinning. A farm for him, in America! What about Tom and the thoroughbreds? Should I go see Esther and Kyle? Do Kyle and Molly need my help too? Finally, he asked Mike, "What do you think I should do?"

"Well, I know you like working with horses and Tom with the hope of someday being a jockey or a trainer. But I gotta tell you, I don't think you can ever be a licensed jockey, and as for being a trainer, I don't think you have enough schooling. You can barely read and write."

"Going to America, I don't know. I know I can book passage right down the road in Liverpool, but what's this Pickaway County and Ohio about? I don't even know what they're talking about."

I think Pickaway County would be like County Cork or County Tipperary in Ireland. It's called the United States of America and I think Ohio is one of those states."

"Well, where is it and how do I get there?"

"You'd probably land in New York and these days there might be a railroad going to Ohio, which I think is west of New York."

"All that costs money and I don't have more than a couple Sovereigns to my name. I know you can book passage from Liverpool for around five Sovereigns in steerage but it's a lot more if you want a cabin even if you join with five or six fellow passengers."

"Tell you what, if that is what you decide to do, I have five sovereign or so I could lend you. Then when you get rich from farming over there in America, you can pay me back. With interest of course." (chuckle)

"What about Esther and Kyle? Maybe I should go with you to help on the farm."

"Mom didn't say bring Hank with you, she just told us about Uncle Francis. I think with the hired men there at the farm, we can handle it. I'll tell Esther you send your love. I think she will be thrilled that Francis gave you this opportunity in America. I think that's what you should do, so I'll go pack up and bring you some money while you go talk with Tom. Here, you keep the letter. You might need it in America."

With that settled, Mike left, and Hank went to find Tom. Thinking to himself that things were happening awfully fast, he wondered if maybe he should slow down and think this through a little better. Finding Tom, he said, "Mike went to pack up. He said he showed you the letter."

Tom replied, "He didn't let me read it. He just told me what it said about his dad being injured and him having to go home and help at the farm. He did mention something about you inheriting a farm too, but mostly I was wondering if I was going to lose two good men at one time. Are you going with him?"

"No, the farm is in America, and I got to do some heavy thinking about that. Mike thinks he can handle things in Moneygall and that I would be a fool not to go to America and claim my farm."

"Well, I would appreciate it if you could stay at least a couple of weeks so I can try to find competent replacement help. Okay?"

"Okay! You ever been to America, Tom?"

"No, but I've read some about it. I'll try to give you a few pointers before you leave. Thanks for helping me out."

Mike arrived with his packed bag and gave Hank some money and said, "Take good care of it, it's kind of hard to come by. You and Tom get things talked over?"

"Yeah, I'm going to stay a couple of weeks or so, until he can find some replacements for his two best workers if that is even possible."

Mike and Tom both laughed, then Mike shook hands and walked away. For the first time since he had left the workhouse with Kyle, Hank felt alone in the world. He buried himself in his work for the next several days, even taking over some of the duties Mike had been performing.

Tom, true to his word, tried to fill Hank in on some of the things he had heard about America: "First off, I've heard some terrible stories about those famine ships hauling immigrants to America. So, take along some of your own foodstuffs. Secondly, I've heard you need to be careful in New York. The swindlers there would make the thieves at the Grand National look like pikers. I've also heard the country itself is beautiful and they practically beg you to take up some land and start farming. I've seen the bales of cotton and the lumber being brought in on the docks in Liverpool and its good stuff. Oh, and importantly, they don't use the same money as we do. They use dollars where we use sovereigns but don't let a money changer rip you off. Go to a bank. Tell you what I'll do, I'll go to a bank in Liverpool and see if I can get you a few dollars so you can maybe get a room and something to eat when you get there."

Tom's two weeks turned into a couple of months plus, but it did give Hank time to plan his voyage and to learn more about America. One of the groom's family had immigrated to America and he had received letters he read to Hank. Also, he had received a letter from Mike which he managed to read by himself with just a little help from Tom. Mike said his father was doing better and expected a full recovery. Esther was also doing better by spoiling Henry's little boy. The surprise was when Mike said he would not be coming back. Kyle had always told him someday the farm would be his, and it was time for him to learn the ropes of running the place.

In January of 1854 Hank went into Liverpool to inquire about booking passage to America. He was surprised to still see lots of poor Irish peasants trying to immigrate. He avoided the runners trying to sell tickets and went straight to a booking office. They told him few ships made the crossing in winter, and it would be better to wait until March when more ships sailed, telling him even in March and April ships had to be aware of floating icebergs when crossing. With that information, Hank decided to wait until after the Grand National scheduled for March 1st.

Tom kept Hank busy and let him ride as a stable training jockey but not in any hurdle or steeplechase races. Baron Goodman was still around and neither Tom nor Hank wanted to stir up any trouble. Toward the end of February, Hank secured his ticket aboard the immigrant ship Washington sailing from Liverpool to New York. On race day, Tom told Hank "I know you're no longer working for Lord Sefton, but you're welcome to come with the crew and watch with us."

Hank readily accepted then went and packed his old suitcase Kyle had given him. He walked alongside for the two-mile trek to the Aintree racetrack. He was feeling a little remorse about watching his last steeplechase. Before the start of the race, Tom pulled him aside and said, "I managed to find a bank that would exchange Sovereigns for dollars so here you go. I exchanged one sovereign and got you four American silver dollars, a half dollar, and a couple nickels. There are twenty nickels in a dollar to tell you their worth. Finally got that off my mind so I can get back to my real job. Trying to win this race."

Hank thanked him saying, "I still have a couple Sovereign if you want me to pay you back."

"Nope, nope, you keep 'em. You'll be needing them along the way somewhere."

With that, Tom was gone. Off to check on the horses and jockeys. Hank wasn't sure he would see him again until after the race, if then. He had to walk the three miles from Aintree to the Liverpool docks and wanted to beat the exiting crowd after the race. His ship was to begin boarding that afternoon in order to leave on the evening tide the following day.

Hank was in search of a good spot to both watch the race and get away quickly after it was over. He was approached by a couple of men who inquired, "Do you have access to the stables? We are in need of a favor."

Hank answered, "Why? What do you need?"

"Well, you see, we and several others have bet a hefty sum on a certain horse, but we're concerned that Miss Mowbray, being the favorite, could ruin our plan. Consequently, we're prepared to offer you the sum of 10 Pounds, 5 now, 5 after the race if you could perhaps find a way for Miss Mowbray to miss the race."

Hank was instantly enraged, saying, "That is the most unscrupulous thing I've ever heard! Get out of my sight before I report you to a steward."

The men did eventually leave but not before rising and giving Hank a menacing look. When they had gone, Hank went to find Tom but was unsuccessful in the heavy crowd so returned to his spot to watch the race. A short while later as the horses began to appear for the start of the race, a murmur went up through the crowd. Less than an hour before post time, Miss Mowbray, a previous winner and the prior year's runner-up, had been scratched from the race. Hank was to never know why but it was reported later that someone had gotten to the horse and rendered her unable to run because of damage to a foreleg.

As for the Grand National itself, it was won by Bourton. The very horse that had banged against Hank the year before, causing his saddle to break and for him to pull up. Bourton won by twenty lengths causing Hank to wonder what might have been had he been able to ride.

Some of the crowd had already left before him as Hank rushed toward the docks at Liverpool. He didn't get to say good-bye to Tom or anyone else in his rush. He arrived in time to see a line had formed for the medical inspection required by the government before boarding. There had been so much sickness and death aboard the famine ships that now you were inspected before boarding. This inspection was by a government appointed surgeon, so in theory if you failed to pass you could get your money back. However, nearly everyone passed this cursory inspection and was allowed to board, including Hank with his old suitcase and a sack with blanket, eating utensils, and a supply of hardtack and jerky.

12

Henry's former boss, Tom Murphy, had read in the newspaper some information about the ship Hank was sailing to America aboard, the Washington, and had read it to Henry:

'The ship had an infamous voyage in the fall of 1850. One of the passengers, Mr. Foster, kept a diary of the trip that he subsequently published in the paper. The Washington was a large packet ship operated by Black Star Line. She had two spacious decks with cabins besides the steerage passengers and could handle up to 700 passengers in total. Mr. Foster found the passengers on the upper decks were treated decently for the most part, but the immigrants in steerage were severely mistreated. The example given was a call for everyone on deck for their daily water allowance and then being ordered back below deck after only 30 or so received their allowance. Also, before ever leaving port and after being on board for one full day, no meal provisions were granted to anyone despite explicit wording on their ticket. Steerage passengers were severely abused during the entire voyage, subjected to abusive language and beatings for the most trivial of mistakes. The captain of the ship was never seen in steerage and the passengers were never informed about their location. The ship left port on the 25th of October and ran into a hurricane on the 22nd of November. Provisions had been hit or miss during the entire trip and on the 25th of November the 12th child to die from dysentery was heaved overboard. There is much more to Mr. Foster's article, but the Washington did finally reach New York on the 2nd of December. The publication of Mr. Foster's diary did cause an upheaval in the British Parliament but in the end, little was done because

of a lack of evidence. Similar or worse complaints were filed against other Black Star Line officers.'

As Tom related to Henry from the article, the land of milk and honey, America, comes into view with the appearance of the lighthouse at Sandy Hook and then the banks of the East River followed by the quayside docks at South Street Seaport. The ship's captain was responsible for listing all their passengers for the immigration authorities. However, with sometimes ten ships a day pulling up to the docks from Ireland and Liverpool, the officials were swamped, resulting in incomplete listings.

In truth, the land of the free would prove to be a very hard and often bitter struggle for the newly arrived immigrants. Work was not easy to find, and the Irish tended to band together in tenement slums subject to petty crime by their own brethren. Besieged by the street gangs of New York, they often lived among packs of wild dogs and feral pigs roaming the streets. Rubbish and worse laid ankle deep in side streets and alleyways.'

Tom said, "Such is the world where you will soon hope to disembark according to the article. I thought you might like to know what I read about it."

"It doesn't sound too encouraging, but I do appreciate the heads up about what I might encounter."

13

Hank managed to secure one of the higher bunks and decided to keep all his belongings with him rather than stow it in the limited storage area. Many immigrants attempted to take some tools of their trade with them or some family memento but more often than not it had to be left dockside for scavengers to find. After the gangplanks were pulled, the Washington was pulled by tugs toward the mouth of the Mersey but made one more stop before entering the Irish Sea. A thorough search of the ship was conducted for any stowaways and the ship's doctor did another inspection of each passenger. Any passenger that was sick was sent ashore along with the stowaways, put out in a little dingy that came alongside the ship. The purpose ostensibly was to prevent sickness to other passengers but also to prevent fines for the captain upon landing in America. Two stowaways, young teenage boys, were found and three sick women and two of their husbands, along with attendant children, were put off the ship with no refund of fare. If they had stowed any belongings, those were also given up because they were put off with nothing but what they had with them.

With favorable tides and a favorable wind, the Washington was soon out into the Irish Sea. Hank chose to stay in his bunk, remembering the slight sea sickness he had endured in the crossing from Ireland to Liverpool. Others chose to go up on deck to get their last glimpse of land. No provisions or water was provided at all clear through the next day. Hank ate a little of his jerky but wanted to keep as much as he could for later in the voyage. He also noticed a good share of the passengers in steerage did not appear to be as destitute and starving as the ones he had seen when he first arrived in

Dublin and Liverpool. He discovered as the voyage progressed that many of these immigrants were Anglo-Irish who had lost their property under the Encumbered Property Act. Thus, they weren't the destitute, illiterate, starving Irish peasants, but educated former property owners who had lost everything at least partly because of their high living and leverage of their former lands.

The following day broke sunny and warm and steerage passengers were told to go topside to get fresh water and food provisions while the crew would swab the aisles below and tend to the toilets. Most passengers including Hank were able to get their provisions before being ordered back below because the crew was done cleaning. Hank did note that the cleaning job was somewhat worse than what was expected of him when he was cleaning thoroughbred horse stalls.

While passengers were getting their provisions, the ship's captain, a fellow named Page who stated he had been the captain ever since the ship had been launched, announced that the ship's doctor would be making his rounds in steerage to check passenger health and to ensure no infectious disease was being spread. The doctor's rounds became an almost daily occurrence, but if anyone needed cough syrup or something to settle a stomach, they were expected to pay for it before receiving it from the doctor.

The next fortnight went without any major incidents. Passengers were allowed to use the small fire brick ovens for baking and firebrick encircled fires for cooking. Provisions were systematically dispensed on most days, and it had been smooth sailing. Toward the end of the third week, they were hit by a late season nor'easter, a violent winter storm with gale force winds, sleet and snow. No one was allowed on deck except members of the crew on the lookout for icebergs. The storm lasted the better part of three days and caused a lot of panic and sea sickness below deck with the resulting fetid smells causing even more discomfort. The seas calmed at the end of the third day, but it remained bitterly cold, so no one spent long on the deck.

It was the following week that trouble began to brew. The passengers were sick, cold, and hungry; the crew was tired and hungry, and the officers were arrogant and belligerent, especially to the passengers in steerage. The winds had gone from gale force to nothing at all so the ship was nearly dead in the water and making little or no progress. To make matters worse, some passengers were becoming sick. The doctor was worried that some of the children could be coming down with pellagra or worse typhus. No one, with the exception of the captain and maybe some of the officers, had any idea where they were other than in the middle of the Atlantic Ocean, and a crew member in the crow's nest had spotted icebergs far off the starboard side of the ship. Hank primarily remained in his bunk through the storm and the later calm days. He had not spoken more than a few words to anyone. He was seriously wondering if he had made a terrible decision but the dream of having his own land where he could raise all the horses he wanted, kept him looking forward. Although, he doubted he would be breaking and training any thoroughbreds in America. Riding and draft horses were more likely to be his stock and trade. Hank was still lost in his own thoughts when a ruddy faced redhead appeared over the side of his bunk and said, "Hi, my name's Markus Muldoon and I'm in the next bunk down, and I just want to say I appreciate that you didn't puke over the side during the storm. If you would have, then I would have, and we would have had a cascading waterfall of up-chuck like I saw in some of the other bunks."

Hank was a bit unsure how to answer but finally said, "My name is Hank Kearney and I'm glad I could be of service. It was quite a storm, wasn't it?"

"It sure was. I'm sailing to America where I hope I can be a blacksmith. I had my tools, but the bastards wouldn't let me bring them on board. Too heavy they said, so had to leave them on the dock. Guess I shoulda been a damn watchmaker. Coulda kept all my tools in a vest pocket. What you goin to America for?

"I inherited a farm in Ohio, so I'm headed there to check it out." He wondered to himself if it was safe to befriend this Muldoon guy, but he seemed friendly enough.

"You traveling by yourself too? I lost most all my family to the famine and the damn Brits hardly let a man survive in Ireland, so I decided to head for America."

"Yeah, both my parents are gone, and I have no brothers or sisters. I have some uncles and one of them left me the farm. He went to America before the famine, and I guess he did well but got consumption. Left me the farm in his will because he had no children and my dad and him were best friends."

"I hope we get to America soon; I'm getting tired of this damn boat. Shall we go topside and see if they're gonna hand out any provisions today?"

Hank replied, "sure," as he climbed down from his bunk. It was then he realized just how big a man Markus Muldoon was. He had to be six foot three or more and weigh around two-sixty and it was all muscle. His arms were thicker than Hank's thighs and he had broad shoulders and a barrel chest. He wore a seaman's shirt that was laced at the top with balloon sleeves, but on Markus the sleeves were skintight.

They reached the deck to find a line of Irish peasants already forming up to receive provisions even though the crew had given no indication of passing any out. A couple of passengers had already started fires in the little firebrick ovens in the hope they would be able to bake some bread. Finally, the crew started to roll out some barrels of food stuff and removed the lids from the water barrels and their line began to move. Hank had just received his provisions when the first mate swung a wooden rod down on the back of Hank's hands, causing him to drop his provisions.

"Kids only receive half portions!" He shouted at Hank. It may have been the size difference between Hank and Markus that caused the first mate's error, but it was nearly a fatal mistake. He had barely uttered the words when Markus grabbed him around the throat and lifted him about two feet off the deck with one hand. Markus looked the now bug-eyed, red-faced first mate right in the eye and said, "Are you a blind man or just looking with eyes that do not see? He's as much a man as you or I and you best not be taking the rod to anymore Irish unless you want to swim with the fishes below."

After Hank had picked up his provisions, Markus continued to stare into the eyes of the first mate as he slowly lowered his dangling legs back onto the deck and released his grip from his neck. It was easy to see that the first mate was furious, but he did nothing as the line continued to move forward.

In the evening of the same day, a crew member delivered a summons to Markus from the Captain. He was being accused of assaulting the first officer and if found guilty would be hung from a yardarm and buried at sea. Hank wasn't sure there were enough seamen on board to even bring Markus to trial unless they used guns or blades. The word soon spread among the Irish passengers in steerage, and they vowed that no hanging of an Irishman would take place if it were within their power to prevent it.

It was the captain's intent to begin the trial the following day but during the night plans changed for everyone. A child had died, and the ship's surgeon said the cause of death was typhus, a mortal disease spread by lice in filthy crowded spaces. The very definition of the conditions for the poor Irish passengers in steerage. Victims of typhus usually succumbed within a week, but they suffered a horrible death. Rashes and sores appeared all over the body. Arms and legs twitched and shook uncontrollably. Fingers and toes turned black, and then just before dying a horrible odor—the stench of typhus. Before the sun rose in the morning, the rest of the child's family were showing unmistakable symptoms. By the time the sun was setting, nearly a dozen more of those who had been confined to bottom bunks, closest to the filth, were showing symptoms.

The captain knew they would never be allowed to dock in New York until the typhus had run its course. Plus, the captain could be fined up to a thousand dollars for each sick passenger that disembarked, a fate he was not about to endure. He quarantined the steerage passengers in the bow where the typhus began and quickly dispatched the dead overboard. Though they were no more than two days from the American shore, he folded the sails and sat dead in the Atlantic waters, hoping no more would contract the disease and they could bury at sea the dead who had.

A passing ship had reported a ship dead in the water to the port authority in New York, so after five days, a skiff arrived carrying port authority officers, a doctor and a harboring captain (a person familiar with bringing the ship to dock side). By the time of their boarding, seventeen passengers had died from typhus and three others were still suffering. The port authority officers, the doctor, and the ships doctor then went one by one through the passenger list and inspected each passenger on deck in the full light of day. The process took a couple of days and two more of the sick died but no new cases appeared. The whole ship was quarantined for another three days during which the last victim was buried at sea. The harboring captain then took the wheel and guided the ship to the American shore. No trial for Markus Muldoon was ever mentioned by anyone. He and Hank stood at the rail looking west to the land that would become their new home.

After the gangway was in place and the steerage passengers began to disembark, Markus and Hank joined the throng. Most of the steerage passengers were entering America with little more than the clothes on their back and with little idea of where to go or what to do next. The teeming throng at dockside didn't help, with boardinghouse runners, moneychangers, teamsters, dockworkers, dray wagons and occasionally family waiting for those coming ashore. Henry noticed a well-dressed younger couple where the husband seemed to be arguing with a moneychanger as he and Markus stepped onto the American shore. He turned to Markus and said, "We know I'm heading for Ohio. Where are you headed?"

Markus replied, "My Mom had some relatives immigrate several years ago and they settled in Virginia. I'm not much for the city life so I'll probably head south down around Richmond or maybe a little further south. One thing about a blacksmith, you show me a forge and anvil and a hammer, and I can make most of the tools I need. Plus, my grandfather was a tinker and taught me a little about tinning. So, if you bring the tea; I can make a cast iron stove and a tea kettle so we can drink it."

With that said, Markus held out his big mitt, shook Hank's hand and with a pat on the back they went their separate ways. Hank again noticed the young couple, now walking past the crowd and up the street. The man carrying two suitcases and his wife a smaller one. Thinking they might be headed to a hotel. Hank decided to follow them and get away from the teeming dock area and its adjacent cheap tenement houses and filthy slum areas. After a few blocks, the couple did indeed enter a corner hotel. As he was close behind them, Hank followed them in, just a few steps back. The husband was inquiring about the price of a room for him and his wife for one night and the clerk responded that with one dollar that included an evening meal of stew and a breakfast of biscuits and gravy plus tea or coffee. When they had paid and left, Hank stepped forward and asked, "How much is a room for a single person?"

The clerk answered, "Seventy-five cents to include the evening and breakfast meals."

"How much if I skip the meals?"

"The same because we still have to prepare the food for the other guests."

Hank took out a silver dollar and handed it over, getting a quarter and a room key in return. He then asked, "Is there a bank close by where I could exchange British money for American?"

"Cattycorner across the street is the one the hotel uses."

"Okay, Thanks! If a person wanted to get to Pickaway County, Ohio, what would be the best way to get there?"

"I don't know about Pickaway County, but if you're going to Ohio, I would take a train."

"And how do I go about doing that?"

"Well, the B & O Railroad, that's Baltimore and Ohio has a relay station I think on about forty-second street. You could probably go there and inquire about tickets to specific places."

"Thanks for the help. It's appreciated.' Hank went up to his room, took out his last two remaining one-pound Sovereign coins, locked the door behind him and proceeded to the bank. He exchanged the coins for nine dollars and a quarter. He now had a total of about fourteen dollars to his name and was wondering how much a train ticket to Ohio was going to

cost him. He went back to the hotel where he ate a very hardy supper, went up to his room and slept his first night in America. And a good night it was, no wave-tossed ship, no groaning or coughing from other passengers. Only sweet dreams of the green of Ireland and horses running free through the tall grass.

The following morning, Hank rose with the sun, ate a hardy breakfast then checked out of the hotel and started walking to the 42nd Street relay station. When he arrived, there was a short line at the ticket window, so he waited his turn. At his turn, the ticket agent offered a friendly, "Good morning! How can I help you?"

"I'm looking to travel from here to Pickaway County, Ohio in the quickest and most economical way."

"Pickaway, County, Ohio huh. Well, let me do some checking here." With that the agent turned and opened a couple of books behind him. Referring first to one then the other, and then back again. Finally, he turned and said, "It appears Circleville is the largest and maybe only town in Pickaway County. There is no rail service going there, but there is to Columbus, Ohio about twenty-five miles north. You have two choices. You can take a train to Buffalo, New York then a ship across Lake Erie to Cleveland and then a train again to Columbus; or you can take the B & O from here to Wheeling, Virginia on the Ohio river. There you can board a steamboat down the Ohio river to Marietta, Ohio where you can board another train into Columbus. The first choice would take a week or so longer and cost you more. The second option takes seven days and would cost you four dollars and seventy-five cents to get you to Wheeling. The steamboat and train to Columbus, maybe another three dollars at most."

Hank thought for a moment. The agent seemed to be kind of pointing him toward the B & O option, but he finally decided he had had enough of travel by ship to last him a lifetime, so he told the agent, "Let's go with the B & O."

"Great! Let me write out your tickets here and I think I can get you to our main terminal in time for you to catch the outgoing train at four-thirty this afternoon."

"Perfect!" Said Hank, then had the agent tell how he was to get from train to train and any details like where he could sleep, and where could he get something to eat. The agent explained that he had bought a seat and not a berth, so he should just sleep in his seat. The train would make frequent stops for water, coal, and to pick up or let off passengers, so many of the stops were long enough to get something to eat.

As he boarded the train that would take him to Ohio and that town—what was it, Circleville, Hank thought that overall, his first two days in America had gone well. He had followed Tom Murphy's advice and avoided the dock area of New York City and successfully exchanged his coins for American dollars. He also had secured his passage to Ohio but was a bit concerned about his money situation.

14

The first three days, all Hank ate was the jerky he had bought just before boarding. He spent most of his time during the day just looking at the passing scenery and the nights trying to sleep though the frequent stops seemed to always jar him awake. The various passengers seated next to him seldom said more than hello, and between some stops there was no one seated there at all. On waking on the fourth day, he felt some of the pangs of hunger from long ago, so at the next stop he bought himself a twenty-five-cent breakfast which included two eggs, biscuits & gravy and coffee. That meal plus his remaining jerky enabled Hank to last until the train reached Wheeling, Virginia.

The last fellow seated next to Hank did more talking than all the others combined. He had no more than sat down when he said, "Hello! My name is Jim Johnson and I'm a harness salesman for the G & R Harness Company out of Columbus, Ohio. I've been calling on the livery stables and other merchants that sell harness on this side of the Ohio river. We're strictly wholesale. We don't try to sell every farmer up and down the Ohio river valley. What's your name and trade?"

"I'm Hank Kearney, recently arrived from Liverpool on my way to Columbus or actually Circleville."

"Yeah, I can here that Irish accent, but you speak much better than most I've heard. Circleville huh, what you got going down there?"

Hank was a little guarded about this whole conversation, so he answered, "I have an uncle down there that's a farmer and I came over to help him and maybe get started myself. The Irish are nothing but slaves to their English overlords. No prospects there, so I managed to save enough for passage to America on one of The English coffin ships."

"I hear you! My grandfather came over from Sweden with a couple brothers and got worked to death in the Pennsylvania coal mines. My father wanted none of that, so he went to work for a carpenter. Tired of that, when he got married, they pulled up stakes and moved to Ohio. He first got a job driving a funeral coach for an undertaker and eventually learned that trade and went out on his own. Furniture business kind of goes hand in hand with the funeral business. You know, making sideboards and dressers ain't a whole lot different than making coffins. He even made his own fancy funeral coach which he had me driving for a while. He discovered the furniture makers in the northeast were a lot better at it than he was, so he started buying theirs and having it shipped out here. Has himself a booming business now but that undertaking stuff wasn't for me. Way too solemn and serious and dealing with those dead bodies, uh uh! So here I am, selling harnesses for the last three years. Got a wife and kid to support so gotta keep at it. We've reached Wheeling, so come with me. I'll show you the way to the steamboat boarding station."

They left the train platform, walked a ways, and then started down a steep hill to the water's edge of the Ohio river. Off to the left, a rear wheeler steamboat was tied to the dock. Hank and Jim Johnson entered a station just to the side of the dock and bought tickets for a dollar fifty each. Jim said, "I think you will enjoy this steamboat ride. You can move around wherever you want. Go up topside and maybe visit with the captain after we shove off or just look at the scenery as we go down river. This level has a bar and a salon where you can get a drink, play some cards, or sit and read a book or newspaper. Ours is a short trip so we don't need any sleeping cabins. These days if you want you can ride one of these all the way to New Orleans. Come on, I'll buy you a beer."

Hank had never had a drink of alcohol of any kind. He had heard the stories that all the Irish were good for was getting drunk and having babies. Plus, he had seen among the starving peasants the drunken sots lying in their own puke next to the gutters and fetid alleyways. He wasn't at all sure he wanted to start now, but decided to try it once just so he could have the experience. He took a sip, and it tasted bitter. He must have made a face because Jim Johnson asked, "What's the matter, don't you like it?"

"I must confess, I've never had a drink in my life."

"You're kidding! I think I had my first beer when I was about thirteen and may have had a nip or two from my dad's whiskey bottle earlier than that. How old are you?"

"I'm an orphan so no one is exactly sure, but I think I'm eighteen."

"Eighteen and never had a drink and probably never been kissed either, right?"

"Well actually no. I was on a coach ride once with the most beautiful girl I have ever seen and I think she kind of liked me, but I was too shy to even talk to her. Other than her the only girls I saw were the whores working around Aintree before the races, or some starving ones at the workhouse in Ireland."

"Boy, if I was a little younger and not married, I could get you a hell of an education right here in Columbus. Take a few more swallows. Beer has a way of tasting better after you drink a little more. Those first couple swallows are just to prepare the throat and stomach for more to come."

Hank took a couple more swallows and decided Jim might be right, as they went down a lot easier. However, he still wasn't convinced he liked the stuff all that much. He did manage to finish the glass and Jim asked, "You want to go up top and watch the world go by? I can maybe fill you in a little bit about girls because one of these days one is going to come along and set her hooks into you and if she isn't the right one, you're set for a life of misery."

"I've already pretty much had a life of misery. Kind of what it means to be Irish. Lost my mother when I was two or three, lost my father to starvation in the famine. Loaded dead bodies onto a hay cart then spent time in a workhouse where dozens were dying every day. A fourth of the population of my homeland either died or left. Then I got a chance to do what I loved,

working with horses, but they told me I can never be a jockey and can never be a trainer because I'm uneducated and can barely read and write. I come to this country on a damn English coffin ship where the Irish are stacked four deep in steerage surrounded by filth and treated like shit by the crew. We couldn't even come to shore until all the Irish dying from typhus had met their maker and then they were unceremoniously dumped over the side of the ship to a watery grave. Misery, yes, I think we've met before."

Jim sat there with his mouth open then said, "Jeez man, that's a lot to endure for a kid of just eighteen. Just let me say this: if you ever think you have found the love of your life and she loves you, make sure she loves you for who you are and not for what you have and will not try to make you into something you are not. Nearly all men need some refining by a good woman, but you've got to be you. I'm done preachin at you and we're nearly to Marietta already. Let's just watch the world go by at the rail."

That sounded like a good idea to Hank because he could feel a slight buzz from the beer and wondered if it had maybe loosened his tongue too much. Hank decided he had enjoyed the steamboat ride with its twin smoking stacks and the big paddle churning the water. The ride was smooth, nothing like a ship on the ocean. Jim had told him later in the summer when the rivers are lower, the boats must be careful about shifting sandbars where they could easily run aground. But as the boat pulled up to the dock, Hank was thinking he wouldn't mind a ride like this again.

Jim led him down the gangway and up the hill to the train station where they each bought a ticket for one dollar, then boarded the train for Columbus. Hank was thinking the agent in New York hadn't steered him wrong—the trip took seven days and the rest of the trip cost less than three dollars. He and Jim had mostly small talk on the trip to Columbus, Jim talking about his wife and two-year-old daughter. They had a house well north and east of the train station and Hank was heading south, so Hank asked if Jim could recommend a hotel. Jim said he was welcome to stay at his house, but Hank thought that to be too much of an imposition. Jim gave him the name of a hotel which he thought Hank could get a bed and breakfast for fifty cents. Jim also told him there should be a signpost outside the hotel pointing the way to Circleville. He said the road follows along the side of the Scioto River all the way there. It was dark when they finally reached Columbus, but the train was continuing to Dayton and Cincinnati. Jim pointed out the hotel to Hank then hailed a hackney cab. They shook hands and Jim wished him luck as Hank turned toward the hotel, still carrying his old suitcase.

Hank arose the next morning before first light. He donned his William Kearney Bootery work boots and a pair of workpants, which would be more comfortable to walk in for the twenty-five-mile trek to Circleville. He went down and ate a good breakfast, found the signpost, and started walking at a good pace. It was a beautiful walk along the river with trees often arching over the roadway, then open meadows with cattle grazing, followed by freshly planted fields, and then again, a canopy of trees. He met but a couple of wagons going the opposite way. One looked like a farmer going for supplies as his wagon was empty. The other maybe a seed salesman or something, as his wagon had a graphic on the side. Both nodded and waved as they passed on the roadway. He did pass one farm where three or four men were felling trees in a flat area, probably to become a field when the stumps were cleared. He wasn't sure how far he had walked when the sun started fading in the west but was pretty sure he was well over halfway. He was a little hungry but nothing like he had been in the past, so he found a comfortable spot next to the river and away from the road and settled in for the night.

At first light he awoke and was feeling a little hungrier. It was springtime so there were no berries to find and eat, but he did find some nettles. He had a cup in his suitcase from his ship crossing, so he got some water from the river, started a small fire, and brewed himself some nettle tea. It wasn't very filling, but it was something. He extinguished his fire, gathered his things, and started walking again. It was early afternoon when he walked into Circleville. On Main Street, he came upon a storefront with a painted sign above the window –Samuel Courtright Attorney at Law. Tom Murphy had told him to find a lawyer, so Hank opened the door and entered. He was greeted by a man about his own age who said, "Good afternoon! May I help you?"

"Are you the lawyer, Mr. Courtright?"

"No, I'm Russell, his secretary and clerk. Is there something we can help you with?"

"I hope so! My name is Henry Kearney and I have a letter from my aunt saying I inherited a farm from my uncle here in Pickaway County. I've come all the way from Liverpool and don't know how to proceed from here, but a friend back in England said first thing you do is get a lawyer, so here I am."

"Take a seat and I'll go ask Mr. Courtright if he can see you today."

The clerk disappeared down a hallway to an office in the back while Hank sat down and stared at a whole wall covered with law books. Momentarily, Russell returned followed by another man maybe in his forties but with a slight greying at the temples. He introduced himself as Samuel Courtright while shaking Hank's hand and said, "Come back to my office, Mr. Kerney, and bring your aunt's letter with you."

"Kar-nee!" Hank corrected. "It's an old Irish name my grandmother said was originally O'Carnaigh. The English dropped the O but used three syllables, Key-R-nee and over time that became simply Kar-nee."

"Well, that was impressive. I stand corrected Mr. Kearney. Have a seat and let me read that letter."

Mr. Courtright perused the letter, then asked, "This Molly that wrote the letter, she's your aunt?"

"Yes, she is the wife of Kyle Kearney, my uncle in Ireland, and Michael is their son and my cousin."

"I see. And Francis is . . ."

Francis is Kyle's brother, as was my dad Thomas, as well as William Henry back in Ireland and Joseph and Fredrick who both immigrated here to America like Francis."

"Okay. Did you or your aunt ever receive any letters or papers from the Pickaway County court?"

"Not that I'm aware of."

"I see. Well, I do seem to remember the passing of a Francis Kearney in the newspaper. I have nothing pressing this afternoon. I think we should go over to the courthouse. The will should be probated by now and we can see what is going on. Come with me."

At the courthouse, Mr. Courtright asked the clerk if he could see a copy of the probated will of Mr. Francis Kearney and the status of the deed to the Francis Kearney farm. The clerk returned with a book containing a transcribed copy of the will and a much larger book from the Register of Deeds office. She handed the smaller one to Mr. Courtright then began turning pages in the larger one to find the farm location and any deed transactions. Hank noticed as Mr. Courtright was reading and moving his hand down line by line he was murmuring, "Yes, uh huh, yes uh huh, yes uh huh." Then glanced over and reviewed the information in the big book, turned to Hank and said, "I believe I can see how the trouble arose. See this section here where it says, 'It is my will if I have no surviving heir of my own to divide my property between my brother Thomas' son and the children of my brother Joseph.' Well. That is where you come in, being the son of Thomas. The problem comes with the section stating if I have no surviving heir."

Hank interjected, "But he had no surviving children."

"Yes, but he did have a wife, Sylvia, that survived him. So, she is the heir to most of his property unless she marries again within three years, and I see over here the deed is now in her name, but she has rented the farm ground to her brother-in-law Joseph."

Hanks' knees felt week and his head was spinning. He grabbed the arm of the bench against the wall and sat down. He could control it no longer. With his hands to his face and his shoulders heaving, he began silently to cry with tears flowing freely. Finally, he turned to the uneasy Mr. Courtright and blurted out through tears, "I have no farm. I have no money. I have no family and no place to go. I traveled thousands and thousands of miles over sea and land for nothing, nothing."

Mr. Courtright, putting his arm around Hank's shoulders, said, "I can understand this news is very distressing. Come with me. We'll get something to eat, my treat. Then we will try to figure out what you should do next."

Hank stood, still shaking his head and rubbing his forehead as Mr. Courtright took his elbow and led him from the courthouse to a café across the street. They sat at a table in the back and Mr. Courtright told the waiter, "Bring us two of the biggest steaks you have, with all the trimmings, not over cooked. Oh, and bring us some water and a couple cups of coffee."

With that out of the way, Mr. Courtright turned to Hank and said, "Son, I was thinking as we walked across the street. You said you have no family, but you do. Sylvia Kearney is your aunt and Joseph Kearney is your uncle, your dad's brother. I think you and I should go out and talk with them in the morning. I'll spot you a room for the night over at Miss Maberly's rooming house and pick you up with my buggy in the morning and head out that way."

Hank asked, "Why are you doing all this? I can't possibly pay you."

"Well, sometimes in life you just see a situation where you can really help someone, and this appears to be one of those times. Besides, I've heard the old platitude about 98% of lawyers give the rest a bad name. I would prefer to be remembered as part of the rest and not the 98%."

That statement even elicited a chuckle from Hank as the waiter was delivering their steaks. Hank couldn't remember ever having a steak since leaving Kyle and Molly's home in Ireland. At Aintree the bunkhouse always served lesser cuts of beef, pork, or lamb. On the trip across the Atlantic aboard the Washington, they were lucky if the cook drug a hambone through the broth.

They finished their meal and then Mr. Courtright escorted Hank to the rooming house. There he introduced Hank, then excused himself saying, "I have a couple things to take care of at the office but, Hank, I'll meet you at the café around seven for breakfast."

Hank spent a fitful night at the rooming house. He kept going over and over his situation and how he could have been so dumb as to ever leave Aintree. Plus, when he did sleep, he had horrid nightmares about traveling with Al to Skibbereen. Al kept telling him to pick up bodies and Hank would try putting his arms underneath them to lift, but his arms just went right through the bodies. They were still lying there, staring right at him with eyes wide open. He'd try to close their eyes, but they snapped right back open. It happened over and over again even when he tried to lift his own father's body. They all just stared at him.

He thought it was around six in the morning when he gave up trying to sleep. He wasn't sure of the time as he had no watch but thought he had counted the chimes from the mantle clock downstairs. He washed his face using the pitcher of water and bowl supplied then started to dress again in his work clothes and boots. Boots and pants on, he sat down on the bed wondering if the trip out to see the widow Sylvia Kearney really made sense. Deciding no other choice seemed available, he washed his face again hoping it would wake him up. Donning his shirt and packing up his suitcase, he went out the front door and walked over to the café. Mr. Courtright wasn't there, at least not yet, so he sat down at the same table to wait, asking the waiter for a glass of water.

Finally, at around seven-thirty, Mr. Samuel Courtright entered the café, came over and sat down while removing his hat. "Sorry I'm late. I had a little trouble with the horse and buggy. Sometimes ol' Grace just isn't in the mood to pull no buggy. Have you ordered? Order whatever you like, I just need a cup of coffee or two."

Hank ordered some ham and eggs with biscuits and gravy on the side, along with a cup of coffee. While he was eating, he and Mr. Courtright discussed how far it was out to the Francis Kearney, now Sylvia Kearney, farm. Plus, they talked a little about Hank's story and toward the end of breakfast, about ol' Grace out front, harnessed to the buggy.

As they left the café, Hank thanked Mr. Courtright as he walked over to pet Grace and scratch her jaw. Grace lifted her head over Hank's shoulder as if to give him a hug and thank you. Meanwhile, Mr. Courtright was telling Hank, "Just call me Sam. We're not in court or anything, so we don't need those formalities."

As they climbed into the buggy, Hank asked, "How old is Grace? She looks like she has some years on her."

"She's in her twenties. Been a great horse but getting a might cantankerous in her old age."

"Probably has a bit of the rheumatism just like people get. Trainer I knew at Aintree said horses grow old about like people do. Just sooner because they don't live as long."

"I suppose that's true enough. Sounds about right anyway. Ol' Grace probably would rather just eat her oats and lay in the pasture all day if she could, but a little exercise like today will probably do her good. We only must go about three miles south of town to find Sylvia's place. Joseph Kearney lives another mile south, so they're close neighbors."

They had already gone over a mile with the road still running next to the Scioto River. Then Hank noticed while the road ran straight, the river made a big bend to the west for a quarter mile or so before turning back south then at a diagonal back to the southeast. The bending left a large open meadow devoid of trees but fenced in and split down the middle with another fence. Sam said, "That consisted of the majority of the old Francis Kearney farm. There was another eighty acres on the east side of the road along the tree line where the homestead was located and cleared field ground usually planted with oats and wheat. Soon as we get around that little bend you can see it."

Hank was lost in his own thoughts. The meadow reminded him of the manor of his youth in Ireland. With thoroughbred horses running free. Oh, what might have been if the farm had been his, but it wasn't. He knew nothing of this Sylvia Kearney and little of Joseph Kearney, other than that he was the youngest son of William and Esther Kearney and had immigrated to America a year or so after his brother Francis. He remembered Esther complaining that Francis was the only one to ever write. All she ever received from Joseph and Fredrick was a note at Christmas and her birthday and even then, not very newsworthy.

As they turned up the driveway toward the house, a woman came out and grabbed the collar of a large dog who had begun barking furiously. "Can I help you? My dog doesn't take to well to strangers entering the yard."

As they stepped from the buggy Sam said, "Why yes ma'am, I take you to be Mrs. Sylvia Kearney. I'm Samuel Courtright, an attorney from town, and this young man is Henry or Hank Kearney the son of Thomas Kearney, the deceased brother of your late husband Francis Kearney. Is that all about as clear as mud?"

"Well, yes I'm Sylvia Kearney but I'm still not clear on the nature of your business here?"

"Ok! Well, young Henry here came all the way from Ireland and England under the mistaken impression he had inherited some farm ground from your late husband. Now he's here with no farm, nearly no money and you and Joseph are the only kin folks he knows of. We're here to try and decide if we can come up with a solution for his problem."

Sylvia, still holding on to the growling dog's collar, asked, "What's your angle in all this?"

"Young Henry simply stopped at my office by random with a letter indicating he had an inheritance. I had him go with me to the courthouse where we determined the letter was in error and told him I would see if together we could find a solution to his predicament. It is all gratis on my part. I expect to receive nothing more than his gentle soothing of my horse Grace."

Sylvia hooked the dog to a chain attached to the porch and said, "Very well, come on in, I'll fix us some tea."

Sylvia was beginning to wonder if what she was hearing was true, perhaps divine providence had answered her prayers. She told Sam and Hank to have a seat at the table while she went to prepare them some tea. While she worked, she inquired, "Henry, can you tell me the names of your grandparents or other relatives in Ireland?"

"Certainly. William and Esther were my grandparents. He was a shoemaker. His son Henry took over that business and another son, Kyle, runs the farm. William died of a stroke and as far as I know Esther is still living. Oh, and there is a daughter Kathleen, married to a Richard Summerfield."

Now satisfied that Henry was who he said he was, Sylvia served them all tea then sat down at the table saying, "I believe you are who you say you are, but why did you think you were inheriting Francis and my farm? That makes no sense to me."

"I can answer that!" Sam interjected: "You recall in your husband's will there was a section that stated, "If I have no heirs then my farm is to be divided between my brother Joseph's children and the son of my deceased brother Thomas,' or words to that effect. Henry and also apparently his aunt Molly, interpreted no heirs to mean no children. Or in Francis' letter about his illness to Kyle and Molly things somehow got misconstrued."

Sylvia, with chin in hand, was contemplating. She could see where perhaps the will had been misconstrued. She and Francis had lost their first baby shortly after birth and she had miscarried twice since. All of which Esther and Molly would have known. She had been lax in not corresponding after Francis' passing so they may not have known anything about her and Francis' situation. Finally, she said, "I've had a rough go of it since Francis died. Joseph and his boys have helped, and I did rent most of the farm to him, but there are a million things around here that Francis just took care of and now they are up to me, and I could use some help. Henry, I'll give you room and board and a modest amount of pay if you will stay and do such things as taking care of the team and harness them up when I need to go to town, milk the cows twice a day, put up the hay in the hayfield and move it to the barn before winter, fix the fences when they need it, help me put up stuff from the garden, butcher chickens, and dig potatoes and move them to the cellar. But first of all, fix the broken sash cord in my bedroom. Joseph had been saying he'd do it for a month now and it still isn't done. Actually, I've been praying to God for weeks to show me a way out of my dilemma. You can be the answer to my prayers and maybe I can be the answer to yours. What do you say?"

Hank was nearly overcome with joy. The good Lord had provided an answer. He jumped to his feet went around to where Sylvia was seated and shook her hand saying, "Yes, yes, yes! We can make that work. Thank you, thank you!'

Sam Courtright, also excited but ever the lawyer, stated: "Are you both okay with me as a witness to this oral contract or do you want me to put something to paper?"

Sylvia responded, "We're family; no written contract is necessary."

Hank nodded in agreement, then asked, "Where's that window that needs fixed? I'm ready to get started."

They all rose from the table as Sylvia started to point to her room but then said, "Come on outside; there's someone I want you to meet."

As they descended the steps, Sylvia called to her dog Rex who came running. "Rex, meet Hank! Hank, meet Rex."

With that, Hank kneeled and patted Rex' shoulder as Rex was trying to lick Hank's cheek.

"That went well!" said Sam, as he withdrew toward his buggy and the waiting Grace.

Hank and Sylvia both shook his hand and thanked him for the help. Hank said, "You are definitely not in the 98%."

Sam smiled and said, "One final thought, do we need to notify Joseph, so he knows what's transpired?"

"He's supposed to be by this evening, so I can fill him in," Sylvia replied.

Hank removed his old suitcase from the buggy and he and Sylvia waved goodbye to Sam as he pulled away. Then they went back to the house so Hank could get after that broken sash.

15

Henry spent the next three plus years working for and living with his Aunt Sylvia. She took to calling him Henry instead of Hank and he was fine with that, but as a result everyone in the area also knew him as Henry. Another big change for Henry was Sylvia was a Catholic and insisted he accompany her to Mass every Sunday. She was also of Irish descent and her family had worked with Catholic charities to aid the Irish during the famine. As a result, this period in Henry's life contributed greatly to his understanding of what occurred during the famine and during England's 700-year domination of Ireland.

Henry's disdain for the English aristocracy and political elites grew stronger, but his feelings for the ordinary Englishman softened as Sylvia told him the English aristocracy had treated their own peasant class little better than the Irish. Sylvia also did an excellent job of explaining the history of the persecution of Catholics and the Irish, so Henry now had a much better understanding of what had occurred in his own lifetime.

However, when it came to religion, Henry was more confused than ever. His grandmother, Esther, had told him one thing and now his aunt Sylvia was telling him another. Both religions said they followed the Bible, Old Testament, and New Testament. Both believed in the ten commandments. Catholics seemed to have a much more hierarchical arrangement with their Pope, Cardinals, Archbishops, Bishops, Priests, Monks, and Nuns. In addition, they had all their icons, paintings, and Latin rituals. He wasn't sure all that was necessary even if you believed they were the original Christian church. Protestants were willing to cede that the Catholics stemmed from the original but had become corrupt. Catholics chose to believe religious teachings or law could be added by the Pope, while protestants believed you could not add or take away from the scriptures.

Henry could not understand, even with their differences, how one could reconcile the slaughter and starvation of the Irish people simply because they worshipped slightly differently to the same God. He chose to believe in God and heaven, and if Christ died for his sins so much the better. He just prayed that he could see his dad again in heaven.

Henry's uncle, Joseph Kearney, also had a substantial influence on him during this period. It was a much more American political influence. Henry had for the most part stayed clear of any political rhetoric. He had no love for the English aristocracy but kept it to himself. His uncle Joseph, however, was very vocal about his political opinions. Especially about the know-nothings or American Party from the New England states. They were a nativist party and fiercely anti-Irish, anti-German, and anti-Catholic. They called for the native born to arm themselves against the Pope and his Irish band of priest- and bishop-led immigrant army. They thought that the Irish were nothing more than illiterate scum unloaded on American shores.

Joseph would rant, "If the Irish were illiterate, it was solely due to the God-damned ancestors of those settlers now living in New England and their enslavement of the Irish and their stealing of all the Irish people's lands. If the damned former Royalists had a lick of sense, they could see the Irish were the workers fueling the American economy, the builders of the canals and the railroads. They were the ones clearing the land and planting the crops."

Joseph also imparted his ambiguous feelings regarding slavery to Henry, saying, "The English have enslaved the Irish for hundreds of years. Even sending hundreds of thousands of Irish women and children to the West Indies. Of the negro I know very little. I've seen a few, but mostly go by what I've been told. They are somewhat less than human, but above all the other apes. They can be taught to talk and are good workers with proper overseers. In the South, thousands of them are used in growing cotton and are housed on plantations much like we were by the English back in Ireland. Now some are saying they are human beings like us, just with dark skin, and as such should not be enslaved to anyone. Consequently, there is a growing movement in the northern states to abolish slavery in any form in the United States. My only question is where were all these abolitionists when the Irish were enslaved centuries earlier? It's more than a little ironic that slavery and the transportation of slaves has now been banned by the British!"

Joseph's constant retelling of his opinions every time Henry went to work with his horses eventually caused Henry to also adopt the same attitude toward the know-nothings and slavery. He also had seen a few dark-skinned people around Liverpool and in the train stations when he first arrived; but had never actually spoken to any.

16

It was in the fall of 1858 when the widower, Evan Hughes, began calling on Sylvia. Originally, he just offered to take Sylvia and Henry to church on Sundays. Then he asked Sylvia to accompany him to a church dinner. After that dinner, Henry noticed that Evan Hughes and Sylvia were seeing each other more and more often. Henry began to worry a little about his own future. If Sylvia and this Evan Hughes were to marry, he could see no reason for Sylvia to need him anymore. He had managed to save a couple hundred dollars in the hope that he would someday be able to buy his own farm. He especially liked that open meadow near the Scioto River he had first seen upon arrival with Samuel Courtright. Sylvia still owned it and rented it to Joseph. It reminded Henry so much of the Ireland he knew as a little boy working with his father and the thoroughbred racehorses. The vibrant green waving grass, the running water, the blue of the bluffs in the distance, they all screamed Ireland to him. Of course, for all he knew, maybe Sylvia intended to keep it forever or Joseph would want to buy it for one of his boys. Plus, now Evan Hughes was in the picture, and he was a farmer. Maybe he envisioned Sylvia and him owning it together.

In the end, Henry decided it was time for him to start thinking about moving on. Joseph had talked of the opportunity further west. He had heard about the gold in California and the recent discovery of the Comstock lode silver mine in Nevada. However, mining held little interest for Henry. He wouldn't know a gold or silver nugget if he tripped over it. His love was horses, but he also enjoyed the planting and harvesting of grain. Corn especially intrigued him. It was labor intensive planting one seed every square foot in a carefully laid out checkerboard pattern, but oh the harvest. With wheat or oats, you could broadcast the seed and could harvest a hand full of seeds from each stem. But with corn, each seed usually produces two ears with around four hundred kernels each or eight hundred in total. It was nutritious, livestock loved it, it could be ground into cornmeal or corn flour, and some varieties were sweet enough that people ate it right off the cob. Henry decided he either needed to find a job working with horses or become a farmhand until he could purchase his own farm someday.

Henry ended up discussing his future with Joseph while helping him shoe horses in the spring of 1859. Joseph agreed with Henry that the thing between Sylvia and Evan Hughes was getting serious and would probably imperil Henry's future. After some discussion, Joseph turned to Henry and said, "I was thinking of going to Chicago for a big agricultural exhibition in a couple of weeks and taking you with me to help choose a team of Belgian horses. Maybe we can see if there are some opportunities for you while we're there. The expo will have all the latest in farm machinery and also a whole contingent of various breeds of work horses and some riding horses. Won't be any of those thoroughbreds like you saw in England, but you might find something you'd like."

"That sounds great to me! How would we go, by train?

"Yeah, we'd take a train, and if we find a good team of Belgians, we'd ship them back here by train too."

Henry was excited about the trip, but on his way back to Sylvia's house, decided it was time he should discuss things with Sylvia.

"Joseph asked me to go along with him to Chicago to help him find a new team of Belgian horses. I thought while we were there maybe I should begin looking for a new job. Seems like you and Evan are getting kind of serious, and I thought there may not be much use for me around here in the future."

Sylvia asked Henry to come sit at the table and said, "Henry, I would never put you out but yes, Evan and I have grown close. I don't know if we will marry. We haven't discussed it yet. But if you want to explore other opportunities while you're in Chicago by all means do so. Take my hand and we shall pray for the good Lord to give us both guidance in our journey forward."

Two weeks later Joseph and Henry boarded the train for Chicago. Upon arrival they took a hackney cab to the Madison Hotel across the street from a field with a huge circus type tent set up for the agricultural exposition. The following morning the field was filled with a myriad of food vendor tents and booths hawking everything from rainmakers, to lightning rods, to float valves, to medicinal remedies for whatever ailed you. The first day or so of the expo was dedicated to demonstrations of new farm implements, while the following day was for showing breeds of work horses and their strength. The last day was reserved for breeds of cattle and hogs. Joseph and Henry spent the first day touring the various booths and watching the demonstrations. Joseph took particular interest in Jethro Tull's seed drill and a new horse drawn sickle mower. On the second day, Joseph wanted to return to talk with the manufacturers. He was still planting his oats and wheat by scattering seeds, a hit or miss proposition for germination which Tull's drill alleviated. The sickle mower and a horse drawn sheaf binder being developed sounded like pure miracles compared to swinging a scythe and bundling the sheaves by hand. Henry, however, knew all this technology was a ways away for him. Consequently, he told Joseph he was going to go over to the livery adjacent to the hotel to see if he could catch an early glimpse of some of the draft horses.

As Henry approached the livery, a well-dressed young man slightly older than he was had his suit coat slung over the railing and had a pitchfork full of hay he was throwing onto a hay wagon. He spotted Henry and said, "Can I help you, young man?"

"Oh, I'm here with my uncle for the expo but got a little bored so thought I might wander over here and see if I could see some of the work horses."

"You're a little early for that and they're fussy about who gets near their horses. You like horses do you?"

"Yeah, I've always been a horse lover. Ever since I was just a kid, and they seem to like me too."

"Well, I can't show you any of those fancy work horses, but I can show you around the livery if you'd like. My family owns the livery. My dad and his brother started a livery in Baltimore years ago and got tied in with the Madison Hotel people. When Madison built a hotel in St. Louis, my father moved there to set up an adjacent livery and now I've done the same thing here in Chicago. You like horses so you might like the livery business. Let me show you around. We're standing by this haystack of fresh hay, over there is our grain bin filled with oats and that windmill down on the far end provides us with water. Other than shelter, that's pretty much what you need in the livery business-- oats, hay, and water. Now come along the side of the barn here and you can see we have row after row of carriages and buggies all fenced in and protected from thievery. Most of these belong to guests of the hotel, and we assign a number to each one, give it to the guest and then enter the number into a ledger by their name. We do the same with the teams of horses and single horses."

"That sounds a lot like the system my uncle used for making shoes back in Ireland."

"An Irish lad huh! My name is Patrick, Patrick Meyer and I've a bit of Irish blood myself. What's your name again?"

"Henry Kearney. Looks like you have a good business built up here."

"Yes, we do. We get a dollar a day for teams and carriage storage and a quarter for riding horses, so we do well. Say you like horses. Do you think you might be at all interested in the livery business? You might be able to help us, my family, with a big problem we have right now."

"Well, yeah it does sound like a good business that I might enjoy. What's the big problem you have?"

"As soon as I'm done here, I was going to meet with a lawyer and a business broker. I told you my dad is running the livery down in St. Louis, well two days ago I got a telegram from my mother telling me dad got kicked by a horse and fell and hit his head against a post and is still in

a coma. Mom says he isn't doing well, and I need to get home and start running that stable. I asked her what am I supposed to do with this livery stable? She said get rid of it, sell it, whatever you need to do, just get down here. Think you would have any interest in buying a livery stable?"

"I don't have the kind of money it would take to buy this stable and probably never will have."

"Don't sell yourself short, Henry. We might be able to work something out on contract. I was thinking the livery is worth in the neighborhood of $3,500 to $4,000. If you can come up with ten percent down or $350, I'll carry the balance on a ten-year contract at 5% interest. This business should generate enough profit to make that payment and provide you with a nice living besides. What do you think?"

Henry's head was spinning. Here he was in Chicago sort of looking for a new opportunity and now this Patrick Meyer was perhaps offering him a chance to have his own business and it was working with horses. "How exactly would we go about this if I was interested?"

I already told you, Henry, I was going to meet with my lawyer. How much money do you have with you? Can you come up with the down payment?"

"I can't by myself. I only have about fifty dollars for our whole trip, but if I can talk to my uncle tonight, I might be able to come up with it by tomorrow."

Tell you what I'll do. I'll go see my lawyer and have him draw up the papers then you and your uncle meet me here tomorrow morning to complete the deal."

"That would be good because I'm sure my uncle will want to read through the contract because my reading skills aren't too good."

"How much money do you have on you right now?"

"Probably about forty dollars. Why?

"Well as a good faith gesture, you give me the forty dollars to apply toward the contract so I can tell my lawyer you are serious about this purchase. You give me the money, and we shake hands on the deal, Henry

Kearney, and meet in the morning to sign the papers. Then I can board a train to St. Louis to see how my dad is doing and please my mother. Henry Kearney, is that spelled Kearny or Kearney? We want it spelled right in the contract."

As Henry dug the forty dollars out of his pocket and they shook hands on the deal he said, "The latter, K-e-a-r-n-e-y pronounced Car-knee."

"Alright! I'm off to see my lawyer. See you in the morning."

Henry was beside himself with excitement as he hurried back to the hotel to talk with Joseph. He was pretty sure he could come up with another hundred dollars or so but would have to borrow at least a hundred from either Joseph or maybe Sylvia. When he entered the hotel room, Joseph was already there washing up before dressing for dinner. He asked, "Where have you been all day? Thought maybe you got lost in the big city."

"You won't believe it. I think I've secured the opportunity of a lifetime." With that announcement, Henry relayed the entire story of his day with Patrick Meyer. Including the part where he might need to borrow a hundred dollars or so and that they were to meet in the morning at eight o'clock outside the livery barn.

Joseph, having dried his face with a towel but still holding it on his hip, was sitting on the edge of the bed just staring at Henry like he was turning several thoughts over in his mind. Then he said, "Buying the livery next door huh? I thought the Madison Hotel probably owned that. It was included with their ad in the circular for the agricultural exposition as the place to stay because they had a livery right next door. Let me finish dressing, then we'll go downstairs and talk to the manager of the hotel. I've got some questions for him before I have some questions for you."

As they continued down the stairs, Henry wasn't too concerned. Patrick had told him his family had an agreement with the Madison Hotels in Baltimore and St. Louis. It made sense for them to have one in Chicago too. At the front desk, Joseph had the clerk summon the hotel manager. The manager appeared and introduced himself as Mr. Nelson and asked how he could help.

Joseph jumped right to it and asked, "Concerning the large livery stable next door, is that owned by the Madison Hotel group or someone else?"

Mr. Nelson cleared his throat and replied, "Yes sir it is fully owned by the Madison. Why do you ask?"

"Is there another Madison Hotel owned by the same people in St. Louis or Baltimore?"

"Not that I'm aware of. The Madison Hotel Group is incorporated in the state of Illinois, and I believe all or nearly all the shareholders are residents of Illinois."

Henry's heart rate increased dramatically. What was going on? Patrick Meyer had distinctly told him otherwise. Joseph looked at Henry then turned to Mr. Nelson and inquired, "Can you put us in touch with a policeman to go with us in the morning? I believe my nephew here has been conned out of a sum of money and the scoundrel may be back in the morning for more. You don't perchance have a fellow named Patrick Meyer working at the stable, do you?"

"No, no, that name doesn't ring any bells. We do have quite a bit of turnover at the stable. A lot of these city kids don't take too well to shoveling manure. But yes, I can connect you with a policeman for tomorrow morning, but I have my doubts about anyone showing up."

Joseph turned to Henry who was standing there red faced with his shoulders sagging, and said, "There you go Henry, you can get a job in the stable shoveling shit, cuz I think you can kiss your money goodbye." He put his arm around Henry's shoulders and said, "Come on kid, let's get something to eat and hope we can catch the scoundrel in the morning. If not, you'll have to chalk this one up to an expensive lesson learned—if it looks too good to be true . . ."

Henry was grief stricken. He had just handed over twenty percent of his total net worth to a con man. Henry didn't feel much like eating but Joseph insisted he go with him to dinner. He was dining with a representative from the company producing the new sickle mower he had bought, and the salesman would probably pay for dinner.

The next morning Joseph and Henry met a plain clothes police detective in the lobby. Together they proceeded to the livery where the detective waited out of sight. Eight o'clock came and went. At nine o'clock they gave up. Patrick Meyer or whoever he was wasn't going to show. Joseph and the detective shook hands as Joseph thanked him for his help. With that fruitless endeavor completed, he turned to Henry and said, "Let's get over to the expo and check out those draft horses. That's something you know a little more about."

The English had their thoroughbreds and now some Americans had crossbred them with horses originally brought over by the Spanish to bring forth the American quarter horse. So named because it was very fast for a quarter mile. It was also very smart and a great horse for working cattle. However, the farmers now arriving in great numbers to settle the expanding frontier needed a more muscular and stronger horse for clearing trees and turning the sod, especially with some of the new farm implements developed during the industrial revolution. Draft or work horses bred specifically for that job included Shires, Clydesdales, Percherons Haflingers, and Belgian Drafts. The Belgian, new to the United States, was derived from the Belgian Black used by knights in previous centuries. It was strong, calm, and easy to train from what Joseph could discern from the literature.

The expo had each breed harnessed to a weighted sled with weight added until a team could pull no further. It gave the patrons a preview of the strength of each breed and how much they could pull. Joseph was impressed with how well the Belgians did against the much bigger Clydesdales and Shires. He decided that after the demonstrations he would go talk to the breeder that had brought the Belgians. He and Henry made their way to the back of the demonstration ring where each of the different breeds were held in individual corrals. Joseph approached a well-dressed man and introduced himself, saying, "Hello, my name is Joseph Kearney, and this is my nephew, Henry Kearney. Are you the owner of these fine draft horses?"

"Yes, I am. My name is Milford Keating and I'm pleased to meet you. I imported a Belgian stud and eight broodmares about three years ago and

more since. My intent is to get the breed going here in the United States, so I bring them to various agricultural shows around the country. They are great work horses. They are docile and travel well even by rail and on the ship coming over. Did you get to see them pulling that sled?"

"Yes, I did, and they were quite impressive for their size. Are the geldings much larger than the mares or can you pair them together?" Joseph asked.

Milford Keating and Joseph continued their conversation about the Belgians, but Henry went into the corral with the horses. He wanted to see how calm they were and how they handled being harnessed or having their hooves lifted and inspected. Applying lessons learned from Tom Murphy, he was running his hand over their back and down their chest and legs, checking their teeth to see what he could discern.

Meanwhile, Joseph had relayed a little of Henry's story to Mr. Keating. How Henry had trained and ridden thoroughbreds in England, and how he loved horses and was in search of a new job. Joseph even related the story of how Henry had been swindled out of his money just the day before.

As Henry exited the corral and approached Mr. Keating and Joseph, Mr. Keating spoke up and said, "Henry, Joseph was just telling me a little about you and your unfortunate event of yesterday. Joseph has agreed to buy a team of my Belgians, but I may have an even better offer for you. I spend a good deal of my time traveling around to these shows or getting ready for these shows and I could use a good man to train and team up my horses at my farm in down state Illinois. If you would like to give it a try, I'm willing also. I'd give you room and board plus ten dollars a month. Might even spot you a few trips to shows like this one, where you could demonstrate how great my Belgian horses are. What do you say? Want to try it? If it doesn't work out, I'll pay your train fare back to Ohio."

Henry could hardly believe what he was hearing. After the previous day's fiasco, he wasn't quite sure if Milford Keating was serious or just toying with him. He glanced at Joseph for some kind of signal to see if this was a legitimate offer or what. Joseph kind of smiled and said, "It sounds like a rather good offer for a kid looking for his next stage in life. If you want to give it a go, I can gather your things from Sylvia's house and ship them to you."

Henry didn't ponder it too long before accepting the offer and shaking Milford Keating's hand. They agreed to meet back at the hotel. The following morning, Henry boarded a train with Mr. Keating, heading from Chicago toward St. Louis. Traveling south through Illinois, Henry saw farmland like he had never seen before. The land was dead flat, and trees were few. Milford, as Mr. Keating told Henry to call him, said Illinois had some of the richest soil in the country. Perfect for growing crops and with ample rainfall. He explained that they weren't going all the way to St. Louis, but would get off at Carrolton, Illinois, where his farm was located.

17

They arrived in the afternoon of the second day. They were greeted by a carriage for Milford and Henry to ride in back to the farm, and there were also some men on horseback to escort the Belgians back. The Keating farm wasn't very far out from the rail station where they had disembarked. They went by a couple of well-manicured farming homesteads before arriving at the Keating farm with its white board fences, a large red barn, and several young Belgian horses eating grass in the pasture next to the driveway up to the house. Henry could see nothing that he would not like about the Keating Belgian Horse Farm.

Indeed, that is the way it transpired for him. The people were great. The accommodations were great, and the Belgian horses were great. The other hired men even treated Henry like the expert horse trainer he had become. Marveling at his ability to tame and ride horses without having to go through the bucking bronco phase. By the end of 1859, Henry thought he had finally found his home.

It was the spring of 1860 and Henry was working with a pair of Belgian geldings to get them to work as a team and not have one slacking while the other did the pulling. He was just finishing when he noticed a one-horse buggy coming up the drive with another horse tied to the back. When the buggy pulled to a stop beside the corral, he saw it was the neighbor from down the road, Thomas Jones, along with his daughter.

"Hello Thomas, what can I do for you?"

"Just call me Tom. Henry, I would like you to meet my daughter, Mary Ann, and we brought over her new Palomino horse. I talked with Milford,

and he said it was up to you whether you wanted to spend the time breaking him to ride for Mary Ann. He's a young gelding broke to halter but that's about it. I thought he should be calmed down a lot more before Mary Ann rides him, and I'll gladly pay you for your time."

With that, Mary Ann stood with one knee on the seat and said, "I told Dad I was big enough to do it myself, but no, let the great horse trainer from Ireland do it. He won't let me do anything I want to do."

Henry walked around the Palomino with his hand on his back then said to Mary Ann, "Pretty good-looking piece of horse flesh. Long neck and long legs. Might be a touch of thoroughbred blood in his line. Do you have a name for him?"

"I wanted to name him trumpet because of his gold color and all the noise he was putting up when we first got him home. I think he was just homesick, but he was neighing all the time and it sounded like a sick trumpet. But Dad said, 'Trumpet? If you look at him from the back with those long legs and that white tail, he looks more like a banjo standing on its neck!' So, he started calling him Banjo and it kind of stuck, so I call him Banjo now too."

"Banjo, huh! Looking from back here that seems to fit."

Henry saw this Miss Mary Ann Jones was a twelve-year-old, freckle faced, tomboy and, as he had heard the ranch hands say, "Full of piss and vinegar." Precocious may have been a better term, but it was somewhat understandable as she had a couple older brothers that teased her incessantly.

Henry turned to Tom and Mary Ann and said, "Tell you what let's do. You leave Banjo here with me for a couple of weeks so he and I can get to know each other. Then, Mary Ann, you can come over and help me break him to ride. How's that sound?"

"Sounds good to me," said Tom.

"Wait, you mean I don't get to see Banjo for two whole weeks? That's not fair!" Mary Ann blurted.

"Okay, okay," said Tom. "Would it be alright, Henry, if she stopped over after school a couple times to see her precious Banjo?"

As Henry untied Banjo from the buggy he said, "Yeah, that should be fine."

Mary Ann jumped down from the buggy, wrapped her arms around Banjo's neck as best she could, and gave him a hug. Tom stayed seated and just shook his head as Mary Ann bounced back up into her seat. Henry led Banjo into a small corral next to the barn and began working with him at once.

The very next afternoon Henry was working with Banjo, holding on to a long halter rope as Banjo went in circles. He would throw a horse blanket on Banjo's back, let him circle, then pull it off. He repeated this time and again until Banjo would no longer shy away but just let the blanket stay on his back. As Henry's eyes were following every move Banjo made, he glanced up to see Mary Ann peering through the fence rails.

"Where'd you come from?" he asked, as he continued to watch Banjo circle.

"School's out, so I thought I'd come over before my chores and homework. You just trying to make him dizzy by going in circles or what?"

"No, just getting him used to having something on his back so some day when you're up there, he won't throw you in the nearest ditch."

"Yeah, that kind of makes sense. What do you do next?"

"Couple of things, I guess. I get him used to more weight on his back and maybe introduce him to a bit and bridle. That may be a few days off yet but one thing I do every day is reward him with oats and a good rub down if he's been good but if he's being stubborn kind of like a certain girl I know, then no oats."

"What's that supposed to mean? You said I could come over!"

"I said a couple times, and this is one. I want to build a relationship between Banjo and me. I expect certain things from him, and I want him to know what to expect from me. After we've established that, then I hope to transfer those expectations between man and horse to you. However, if you are over here all the time, it interrupts the flow of understanding between horse and rider."

"That's better! Horse and rider. Before you said MAN and horse, but you should say rider because women ride horses too."

"Did you not hear the part about interrupting?"

"Yeah, I heard you. I'll try to stay away for a few days."

Either true to her word or her dad laid down the law, Henry didn't see Mary Ann again until the second weekend. On Saturday afternoon as he was working with Banjo, he saw her approaching. She hopped up on the corral fence and said, "Good afternoon Mr. Kearney. How are you today?"

"I'm fine Miss Jones but we don't have to be so formal. You can just call me Henry and I'll call you Mary Ann, okay?

"Yeah, that should be fine Mr. Ke—er, Henry. Henry, how you coming along with Banjo and that relationship thing you talked about?"

"We're progressing well. Banjo is a pretty smart horse. He took to the bridle and bit quickly. Rather than having to pull on the right rein to get him to go right or the left for him to go left, he learned as soon as that left rein wasn't just resting on his neck but hitting against his upper neck, he should turn right to avoid a jerk on the right rein on the bit in his mouth. He's still not comfortable with a man on his back, er I mean a rider on his back, but is getting used to being saddled. A lot of progress for a week or two."

"When am I going to get to ride him, Henry?"

"Well, we're a week or two away from that yet, but we'll see how it goes."

"That reminds me. Dad said he heard when you were in Ireland you used to train horses to jump over fences, hedges, or puddles of water, is that true?"

"Steeplechase racehorses. Yeah I used to do a little of that back in England, but they weren't puddles, they were shallow pools or sometimes running creeks of water."

"Well, I've been thinking. Right now, every afternoon I have to saddle-up or bareback ride ol' Nig and ride out and round-up the milk cows and bring them back for milking. To do that I have to open the corral gate, lead Nig through then shut the horse corral gate. Then I ride to the outer corral

gate, hop down and open it and lead Nig through and close it. Mount up again and ride to the cow pasture gate, get down and lead Nig through again and close it so the two yearling steers we're going to butcher don't escape. Then mount up again to go after the milk cows. And after all that, I have to repeat the whole darn thing to put Nig away. So, I was thinking if you could just teach Banjo to jump over some of those gates, I wouldn't have to do all that gate opening and closing. What do you think?"

"Couple of things. First of all, that hopping down to open and close gates is probably good for you. It not only gives you some exercise, it teaches you discipline. Not closing a gate has consequences. Secondly, if Banjo knows how to jump gates and fences, what's to keep him from jumping the gate and just going back to where you got him. Or worse yet, getting a whiff of ripening oats and jumping the fence to eat his fill. Then he founders and isn't good for anything and has to be put down."

"Oh yeah, I see what you mean. Maybe you could teach him to jump only when I'm riding him. How about that?"

"I think perhaps you should forget about teaching Banjo to jump and just be thankful you're getting a horse of your own. And that you don't have to milk all those cows you bring in."

"I do help with the milking sometimes. Dad comes in and says, 'I need you to be a milk maid because so-and-so can't help tonight.' Then I have to help milk and feed the calves."

"Glad to hear it. Does you good."

"Henry, sometimes you just don't see things the same way I do at all."

"Well, Mary Ann, I think that is probably a good thing. Maybe I can keep you out of trouble and someday maybe you can keep me out of trouble." He could hear the Jones' dinner bell ringing, so told her, "You better skedaddle on home, or you'll miss your supper."

It didn't happen quickly enough for Mary Ann, but eventually Henry taught her how to bridle, saddle, and ride Banjo. Getting in the saddle was a bit of a problem. If the saddle stirrups were the right length for Mary Ann to ride, she had to leap off the ground while holding the saddle horn to get her left foot in the stirrup. It was often easier to just lead Banjo along the corral fence, then climb the fence before getting in the saddle. Henry rode along beside her for the first several rides to ensure things went smoothly. Both he and Mary Ann noticed Banjo enjoyed running rather than walking or trotting. Mary Ann was thrilled because she loved the wind blowing through her hair while going at a full gallop. Henry had to caution her it may be all right to go after the milk cows at a gallop but under no circumstances was, she to bring them in any faster than a leisurely walk.

The rest of that summer and into the fall, occasionally Mary Ann would ride over on Banjo and if Henry wasn't too busy, they would go on longer rides along a creek that ran into the Illinois River. Mary Ann loved showing off her knowledge of the local flora and fauna, telling Henry such and such was goldenrod and that's a sunflower. Followed by things like, "Hear that? That's a quail, or that's a killdeer. Or look over there, those are prairie chickens."

Henry would think to himself, she really does know a lot about the local birds and stuff, but mostly she enjoys thinking she's teaching me a thing or two. So, on occasion, he would disagree with her saying things like, "That was no wren! It was a common sparrow."

Mary Ann would come unhinged, screaming, "No it wasn't!" Then go into great detail about the difference between a wren and a sparrow and how he should pay more attention to the size difference and the different coloring of their feathers.

It was after one of these rides when Henry was met by Milford Keating, who asked, "You and the Jones girl enjoy your Sunday ride?"

"Yeah, I get a real kick out of her. She no sooner gets a question out of her mouth than she's telling me the answer. What's up?"

"Well, the results of the election are in, and Abraham Lincoln, our Illinois native son, will be our new president. Not only that, but the southern states are also talking about seceding from the Union and forming their own country over the slavery issue. I'm sure the northern states don't want to let that happen. So, we may be talking about a war between the states.

It's mostly an issue between the coastal states right now or over in Kansas on whether Kansas should be a slave state or not but could end up involving all of us. I've never even considered owning slaves and don't know that I've ever met anyone who did. The southern people that I've met are pretty much the same as you and me. Poor Irish or German immigrants that came here to start a new life and get away from some bastard in London or Berlin telling them how they've got to live. Hell, the Irish have been slaves to the English for hundreds of years, but nobody seems to give a shit about that. I read the English even sent thousands of Irish women to the West Indies to use as breeding stock for those negro bucks. Hoped by cross breeding they could get a more manageable slave. Anyway, I'll try to keep you informed about what's going on in our country. Things are happening too fast. Now we have trains going everywhere, faster and faster all the time. Same goes for steamboats, faster and faster. Hell, you can go from St. Louis to New Orleans in less than a week and not much more than that coming upstream."

All Henry could say was, "Wow! Yeah, keep me informed."

It didn't take long for things to heat up. On December 20th South Carolina seceded from the Union and was quickly followed by six other southern states early in 1861. These states held a convention in Montgomery, Alabama and formed the Confederate States of America, wrote their own constitution and elected Jefferson Davis as their president. They were later joined by four other states including Virginia, and the Confederate capital was moved to Richmond.

18

In early May of 1861 Milford Keating entered the horse barn and summoned Henry to his side, saying, "I've just returned from an agricultural show in southern Missouri and a fellow down there has just imported a Belgian stallion and wants to buy eight of our broodmares to start his own breeding program. I agreed to the sale, but we need to get them down there as quickly as possible before this Civil War stuff gets too carried away around here. Tomorrow morning you and I and a couple of the men will take them over to the Illinois River where we will load them on a livestock barge. Then you and I will ride down the Mississippi to New Madrid where he will pick them up. I'm not sure how the horses will take to a boat ride, so I thought you could go along to keep them calm. Pack up to be gone for about a week. We'll ride a steamboat back home when we're done."

Henry once again packed up the old suitcase he had gotten from Kyle and at the last minute threw in the little leather-bound New Testament that Esther had given him. He thought he might try to read a few passages while floating down the river.

Even before sunrise, they had gathered the horses and were heading to the boarding point on the river. Much as Henry expected, the Belgian horses gave them no problems and were content to board the barge four to a side. Their halters were clipped to a rail, and they were given some hay to feed on as the trip began. The barge was just a rather large rectangular flat-bottom boat with corrals built on it. There was a small pilot house on the back for controlling the rudder and feed storage in the front. River currents propelled it down stream and it was towed back upstream by steam power. For this trip the crew consisted of just the pilot and his helper copilot.

Henry and Milford Keating spent the day on a bench at the front of the pilot house watching the shoreline pass by. In the afternoon, they passed St. Louis and then headed on south toward New Madrid, Missouri. They spent the night in shifts; alternately watching the horses and sleeping on the hay at the front.

At mid-morning of the following day, neither Milford nor Henry noticed, but two boats each with seven men aboard were rapidly approaching the barge. Each boat had six men rowing and another man kneeling at the front holding a firearm. A shot rang out and Henry peered back and saw a man aiming a musket right at the pilot while another held a revolver and was motioning the pilot to take the barge toward the eastern shore. As the boats came alongside the barge, three men from each boarded and drew their pistols on Milford, Henry, the pilot, and his helper. The pilot was instructed to steer the barge toward a small dock at the river edge. More men on horseback were riding quickly along the shore toward the dock. Some had already dismounted and were waiting for the ropes to be thrown to secure the barge to the dock. Once secured, Milford, Henry, and the crew were ordered off at gunpoint. They were taken across the river road to a little clearing among the trees and ordered to sit down on a log while two sentries stood guard over them.

There seemed to be some kind of meeting going on at the far end of the clearing and eventually, as the meeting broke up, a man came to them and said, "We are all supporters of the new Confederate States of America. We got word from New Orleans that the Confederacy was in need of draft horses for pulling supply wagons and cannons. We saw the horses on your barge and not knowing if you were Yankees or not; decided it was an opportunity to obtain some draft horses one way or the other. We will all continue down the river to Memphis where there is a unit of the Confederate army and we'll let them decide how to proceed. You have any questions?"

Milford spoke up, saying, "But, we were only going to New Madrid to deliver these broodmares which I've already sold. These horses aren't draft horses. Most of them haven't been broke to pull anything. Memphis is way past where we were headed. I understand you need draft horses, but these are not what you want. Why don't you just let us go and we can let bygones be bygones?"

"Nice try, but if it looks like a draft horse, it can be trained to be a draft horse. We'll all be heading for Memphis in a couple hours, and we'll let the commander there decide how to proceed." With that said, he turned and walked away.

At noon, they were given a plate of beans to eat and then ordered back to the barge. Now there were maybe fifty or sixty additional men on board. Someone explained that they were all recruits for the army but without horses. Those with horses would ride to Memphis, probably arriving days after the barge but hoping to be in the cavalry rather than the foot-marching infantry.

The four original barge occupants were all kept separated for the entire trip to Memphis. Once the barge was emptied at the dock, everyone was questioned as to name, address, and their purpose for being there. Henry had no idea what happened to the horses or the pilot and co-pilot, but he and Milford were loaded into a wagon and taken to a Confederate encampment at the edge of town. They were taken to a command tent and introduced to Colonel McNett, who asked them to take a seat on one of the stools inside.

The colonel stated, "I understand you, Mr. Keating, are the owner of the eight draft horses unloaded from the barge. Is that correct?"

"They are not draft horses; they are broodmares but yes, I am the owner, and I would like to have them returned to me and my trainer, Henry, here so we can be on our way."

Mr. Keating was getting angrier and angrier. His face was flushed, and his hands were held in tight fists at his sides, as if he was ready to fight.

Colonel McNett said, "That is not going to happen. I don't know the price you sold them for, but if you'll tell me the amount, the Confederate army will pay you the same in Confederate currency."

Hearing that, Mr. Keating rose to his feet, eyes flashing and said, "Confederate currency would not be worth the paper it's printed on back in Illinois! You guys are nothing but a bunch of horse thieving bas . . ."

BANG

Colonel McNett had drawn his revolver and put a bullet in the middle of Keating's chest. Keating stumbled and fell backward as two sentries rushed in. McNett motioned for them to take the still-twitching body away. He then turned to Henry and said, "Your boss said you were his horse trainer. If that's true, do you want to continue down the Mississippi with the horses to New Orleans or do you want to join him floating face down in the river?"

"I think I'd rather go with the horses."

"Good answer." Summoning the corporal outside, the colonel said, "Take this man back to the barge, and along with all the recruits and draft horses, send them down to New Orleans and have them report to Camp Walker."

Four days later, the barge docked at New Orleans with well over a hundred jubilant rebel recruits, many from northern Louisiana, a dozen draft horses counting the Keating horses and one very nervous and anxious Irishman named Henry Kearney. However, they weren't sent to Camp Walker, but instead by railroad to a new encampment at Camp Moore along the Tangipahoa River in St. Helena Parish. 75 miles north of New Orleans, but beside the New Orleans, Jackson & Great Northern Railway station. The camp had been cleared of pines for a parade ground, with the Tangipahoa River to the east, and Beaver Creek to the south used for both bathing and drinking water. The southern end of the camp was devoted to campsites for the troops, organized into companies.

One by one the new recruits went through a cursory physical and then the enlistment process. After enlisting they were given their uniforms, accoutrements, and weapons. Much of the latter had been captured from the Baton Rouge arsenal at the beginning of the war. Henry, being toward the end of the line of recruits, was told to enter a tent with Captain Sunderman to complete his enlistment after his physical. Captain Sunderman started through a list of questions, starting with his full name and most recent address. When Henry answered with Carrolton, Illinois, the Captain put down his quill and asked, "Illinois? How did you end up down here?"

"Well, six years ago or so I arrived from Ireland thinking I would be a farmer in Ohio. Through time and circumstance, I ended up training draft horses for a fella in southern Illinois. He and I were delivering some to a guy in Missouri when we got diverted to Memphis then down here because the Confederacy needed our horses. I've never been political so I'm kind of at a loss about this whole Civil War and just want to go home."

"Irish, huh! My wife immigrated from Ireland, and she told me all about how the damned English took all your land, forced you live under their laws, and damn near starved you all to death. Let me tell you that is about the same thing the northern states are trying to do to the Confederacy today. Trying to tell us how we gotta live. Gotta do it their way or not at all. I think if you thought about it, you'd be a fine Confederate soldier like a lot of other Irishmen."

"What if I don't want to be in the army, but just want to go home?"

"Well then, you being from Illinois, we would have to assume you are either a Yankee sympathizer or a coward. Either way you'd probably be shot!"

"Given those choices, I guess I might be inclined to be your newest recruit."

"Good, good! Sign your name or make your mark there at the bottom. Corporal, you sign there as a witness, then show private Kearney where to get his uniform."

The uniform he received was little more than a shirt, a hat, a haversack with eating utensils, and a rolled-up blanket and shelter half that he could wrap around any extra clothing. There were no shoes or boots in Henry's size, so he was told to keep his own; it was the same thing with pants. Henry was glad his old boots made by his uncle in Ireland and recently resoled were holding up well.

Henry's mind was a blur. In little more than a week he had gone from a content horse trainer in Illinois to a soldier in the army of the Confederate States of America at Camp Moore, Louisiana. He worried that no one in Illinois knew where he was or what had happened to Mr. Keating. He was assigned to Company A of the Second Louisiana Infantry. He was happy to find that he wasn't the only Irishman in Company A, and surprised to find he wasn't even the only Kearney. A pair of brothers named J.S. or Sam Kearney and G.W. or George Kearney from Natchitoches Parish were also members of the company. Henry was quick to bond with the brothers and both proved helpful to Henry as he began his military training, George especially because he became the Company A comedian. Everything was okay as long as he got a laugh. He was lucky in the sense that his levity convinced others to keep his hijinks mostly anonymous.

The first week in camp was spent learning and memorizing military procedures, protocol, and chain of command. George lightened the mood by feigning to misunderstand by saluting sergeants and ignoring lieutenants. That got him some extra drill time and latrine cleaning duty.

The topper, though, was when they were learning the proper procedure for loading and firing their muskets. The lieutenant leading the instruction was very intense and just as he had finished inserting the bullet with the ramrod and was bringing the gun to his shoulder to show firing stance, George set off a firecracker. Everybody hit the ground, including the instructor. Several of the trainees, including Henry, had a fairly good idea who had done it, but no one was willing to snitch on George. As a result, the whole company had a significant amount of extra time on the parade grounds doing marching drills, not to mention the hundred pushups the lieutenant required because no one would name the culprit.

Camp Moore was a hot and humid place and rife with flies and mosquitoes. After weeks of constant drills and marching with the army, trying to make a cohesive fighting unit from a bunch of farmers and merchants, the troops were growing tired of it all. Some of the luster had worn off the initial adrenaline rush of fighting to preserve the South. On a sultry Sunday afternoon when Henry finally had some free time, he was contemplating how all this training was becoming arduous and wondered- what was the usefulness of it all. He was looking for a shady spot where he might be able to read some of his New Testament, when he spotted a chaplain apparently writing a letter for a soldier who was unable to write. He approached the pair and asked, "Sorry to interrupt, but are you perhaps writing a letter home for a soldier who is unable to write it himself?"

"Yes, yes I am. I enjoy being able to keep families in touch with each other. It brings such happiness to both parties."

"Would you be so kind as to help me write a letter?"

"Certainly. Give me a few minutes to finish up here and I'll be with you."

Henry managed to find a shady spot under a pine tree and sat down to wait for the chaplain. Shortly, he arrived and said, "Okay soldier, what is your name and with whom do you wish to correspond? Your parents, your girlfriend, or perhaps someone else?"

"Well sir, that has been part of my problem. I didn't know who to write to, but after thinking on it these last few weeks, I think I need to write Miss Mary Ann Jones in Carrolton, Illinois."

"Illinois? Well, that causes me to wonder, but I'm not here to judge anyone and will gladly write whatever it is you want to relate. Is Miss Jones your girlfriend?"

"No, she's just the only person I can think of that might be able to read and understand the circumstances that brought me to this place. My name

is Henry Kearney, and I was a horse trainer in Illinois, and I trained a riding horse for Miss Jones and taught her how to ride."

"An Irish horse trainer. Well yes, you Irish have a reputation for being good at that. I could tell you were Irish by your accent as well as your name. Shall we begin?"

June 16, 1861

Dear Mary Ann,

I could think of no one else to write about the happenings to Mr. Keating and myself since leaving by barge down the Mississippi River. I am certain the neighborhood is wondering what happened to us. Especially since the whole country is now involved in Civil War. Our barge was way laid by a bunch of men south of St. Louis and we were forced to go with them to Memphis. Unfortunately, while we were there, Mr. Keating became irate and was shot and killed by a Confederate officer. I was given the choice of continuing down the Mississippi with the horses and a bunch of Confederate militiamen to New Orleans or to be shot like Mr. Keating. After arriving in New Orleans, I was thought to be just another recruit for the southern cause and was taken to an enlistment site where they convinced me it was better to join than to be shot as a coward or Yankee. As a result, I'm now a private in the Confederate army being trained at Camp Moore, Louisiana. Rumor has it that we will be moving out shortly but to where, I do not know.

You probably know me as well as anyone and know because I neither read nor write well, I've never been political. Yet here I am, caught up in a conflict I don't understand and never wanted to be a part of.

I know Mr. Keating had no kin so I wonder what will happen with his farm. I hope and pray your family is well and when this is over, perhaps I can see you again.

A chaplain here at our camp has been kind enough to put my words to paper and to see to its proper mailing. If an opportunity presents itself in the future, I may correspond again and to hear from you would bring me great joy. So far being in the army brings a lot of loneliness to those of us who can't read or who don't wish to gamble. I have, however, developed a friendship with some of my fellow recruits.

Yours truly,
Henry

"I think you have written a rather good letter here, Henry. I will see to its proper mailing to Carrolton, Illinois, although I'm not sure how that all transpires now between the North and the South."

"Thank you! I owe you a debt of gratitude."

Two weeks later the Louisiana 4th Infantry Company shipped out on the Steamer "Rapides" and shortly after that the Louisiana 1st and 2nd Infantry Brigade departed for Northern Virginia by railroad. Traveling first to Jackson, then northern Alabama, then north to Richmond, Virginia, the Capital of the Confederacy. The trip was not made in comfortable passenger cars, but in freight cars, cattle cars, and flatbeds that hauled men, supplies, and armaments. The trip took well over a month because of frequent stops to feed and water horses and drills on setting up and breaking camp. Upon arrival, the troops were dispatched to Yorktown to build defenses along the York River.

It was a few months later when they were moved to Williamsburg to winter quarters. The company's time at Yorktown was very tedious and boring. They heard reports of other battles or skirmishes with Union troops while they were stuck building barricades and not even getting a taste of warfare. Then they were stuck in winter quarters while both sides prepared for spring offensives. No extended leaves were granted, so free time was spent gambling, writing letters, reading, and the occasional snowball fight or ball game. One of the highlights was they finally received some of their back pay. But, for Henry, the highlight was finally receiving a letter from Mary Ann. He struggled through reading it himself, so went to find the chaplain to read it to him to ensure he had read it correctly.

December 7, 1861

Dear Henry,

I finally received your letter in October and was thrilled to hear from you, although in reading it I became upset both with your circumstances and the unfortunate death of Mr. Keating. It took some time for me to decide how and what to write in answer. I do miss you and our rides. This war has caused everyone to suffer. My two older brothers have left the farm and joined the army, leaving my father, my sister and me to tend to all the farm work. There are no young men left in the area as they have all gone off to war. A couple of sons of families in the area have already been lost in war. It is heart wrenching for the families, knowing their son was lost in some faraway place, and they have no body for a proper burial. They may never know where he lies or the circumstances of his death.

I hope you are doing well, as I think of you often. I was unsure how I was to mail my letter so used the address on the envelope of your letter to me. I hope you receive it and I hope this dreaded war is over soon and you can return. I am uncertain what will happen with Mr. Keating's farm. It looks a little forlorn as no one is living there now. My father expressed an interest in buying it, but I don't know if it is possible with the war and nobody to help with the work.

Please write to me again if you get a chance. I have no one around here of any interest. All that is left are some juvenile boys with no brains and some silly girls that chase after them.

Sincerely yours,
Mary Ann

Henry was unsure which army Mary Ann's brothers had joined but suspected it was the Union army and was glad Mary Ann hadn't said. He asked the chaplain if he was available to write an answer, but the chaplain told him not at the moment, maybe this evening if he came back then. Henry spent the afternoon composing a letter in his head and trying to determine what he could actually tell Mary Ann, finally deciding not much. The troops had been given orders not to divulge exactly where they were or what they were doing.

December 8, 1861

Dear Mary Ann,

I was so glad to finally hear from you. It was probably the happiest day since I've been in the army. My company shipped out from Louisiana and I'm now in Virginia. Hopefully I can tell you that much, though the army will not let me divulge much more. I can tell you that I am fine although the food we are fed is terrible. It is awfully boring here and I have taken to smoking a pipe just to while away the hours. Some of the guys stop the boredom by gambling and playing cards but that has never interested me.

I hope you are doing well and treating Banjo well. Until we can meet again, take care.

Sincerely yours,
Henry

That was Henry's last letter for a while. His company moved out for the spring campaign in March of 1862. He had received a short note from Mary Ann wishing him a Merry Christmas and a peaceful New Year but failed to receive it until February.

Rumors abounded when the order came down to break camp and prepare to march. Large wagons were loaded with everything from tents, stoves, and commissary equipment to officer's furniture. Rations were issued while ordinance officers issued cartridges and firing caps-- sixty of each to the troops. Rumor became fact when it was learned that Union troops were on the march toward Yorktown on McClellan's Peninsula Campaign. McClellan believed Confederate troops were primarily engaged in the defense of Yorktown, but in fact had built defenses all along the Warwick River. The battle was joined with troop losses on both sides, but McClellan thought the Confederate line was too strong to assault and disengaged from the battle. Henry's company was there but saw little action as they were held back as reinforcements if needed.

19

Henry's company, the 2nd Louisiana, was assigned to General Howell Cobb's Brigade in its frontal assault of Malvern Hill in the Seven Days Battle. The Union forces had cut all the trees in a wide swath going up the hill so any attacking forces would be completely exposed as they charged up the hill. In addition, they had aligned their cannons along the hilltop so they could bombard the attacking force with cannonballs and cannister shot, which was basically a shotgun shell shot out of a cannon. When the order was given, Henry marched with the others shoulder-to-shoulder into the maelstrom. The 2nd Louisiana had been in some minor battles before and had seen the carnage when marching past hospital tents, but they had experienced nothing like they were facing now. As they marched up the hill and even before they reached the cleared area, Union forces let loose an artillery barrage including skip shots of cannister loads. Thousands of projectiles of lead, iron, rock, and flying debris tore the advancing troops to shreds. Henry's troop was not in the lead so when the firestorm came, they were not the ones directly hit. Henry could see the troops falling in front of him, in fact, many were blown to pieces with body parts and torn flesh flying around him. For once he was thankful he was small. He ducked behind a tree stump and fallen tree and began firing his musket up the hill. At what, he wasn't sure, because he could see nothing but smoke and dust. Some of the troops tried to move forward into the open area, but the Union sharpshooters were picking them off. Henry started to move up, but when he saw what was happening, he thought better of it and remained where he was, firing up the hill. Eventually, he heard the order to fall back and even that was tough, stepping over the remains of the dead or the screaming agony of the wounded, with cannister shot still flying overhead. Behind the battlefront, the 2nd Louisiana gathered again. Henry's temples were pounding, and his ears were ringing. His uniform was torn and spattered with blood and bits of human flesh. He wanted to throw up as some men were, but all he could do was gag. The whole brigade bivouacked for the night. Henry's sleep was fitful as he kept reliving and seeing the day's battle. Men he ate with the night before were now dead, blown to pieces and shredded beyond all recognition. He now realized that every morning he got to see the sunrise was a precious gift, a gift many others would no longer get. He was relieved to discover both Kearney brothers had survived.

The following day, fate stepped in on Henry's side for once. At least he felt that way. Henry was detailed as an orderly to the company's Colonel Levy and removed from serving in the infantry. As an orderly, he served to fulfill whatever need the colonel had, but his primary duty became as a horse-bearer. He was in charge of the colonel's horse, ensuring he was properly fed, moved, corralled, saddled, and ready to ride at the colonel's command. Henry was thrilled to be working with horses again. In addition, he could be assigned as a courier to deliver orders or communiques to the lines or back to general headquarters primarily on horseback. In fact, the previous orderly had been killed the day before either by an errant bullet or canister shot while delivering orders to the front on horseback.

Henry, thrilled to be out of the infantry, felt he needed to tell someone and the someone who came to mind was Mary Ann. He cornered a chaplain and asked him to pen a letter to her.

July 6, 1862

Dear Mary Ann,

In the last week I have seen and experienced the hell of this war, but this morning I was the recipient of good news. I am no longer in the musket carrying infantry but have been assigned as an orderly to the colonel, primarily as a horse bearer. This means I get to be with horses that I love and keep them at the ready for the colonel.

I so miss those evening rides where you and I rode along the creek leading to the Illinois river, you naming every bird, flower, and tree for me as we went. The birds chirping their happy songs. The insects buzzing in the tall grass. The cicadas with their chorus at this time of year. I pray that this war can soon be over and that we may ride together again.

Sincerely,
Henry

After the Seven Days Battle, both North and South were exhausted and ready to escape the July heat and humidity around the swamps and lowlands of the James River. Henry heard various opinions among the troops. Some said General Lee was reorganizing the army to prepare for an attack on the North. Others said President Davis wouldn't do that because he wanted the North to be perceived as the aggressor so that European powers, especially England, may then recognize the Confederacy and convince the northern states to end the war. At any rate, on July 26th the 2nd Louisiana was combined with several other regiments by General Lee into the "Coppens Zouave Battalion" and assigned to General Richard Ewell under General "Stonewall" Jackson's command.

As the war moved to northern Virginia, they were involved briefly in the battle at Cedar Mountain in Culpepper County, Virginia on August 9th. This was followed by the 2nd Battle of Bull Run or 2nd Manassas on August 29th and 30th. Both armies suffered heavy casualties at Manassas, with the Union suffering over 10,000, and the Confederacy 8,300, of which 130 were from Henry's old 2nd Louisiana.

The order came down in the afternoon of August 24th for Jackson's army, along with Jeb Stuart's cavalry, to move out heading north. They *were given three days rations, but no one seemed to know where they were going. They marched over the dusty and rocky road, many in bare feet, under the hot August sun. They finally stopped late at night, but after a short rest were ordered to march again. The only sound was marching feet and the clank and creak of the harnessed wagons following. Finally, they turned east, and the troops knew where they were headed—back to the railroad junction and huge Union supply depot at Manassas. At Bristoe Station they cut the telegraph lines and tore up the railroad tracks, causing a huge train wreck by Union trains coming to the depot for supplies. General Jackson left General Ewell and three brigades at Bristoe Station, including Henry. Jackson then took the rest of his army and captured the lightly guarded supply depot with its treasure trove of supplies. The depot contained sheds and warehouses with arms, boots, clothing and uniforms, and tarpaulin covered foodstuffs. There were also sutler's wagons full of luxuries including whiskey, wine, and fine cigars. The soldiers helped themselves, but General Jackson, taking no chances, poured all the liquor on the ground. By the afternoon of the 27th Ewell and his troops saw Union forces approaching Bristoe Station, so he withdrew toward Manassas.*

General Lee's plan was to defeat General Pope's army of Virginia before it could be reinforced by McClellan's troops exiting the Virginia Peninsula. In the end, Lee's army of Northern Virginia claimed victory at Manassas, but was unable to destroy the Union army. General Pope was replaced as commander of the army of Virginia by General McClellan who promptly combined it with his Army of the Potomac. While General Robert E. Lee planned for an incursion into Maryland, but feared a march on Washington, a mere twenty-five miles away, which would be too costly with the Union's huge advantage in troop numbers.

Henry's participation at Manassas was limited to delivering orders and communiques from general headquarters to the front and carrying messages back. At headquarters, he not only was horse bearer for his colonel but also for General Stonewall Jackson and General Ewell while the generals conferred about their next course of action. At the battle's end, he was concerned about his old company and was relieved the Kearney brothers were unscathed once again. Henry had no idea how the letter found him, but on the first of September at mail call he received a letter from Mary Ann.

July24, 1862

Dearest Henry,

Your letter was my one ray of sunshine in what has been a horrible summer. With my older brothers away with the war, father and I were left to get the fieldwork done. With his age, his heart simply wasn't up to the task. I found him at the end of the field, his team patiently waiting for instruction. I was too late, he was gone.

Mother and I are at a loss on how we are to handle the fall harvest, but I am determined to find a way. We met with the lawyer yesterday and apparently father had not updated his will for several years. He left the farm divided between my older brothers. The house to mother as long as she lives and then to me. Everything else went to my mother with no provision for any of my younger brothers and sisters.

I too miss our rides and assure you that Banjo and I occasionally still take that now-lonely trail. Please take care of yourself that we may ride together again.

Yours truly,
Mary Ann

The Confederate forces, Lee's Army of Northern Virginia, then moved into Maryland, capturing Harper's Ferry on September 14, 1862, but with a problem. Henry learned after the war that General Lee's plans had been discovered by Union forces because a soldier dropped the detailed plans accidentally. When Union general McClellan learned of the plans, he sent six of his eight corps to intercept and defeat the Confederacy. The two armies clashed at Sharpsburg, better known as Antietam, on September 17, 1862, in the bloodiest day of combat in American history.

Henry was aware of none of this at the time. He was just thankful he was away from the carnage suffered by infantry soldiers. He was still an orderly in Stonewall Jackson's army and mostly tending to officers' mounts. He was with Jackson on his circuitous route from Frederick, Maryland to the west, and then back to Harper's Ferry. After Harper's Ferry was secured, General Lee ordered all confederate units to Sharpsburg, including Stonewall Jackson's army. With all the Confederate troops amassed around Sharpsburg, it didn't take long for word to spread among the troops that a major battle was coming. In fact, they could see and hear the massive buildup of Union troops on the east side of Antietam Creek.

The battle began in the early morning of the 17th with artillery fire from both sides, but from the Miller farm cornfield and the north woods to the sunken road and then the lower Burnside Bridge, the two armies clashed until darkness prevailed. Casualties for the Union were over 12,400 and for the Confederates over 10,300 in a single day. Among the casualties for the Confederates was Henry. He was sent with a dispatch down the Hager-stown Pike toward Lee's headquarters when he felt a sharp pain in his left arm then a blow to his chest that knocked him off his horse. A bullet had pierced his arm then penetrated the courier's pouch and lodged in his haver sack. Both were hanging from his right shoulder and under his left arm. He wrapped the bleeding arm wound with a handkerchief using his teeth to pull it tight, remounted, and completed his ride.

The two armies reached a semi-truce so each could retrieve their wounded from the battlefields. The following morning General Lee gave the order to return to Virginia. Henry and the other wounded who were able to travel moved out. Those unable to travel were left behind to hopefully be cared for by Union doctors. There were minor battles and skirmishes as the Confederates retreated across the Potomac and to the Shenandoah Valley of

Virginia. Henry was sent to the hospital in Winchester, Virginia. They reset his broken arm, sewed up his wound, and assigned him to one of the hundreds of tents surrounding the hospital. Henry expected to be sent back to his unit in a short time, but that failed to happen. First his wound became infected and for a while they contemplated removing his arm. Just when the infection started to subside, he came down with dysentery from the lousy food and sleeping out on the ground. Sleeping on the cold ground contributed to his next malady, pneumonia. Finally, when the spring of 1863 arrived, he started feeling better just in time for another bout of dysentery.

It was a beautiful, early June morning when Henry, feeling better than he had in months, peered out the tent flap and saw a giant of a man sitting on an old hardtack crate. Henry looked again as his mind raced, trying to place the familiar figure. Then he recognized him. It was Marcus Muldoon from the Atlantic crossing, his shipmate. Henry climbed from the tent and said, "Markus, Markus Muldoon is that you?"

As the man turned toward Henry, he stared then said, "My god, if it ain't Henry Kearney. Still ain't big enough to deserve more 'en half rations!"

But when Markus turned toward him, Henry almost stopped in his tracks. Markus had no left arm, no left ear, and no left eye. The left side of his head was all bright pink scar tissue. Henry, wide-eyed in disbelief, blurted out, "My God Markus! What happened to you?"

"I don't rightly know. I was knocked unconscious at the time, but some guys in my unit said a cannon ball exploded on my left, killing six or seven and I guess they wanted to share a little of the blast with me. I woke up a little later with all the bells on earth ringing in my head. Felt like I had a glob of mud in my left eye, so I reached up with my left hand to remove it, but nothing happened. So, I opens my right eye, and I can see I have no left arm. Just a bloody remnant of a shirt sleeve and blood spurting out of what was left of my arm. I grabbed the bloody sleeve and wrapped it tight as I could around the stump, then I passed out again. When I awoke again, at first, I didn't know if I was dead or alive. Bells was still ringing in my head, and it was pitch dark. But then I could smell

the gun smoke and thought I could see a lantern off in the distance, so I let out a scream, or thought I did. I still couldn't hear nothin'. But then I kinda heard a muffled yell sayin' 'Hey you rebs! You got a live one over here.' Sure enough, they comes over and load me up an' that's all I remember until the next morning. Coupla guys pick me up and go dump me on some kind a table. There's a surgeon there in a nice clean apron with saw in hand and he says, 'Well this is a hell of a way to start my morning. This poor guy doesn't look like he has a chance in hell of surviving. Ok, let me sew that eyelid shut. His eyeball is gone. Then you wrap his head with bandages, and I'll see what I can do with this left arm.' Now, here we are a few months later and I'm still kickin' and runnin' into old friends. How about you? Why you here?"

"I got wounded in my left arm but that was a hell of a lot easier than the hell I've been through since. First infection, then the shits, then pneumonia, then the shits again. They think they finally got me put together good enough that I can rejoin my outfit in a week or two."

"Not me! They're sending me home to South Carolina, but to do what I don't have a clue. Henry, what the hell kinda smithy can I be with just one arm? I got a wife and two little boys back there and I'm sure they're gonna be wanting me to put some food on the table. Henry, I just don't know what I'm supposed to do. Heard Lincoln's gone and told the slaves they're all free men. Nobody to pick the cotton soon. No cotton, no need for any blacksmiths anyway. Damn Yankees are doin' just like their damn ancestors in England did to Ireland. 'You do it our way, or we take all your land, kill you off, and do it our way anyway!' The bastards! We Irish have been fighting this same damn war for nearly a thousand years."

Henry was a little concerned that Markus was getting too riled up but saw the wagon pulling up to take Markus on his way. He stood from where he was kneeling and gave Markus a bear hug and said, "God it was good to see you again Markus, though I wish it was better circumstances. I want to wish you all the good fortune I know you so richly deserve. Maybe it will all work out."

"I have my doubts, Henry. You take care of yourself and give them Yankees hell." With that he stood, grabbed his belongings with his right hand and threw them on the wagon. He extended his hand to the wagon driver, put his boot on one of the wheel spokes and hoisted himself onto the wagon seat and was gone without looking back.

Henry was feeling very lonely. He had checked with the hospital to see if they had admitted a George or Sam Kearney but no one with those names had been admitted. He hadn't written to Mary Ann because he had been too sick most of the time. Nor had he received any letters from her. He decided to look up a chaplain to see if he would help him write a letter to Mary Ann to at least inform her that he was still alive.

June 10, 1863

Dear Mary Ann,

It distressed me greatly to hear of your father's passing. He was a good man and an excellent provider for his family. I am truly sorry for your loss. I do hope you were able to complete your fall harvest somehow. So much time has passed since your last letter I hardly know where to begin.

First, I received a minor wound at the battle outside Sharpsburg along Antietam Creek. I was sent to the military hospital in Winchester, Virginia where they tended to my wound. However, a variety of ailments kept me here until this spring. I am feeling much better and expect to be sent back to my unit soon. I hope you and your family are all doing well. It does get lonely here because there is no one that I know and a lot of the sick and wounded can't talk anyway. I would treasure receiving another letter from you, but I know your circumstances have changed now without your father.

Sincerely Yours,
Henry

By the end of June, Henry was released from the hospital and sent back to his unit, finally arriving on July 17th, 1863. He kept his old job as an orderly and horse bearer for the colonel but practically the only enlisted men he recognized were the Kearney brothers. Sam was now a sergeant and George a corporal. Even after all they had seen and been through, George was still the happy-go-lucky character he had been. Always ready to pull off a joke to keep the troops' spirits up and have them laughing. Lee's Army of Northern Virginia was now back in Virginia behind the Rapidan River, returning there after the Battle of Gettysburg, which Henry was glad he missed.

In early September, Lee sent General Longstreet and his two divisions to Tennessee to help the Confederate Army of Tennessee. When Meade, now the commander of the Union forces, learned of the departure, he massed his forces along the Rappahannock River in preparation for an attack. However, in late September he too had to send troops to Tennessee. Lee, learning of the departing Union troops, mounted a campaign to attack Meade's right flank around Cedar Mountain. Henry's unit, still part of General Ewell's corps, was sent in defense of J.E.B. Stuart's cavalry, but was not needed because the cavalry had hidden and let the Union III corps pass. The Union forces were withdrawing toward Manassas Junction. On October 14, Maj General Warren fought a rearguard action against Stuart and Brig. General Hays division. On the same day, Confederate General Hill's corps ran into the withdrawing Union II corps at Bristoe Station and attacked, but the Union troops held their line from behind a railroad embankment, then continued their march toward Centreville and winter quarters. Lee took his forces behind the Rappahannock, leaving a fortified bridgehead on the north bank which were breeched by Union forces on November 7th capturing two brigades of General Jubal Early's division. Lee's army then retired to Orange County, south of the Rapidan, for their winter quarters, leaving Culpepper County to Union forces.

Meade was under pressure from President Lincoln for better results, so he mounted one more campaign at Mine Run, Virginia in late November of 1863. The plan was to try a surprise attack on Lee's right flank by crossing the Rapidan south of Stuart's cavalry screen, then attack General Ewell's II corps which included Henry's brigade. The Union forces under General William French became bogged down fording the Rapidan, giving Lee's forces time to mobilize and slow the advance. Meade planned an artillery barrage and attack for December 2 and Lee likewise planned an assault on the Union's flank. The artillery barrage began on time, but no major attacks occurred because Meade concluded the Confederate force was too great, so it was cancelled and both forces retired to winter quarters. The one unfortunate consequence was that Henry, along with several others, were captured by Union forces during General French's initial contact along Widow Morris Road.

20

As a prisoner-of-war, Henry was first sent to the Old Capital Prison in Washington, D.C. for processing. He was transferred to Pt. Lookout, MD for a month and then was transferred to the prison at Ft. Monroe, VA on March 2, 1864. The treatment of prisoners was rough and the food abominable. At Pt. Lookout, the food was described as "a half-pint of slop water coffee for breakfast and a half-pint of greasy water soup for supper." Prison barracks were wet, cold, and unsanitary. Drinking water was disgusting and toilet facilities rank with filth and vermin. Henry's hope was that he would be released in a prisoner exchange but had to be satisfied with fending off sickness and disease and dreaming about the beloved Ireland of his early childhood, or chase races with thoroughbreds, or occasionally the rides with Mary Ann. Some prisoners did write to their loved ones, but Henry had no access to paper or pen, let alone a chaplain to put his words to paper.

As the number of prisoners mounted, new prisons had to be built and finally in May of 1864, Henry was being transferred to New York. He was forced to help build his own prison in Elmira, New York, built with cheap lumber and having a stagnant cesspool of flood water and sewage at its center. With the arrival of winter in 1864, Henry was very thankful that his old boots made by his uncle were still holding together. Hundreds of prisoners had to endure the cold and snow barefooted. Henry was sure if his feet had been any bigger, he very well may have been killed for his boots. That winter, as many as 10 prisoners a day died from the cold or sickness. By the end of the war, 3,000 of the 12,000 that were imprisoned at Elmira had died.

After placing his X on an oath of allegiance to the United States and being practically nothing but skin and bones, Henry was released in May of 1865. He was given a small stipend and a free pass on any federal train or boat to go home. Henry wasn't at all sure where home was, but finally caught a train to Chicago and by August had made his way to Carrolton, Illinois, spending his first night in the old horse barn at the Keating farm.

He arose the following morning at sunrise with what seemed to be his lot in life, hunger pangs. He hadn't eaten for a couple of days except for some berries he found along the road. He looked across the way at the Jones farm and could see it was still occupied and neatly trimmed and painted. He wasn't at all sure if Mary Ann and her family still lived there as he had received no letters and sent none for over a year. He decided the only way he was going to find out for sure was to go knock on the door. Thinking it was a little early yet, he did a little exploring around the old Keating barn, finding his training halter and ropes right where he had left them years before. Even a small pile of oats was still in the granary, so obviously no one had been using the barn since he left. As he closed the granary door, he noticed an aged piece of paper with writing on it hanging from a nail to the side. His reading ability was mediocre at best, but he could clearly read HENRY at the top and Mary Ann at the bottom. The rest he wasn't too sure of, but thought it was something about Banjo and would he come over when he got back. He took the note from the nail and began the short walk over to the Jones farm.

The sun was up and shining brightly as Henry passed through the yard gate. He was greeted by a friendly collie dog and Henry reached down and patted his side as he knocked on the porch door with his other hand. Shortly, the inner door opened a thin man with a stiff leg and using a cane opened the porch door and looked down at Henry saying, "Can I help you with something?"

Henry recognized him as Mary Ann's older brother Bill, but he didn't seem to recognize Henry at all so Henry said, "I don't know if you remember me, my name's Henry Kearney. Your sister Mary Ann left me this note over at the Keating place to come and see her when I get back. Something about her horse Banjo I think."

Finally with a look of recognition, Bill said, "Oh my God, it is you, Henry! Come on in. I think Mary Ann is just doing up the breakfast dishes."

As they entered the kitchen, Henry saw a woman at the sink washing dishes as Bill said, "Mary Ann, there's a guy named Henry here says you left him a note at the Keating place to come over when he got back."

As Mary Ann turned, her and Henry's eyes met, and sparks flew. She rushed toward him, wiping her hands on her apron as she came. She wrapped her arms around his neck and gave him a huge hug and held him tightly. Henry hugged her back, not knowing what else to do. He couldn't believe his eyes; he had left a know-it-all young girl and now a beautiful young woman of eighteen was standing before him with tears welling up in her eyes.

"I thought you were dead! My God you're just skin and bones. Where have you been?"

As tears welled up in his eyes too, he could only mutter. "Prisoner of war. Got out end of May."

Mary Ann, still holding his hand, said, "Well sit down and let me fix you something to eat! You must be starving."

"Yes, I am a mite hungry. It's been a couple days."

As Henry was pulling a chair to sit down, Bill had already gotten a cup of coffee and was seated, his stiff leg stretched out under the table and his cane hanging from his chair. Mary Ann's mother, Jane, had also pulled up a chair and had both hands wrapped around a cup of coffee Bill had brought her. Mary Ann started to cook Henry some breakfast as Henry's eyes met Bill's. Bill said, "You can relax. Mary Ann told us the story of how you got hoodwinked into being a rebel soldier. Yes, I was a Yankee. Took a bullet to the knee at Missionary Ridge in Tennessee They fixed me as well as could be expected, I guess. Lot a guys died from gangrene or bone infections, so I count my blessings."

"What about Tom?" Henry inquired.

"Little different story there. At first, he just wanted to avoid the whole damn thing and go about his business. But the more some of his friends talked, the more, in his opinion, those damn Yankees in New York or Boston were messin' where they had no business. Somethin' been working for nearly a hundred years, leave it alone. He and some others from around here joined up with some Missouri rebels just to raise hell with the Federals intentions. He came through it all okay, but he and I no longer see eye to eye. We agreed to split the farm. He and his wife took the west part, closer to the river, and I got the part next to the home place. He's pretty bitter and I guess I am too. Haven't seen or talked to him in months."

Henry was unsure how to respond, so as Mary Ann set his breakfast before him, he turned to her mother and said, "Mrs. Jones I was sorry to hear of your husband's passing. He was a good man."

Jane replied, "Yes, he was, and he'd be just sick about the boys not getting along. There's been enough dying around here for everybody lately to last a lifetime. Nearly everyone that lives around here lost somebody in the war or because of it. Henry, what do you plan on doing now that it's over? You going to try to take over the old Keating farm?"

"If I had a dime to my name, that might be an option, but I don't."

Bill spoke up, saying, "Well, you can damn sure come to work for me. Tom was of the opinion those last two teams of Belgians you broke went with his farm, so he took them. I had to buy a couple of new teams and they are in sore need of some of your training. Does that sound like something you'd be interested in trying for a while?"

"Sure does!" said Henry as he wiped his plate clean with the last of his piece of fresh baked bread before devouring it. "In fact, I'm ready to start today. Thank you, Mary Ann; that breakfast was delicious."

As Mary Ann and Henry's eyes locked once again, she said, "That's wonderful! Bill can get you settled in the bunk house, but later this afternoon I want to take you by the corral so you and Banjo can get reacquainted. Maybe we can go on a ride Sunday afternoon like we used to."

"That would be fine. I'll meet you at the corral around seven this evening if that will work."

"Should be fine," answered Mary Ann. With that settled, Bill and Henry left so Henry could get a tour of the farm, where he'd be living, and what his responsibilities would be. Henry inquired about his meals and was told he could fix his own at the bunkhouse, but occasionally he'd probably be asked to eat with the family. It was after 6:30 when Henry wandered over toward the horse barn, but saw Mary Ann was already at the corrals gently stroking the nose of a palomino horse—Banjo.

"Well, hello Banjo. Long time no see." Henry said, as he walked up beside Mary Ann. Banjo's ears pitched forward then he raised his head and put it over Henry's shoulder as Henry began scratching his neck, as if long-separated friends were reunited.

"I think he remembers you!" said Mary Ann.

"I do believe he does. Looks like you've been keeping him well fed, but maybe not riding him enough. He looks a little heavy."

"We can start working on that Sunday afternoon if you'd like to go on a ride with me down by the creek like we used to do."

"We can certainly do that if Bill doesn't have work for me to do and if you can come up with a horse for me to ride."

"You can ride Martha's old horse. My sister was of the opinion she was all grown up and eloped with the first returning soldier that looked her way. Mom was certainly upset about it, but they're gone now. They moved up north someplace but are still in the county. Bill usually takes Sundays off unless there's down hay and it looks like rain or some emergency like that."

"Well, you clear it with Bill and if he's okay with it, we can take that ride and you can once again tell me the names of every tree, plant, or animal we happen to come across. Just like the old days."

21

On Sunday, as the sun rose, it was a clear, warm, late August day. Mary Ann, her mother, Jane, and her younger sisters and brothers rode with Bill to church while Henry went to work with one of the new Belgian teams Bill had bought. It was past three in the afternoon before Mary Ann arrived at the corrals wearing her riding clothes and a wide-brimmed ladies straw hat. Henry wasn't sure he had ever seen a more beautiful woman when she asked, "You think you could saddle up Banjo and Socks so we can go for our ride?"

"I believe I could manage that. Socks is the sorrel over there by Banjo?"

"That's the one. I'll wait here until you get them saddled up."

A few minutes later, Henry came out of the barn leading both horses. He helped Mary Ann up on Banjo, then mounted Socks. They rode off toward the distant creek at the other end of a field of corn. Grasshoppers buzzed and hopped out of their way as they rode along the dusty road, chatting about nothing in particular. At the end of the field, a wagon trail wound down toward the creek with its small stream of flowing water. As they rode down the slope, it seemed like they were entering a different world. A slight breeze rustled the leaves in the giant cottonwoods along the creek that provided shade from the afternoon sun. Willows, wild plum, raspberry, and chokecherry bushes grew along the edge of the creek. The creek itself had a melody as it flowed over the stones and rocks in its path. Robins, finches, sparrows, and birds of all kinds chirped among the branches as squirrels hopped from branch to branch. A redwing blackbird scolded them from the cattails as they rode close to its nest. As a fluffy white cumulus cloud briefly blocked the sun, Henry looked at the verdant green grass along the stream and was carried back to his childhood in Ireland. Mary Ann broke his daydreaming by saying, "We should stop here. Maybe sit on that fallen tree and just enjoy natures beauty around us for a while."

Henry nodded, pulled back on the reins, and dismounted. He walked around Banjo and helped Mary Ann dismount then let both horses start munching on the abundant grass as Henry and Mary Ann sat down. Henry glanced up to see a hawk circling high above as a meadowlark sang from atop a post on the hillside. Turning to Mary Ann, he said, "This place is so beautiful and tranquil. Being here with you, Mary Ann, I can't remember being this at peace or happy ever in my life."

Tears welled in Mary Ann's eyes as she responded, "Henry, I'm just so happy that you are back. I've missed you terribly."

"What I don't understand Mary Ann is with your obvious beauty, why aren't there ex-soldier boys beating a path to your door? You surely have a beau or two, don't you?"

"Let me tell you Henry Kearney. There has only been one man who ever held the key to my heart and I'm riding beside him today. Ever since your first letters, I've known you were the one for me."

Henry was aghast. "I, I had no idea! Yes, I care for you deeply. You got me through my roughest times during the war and thoughts of seeing you again kept me going when I was a prisoner. But, Mary Ann, I'm twelve years older than you. You are a gorgeous young woman, why would you want to tie yourself down with a wreck like me?"

Mary Ann leaned over and gave him a gentle kiss. "It's in this girl's heart, Henry. I know you're my one and only love."

Gently holding her shoulders, he said, "You say that now, but you're so young. We need to give this a little time to ensure that it is right. Right for both of us."

Mary Ann, trying to hide her disappointment that Henry hadn't quite professed his love for her, said, "I suppose you're right to wait a while. You being so much older and wiser. But I'm telling you now, you're the only one for me. You of all people should know when I make up my mind, it's impossible to convince me otherwise."

Both sat quietly, lost in their own thoughts, but when a cicada began his mournful cry high in the cottonwoods, Henry rose and gathered their horses and said, "I think we both have some thinking to do but we better start heading back."

Mary Ann nodded in agreement, arose, clasped Henry's hand, and stared straight into his eyes and winked.

"What is that supposed to mean?"

Means I'm right and I know it, but I can wait until you come around."

"Oh, you think so, huh!" He said as he helped her up into the saddle then mounted up himself for the ride home.

Mary Ann may have been convinced, but Henry wasn't too sure. First of all, there was the issue of his job. If Bill was made aware of a relationship between him and Mary Ann, might he fire Henry on the spot? Secondly, was Jane, Mary Ann's mother. How would she feel about her daughter carrying on with a man twelve years her senior? Henry was very worried about how those two would react, but he had other concerns too. Among them, how would he support a family? Even if Bill kept him on, he wasn't being paid all that much. Definitely not enough to support a family.

Through the fall harvest, the winter, and into the next spring, Henry continued to ponder all the questions that were running through his head. Mary Ann and Henry continued to take their rides and she would invariably ask if he was ready to be her intended. Henry would smile, shake his head in wonderment, and try to change the subject. One thing that kept going through Henry's mind was the advice he had received from Jim Johnson all those years ago on his first steamboat trip down the Ohio River. "One of these days, some girl is going to get her claws into you. So just make sure she wants you for who you are and doesn't want to change you into something else." It seemed like Mary Ann fit the bill. She wasn't trying to turn him into anybody else and accepted him as he was. Still, that twelve-year age difference bothered him.

Toward the end of July of 1866 Mary Ann approached him as Henry was turning some horses out. "I have a favor to ask of you Henry Kearney."

"Oh yeah, what's that"

"Well, I was in town today and saw where the county fair board has built a half mile oval racetrack at the fairgrounds. They intend to hold a horse race during the fair and are looking for entries. You've always said Banjo looked like he might have some thoroughbred blood in him, so I entered him in the race. However, this is where you come in. They won't let ladies ride, so I thought you could be his rider because you told me you used to race horses back in England?"

"Yeah, but that was a long time ago. Don't you think it would have been prudent to perhaps ask me before entering the race?"

"Well, yes but it was a spur of the moment thing. Oh, please, please tell me you will do it."

"How much time do we have?"

"Two weeks. You said we, does that mean yes, you'll do it?"

"Let me ponder it overnight. Come at it from a couple different directions. If we do this, Banjo is in for a couple of weeks of hard work and so are you. I can't shirk my duties around here, so you're the one that has to get him in shape."

"I can do that. Oh, thank you thank you! I know we can win this race!"

"I didn't quite say yes yet."

"I know, but you will."

The following morning, Henry did acquiesce, and Mary Ann did start exercising Banjo every day to get him in shape. By the time the day of the big race came around, everybody at the farm was excited about it including Bill and Mary Ann's mother, Jane. In fact, the big race was the talk of the county when Henry mounted up and rode Banjo into town.

At the fairgrounds, Henry learned there were twenty-four entries so far, but some late entries might be accepted. The rules for the race were read to everyone including that the race would be one mile or two laps around the track. Also, no chicanery would be allowed, like whipping an opponent's horse or trying to unseat another rider. Also, no spurs would be allowed.

Henry noted that a few of the other riders appeared to be riding purebred quarter horses, but most were aboard ordinary riding horses. He also noticed that Banjo appeared to be a good two hands taller than all the other horses except for Slim Martindale's entry. Some of Slim's buddies down at the bar had told him if he would enter, they would pay his entry fee. So here was Slim with his always attendant bottle of hooch, aboard his old Clydesdale, Thumper. Some of the cowboys were teasing Henry about his use of Mary Ann's riding saddle and not lengthening the stirrups so his knees appeared to be up around his chin.

Finally, the starter told them to line up for the start as the huge crowd in the grandstand and along the outside rail let out a yell. When the starter's pistol fired, they all took off in a mad dash except for Slim and old Thumper, clear on the outside. Slim hadn't quite got Thumper turned around yet when the gun fired so they were facing the wrong direction. By the time Slim got turned, the others were already rounding the first corner. Not that it made a lot of difference because Thumper's top speed was a slow saunter to the other end of the grandstand, hopefully with Slim able to stay aboard.

As the horses entered the back straightaway, the cowboys on their quarter horses had a sizeable lead. Henry and Banjo were caught up in a bunch of riding horses, so Henry maneuvered to the outside. Henry was riding with his head down, seat up and his weight squared over Banjo's withers, while all the cowboys were sitting back on their saddle and using their reins to whip the horse to go faster. As they came around the final turn and down the straightaway in front of the grandstand, some of the quarter horses were starting to fade. When Henry and Banjo went by the grandstand, they were still several lengths behind the quarter horses, but had separated themselves from the other riding horses and were gaining on the leaders. Meanwhile, Slim and Thumper were getting close to the far end of the grandstand where they would turn around and head back to the start, much to the entertainment of the crowd.

On the back stretch, Henry and Banjo began passing the quarter horses and when they entered the final turn of the second lap had taken the lead. Mary Ann in the grandstand was beside herself with excitement and was screaming at the top of her lungs. Even her mother, Jane, had risen to her feet and held a hand to her mouth while raising the other arm yelling, "Go Banjo go!"

As Henry and Banjo came down the final stretch toward the finish line, they were twenty lengths ahead and stretching it too more. When they crossed the finish, the closest horse to them was old Thumper heading in the opposite direction. As Henry pulled up and then turned Banjo back toward the announcers stand, Mary Ann nearly ran down the grandstand stairs and ran out onto the track. As Henry dismounted, Mary Ann threw her arms around his neck and kissed him long and hard right on the lips. The announcer yelled loudly to the crowd, "If the other riders had known that was going to be their reward, they damn sure would have rode a little faster."

Henry received twenty dollars as the winner of the race which he tried to give to Mary Ann, but she insisted that he keep it. "You earned it," she said.

Henry stuck the money in his pocket and started to remount Banjo to take him home, but Mary Ann stopped him, saying, "Wait Henry, what time do you want to pick me up to go to the dance?"

"Dance? What dance? I don't know how to dance."

"We won the big race, so we just have to go to the big dance at the fairgrounds tonight. It would be an affront to the people of the county if we weren't there to receive their congratulations."

"But I don't know the first thing about dancing!"

"Well, we'll mostly mingle and talk to people, but come to the house about six and I'll show you some of the basic dance steps before we go. You'll do fine. A lot of these cowboys around here aren't too sure about their dance steps but rather enjoy holding young ladies in their arms."

Henry wasn't totally convinced, and again had thoughts of Jim Johnson's advice about women trying to change you running through his head.

But, in the end, he once again agreed to bow to Mary Ann's wishes and go to the dance, saying, "Alright, alright, I'll see you at six with bells on."

Henry got on Banjo and started to head back to the farm when it occurred to him that Banjo deserved a reward for performing so well in the race, so he turned and went uptown. At a grocery he went in and using some of the twenty dollars, he bought Banjo an apple and some sugar. Banjo eagerly licked some sugar from Henry's hand. Henry thought he would save the apple until they got home, and Banjo was unbridled. As Henry was about to remount, he noticed the jewelry store next door. Thinking Mary Ann would probably appreciate some kind of bauble from his winnings, he entered the store to see what he could find. He finally decided on a heart-shaped gold necklace that you could open and put a picture in each half. He would give it to her before the dance so she could wear it that night.

At six o'clock Henry arrived at the Jones house with the horse and buggy and his best duds on. Jane invited him in and escorted him to the parlor where Mary Ann was waiting along with her younger sister Violet. Mary Ann explained, "Violet has been taking piano lessons and she will play some music while I show you some basic dance steps. In square dancing there is a caller, and you can kind of just do what he is telling everyone else to do; Do-si-do and promenade and all that. You can pick that up by just watching for a while. Some songs are slower, and couples do the waltz or two-step depending on the beat. Okay, put your right arm around my waist and hold your left arm out like this holding my right hand. Now, Violet will begin playing and I'll show you the steps."

After an hour or so of practice, it was time to leave for the dance. Henry turned to Mary Ann while reaching into his pocket and said, "I thought you deserved a little something for lending me Banjo to win that race today, so I stopped at the jewelry store and bought you this necklace I thought you might wear tonight."

"Oh Henry, it's perfect! Help me fasten it in back, then we can go."

Henry had a much better time at the dance than he thought he might. Even learning what do-si-do and allemande left meant. In addition, it was the first time he had heard that kind of fiddle music since boot camp before the war. He and Mary Ann even enjoyed the attention and congratulations for winning the race, but at midnight the music stopped, and it was time to head back to the farm. Henry helped Mary Ann into the buggy and as they started out, she held his arm and leaned her head on his shoulder, saying, "I had an absolutely marvelous time tonight, Henry."

"Yeah, it was fun, wasn't it?"

Raising her head and gently turning Henry's head to face her, she looked deep into his eyes and said, "Henry, I think we should get married."

"You're asking me to marry you? How did you arrive at that decision? What will Bill think and your mother if this old man up and marries their precious sister and daughter?"

"Bill has been expecting you to ask me for some time. As for Mom, she said you were a hard worker and a gentleman. Let me think how she put that. Oh yeah. 'He's kind of a runt but still the pick of the litter.' She even said we could have her bedroom and she'd move upstairs into mine."

"Well, since you have it all figured out and it does kind of match up with my future intentions, I'll say yes. We can get married."

"Good! So, we can tell everybody you asked me to marry you and I said yes." She turned and gave him a passionate kiss. The trip back to the farm took a little longer that night.

22

Mary Ann and Henry were married on February 28, 1867, and their first son, William Thomas (Tom), was born in January of 1868. With a growing family, Mary Ann had less time to write stories, but she did continue to keep a journal or diary of their life together, and the balance of the books in the black metal box were these journals. As I read through the journals, Mary Ann recorded notable events in their lives. The births of their children, after Thomas, was Frances in May of 1869, followed by my grandfather, Samuel in July of 1873, then two more daughters, Annie in 1875 and Nettie in 1878. They first rented the old Keating place and attempted to restart the raising of Belgian draft horses but were unable to make a go of it. It was extremely tough for a confederate veteran in the land of Lincoln even if he was the best horse trainer around. It was the spring of 1868 that they first considered homesteading. The homestead act or it's official title, "An Act to Secure Homesteads to Actual Settlers on the Public Domain," was passed in 1862 and was a boon to the settlement of the west after the Civil War. In reading the first line of the act, Mary Ann had given up hope for them as it read, "Any citizen who was the head of a household or a single person over 21, who HAD NOT TAKEN UP ARMS AGAINST THE US GOVERNMENT could apply for a quarter-section of land. Precluded from homesteading, they moved first to Virden, Illinois, then to a leasehold farm in Raymond, Illinois. There were then moves to Girard in 1879 and back to Virden, Illinois in the early 1880s. As their children grew up, Henry and Mary Ann had secured a small acreage where Henry continued to break and train horses. Through the years they had made numerous attempts to buy a farm but with little money and no land to use as collateral, they were continually outbid by existing farmers. The discovery of a large vein of coal and being near the Alton-Chicago Railroad tracks had put Virden on the map. To supplement their income, Henry had been forced to go to work for the Chicago-Virden Coal Mine. The mine was the largest employer in the area but paid meager wages.

It was Henry and Mary Ann's oldest son Tom who informed them they were now eligible to homestead as he had learned it in school. It had been part of the total amnesty granted by President Johnson in 1869 but had remained unknown to Henry and Mary Ann for over a decade. This knowledge revised their interest in trying to homestead, but where and when remained unanswered. In the autumn of 1886 Henry had delivered his last trained team of draft horses and it was decided that he along with his son, Tom, because of his ability to read, would make a trip by railroad to Kearney, Nebraska to determine the feasibility of homesteading there. Their eldest daughter, Frances, (perhaps named after Henry's uncle and his father's best friend) was now working in a millinery store and Mary Ann was taking in laundry and mending clothes for patrons which would enable the family to buy groceries while Henry and Tom were absent. Mary Ann insisted that Tom keep notes of their entire trip so she could record the story of their adventures.

23

On the morning of the 17th of September 1886 my dear Henry and our oldest son, Tom, boarded a passenger train bound for St. Louis. From there they were to board a branch of the Union Pacific Railroad, a train to Kansas City where they would cross the Missouri River before heading for Nebraska. In two days, they had crossed two of the biggest rivers in the entire country, the Mississippi and the Missouri. The rail line meandered through the northeast corner of Kansas before entering Nebraska northwest of Marysville, Kansas. From there it went through Hastings to Kearney, Nebraska, where it junctioned with the main Union Pacific line. Where else would Kearneys go to begin their search other than Kearney, Nebraska? It seemed like destiny had pointed us there with the postal service even adding the extra "e" so it matched our name, rather than the name of the nearby Fort Kearny named for Steven Watts Kearny.

I had asked Tom to take notes but he did a masterful job of recording their trip so I inserted his pages into my journal here just as he had written them.

Henry and I arrived in the wide Platte River Valley and the city of Kearney early in the day and determined we should first make our way to the Buffalo County Courthouse (Kearney being located in that county) to determine what lands were still available for homesteading in the county. The conductor aboard the train had already informed us that Kearney was a fast-growing, bustling city. With the junction of the railroads and being on the north side of the Platte River, adjacent to all the public free range available for homesteading, its population was nearing 10,000 people. In addition, it was promoting itself as the jumping off place for those heading to the Black Hills of the Dakota Territory where gold had recently been discovered.

We made our way to the courthouse and the Register-of-Deeds office. There they informed us that the Land Office for this part of the state of Nebraska was in Grand Island, forty miles to the east and that is where our claim would have to be filed. However, they could tell us that nearly all the land in Buffalo County had already been homesteaded. There were but a few homestead relinquishments available. They did tell us that going to the northwest up the Wood River Valley into Dawson County there may still be some open range available. There was a good trail heading that way along the Kearney Black Hills Stage line route. They also told us that route was presently being surveyed for a railroad line clear to Deadwood in the Dakota territory. A young man working in the office also told us if we went straight north out of Kearney and through the hills, we would arrive at Pleasant Valley. and northwest of there, along the South Loup River or the low hills bordering it, were some available public lands suitable for homesteading.

Armed with this information and a map, we decided we would get a room for the night, either rent a rig or a couple saddle horses, buy a few provisions, and head to the northwest in the morning. We went ahead to a restaurant along Central Avenue and entered to get a bite to eat. The place was very crowded, so we sat down at a table with another gentleman whose name we learned was Gaslin. In engaging him in conversation we learned he was a circuit judge and was currently setting up a law practice in Kearney. We told him we were in town to possibly look for a place to homestead and he volunteered to help us with our endeavor and relayed the following information. I asked if he minded if I took some notes while he was talking and he agreed that was fine.

"Gentlemen, through hard work and sacrifice I worked my way through law school in Augusta Maine. After losing my entire office to a fire in 1865, I decided to make my way west. The Chicago & Northwestern

being the only railroad across Iowa at the time, I made my way to Omaha after a short stint in Michigan. It was March of 1868 when I rode the ferry across the Missouri into Omaha, which was then a rather small and struggling place. It was full of desperados and a total of seventy-five men were killed in the first year I was there, but I remained until the spring of 1871. In that year, along with a party of two or three others, we struck out for southwestern Nebraska and the Republican River valley. There was little settlement west of Red Cloud in Webster County. We saw huge herds of buffalo, elk, deer, and antelope, plus wild turkeys and prairie chickens on all sides as we went. On the return, we crossed over the divide between the Republican and the Platte rivers west of what is now Grand Island where nearly no one was living at the time. I returned to Omaha and filed a homestead in Harlan County along Nebraska's southern border at the land office in Beatrice, Nebraska. I lived on the homestead through the dreadful winter of 1871-72. In 1875, I was elected as circuit judge of the sixth judicial district in a convention held in Plum Creek by the Republican party and then I won over the Democratic candidate. My district embraced Webster, Adams, Buffalo, Dawson, Lincoln, Custer, Sherman and all the unorganized county of Sioux extending to the Northern Nebraska border. In my first term of office, I oversaw 26 murder trials and have presided over 68 to date."

Henry Inquired, "Is the country around here still that lawless? Do we need to be armed?"

Judge Gaslin replied, "No, it's a lot calmer now. Back in those days, the terminus for the Texas cattle drives was at Ogallala, Nebraska and those Texas cowboys were intent on letting off some steam after weeks on the trail. You know all the men coming into this country back then had gone through the Civil War so killing a man is something a lot of them had done before. Try pushing a man too far and he's going to do what he was taught to do just a few years ago. Plus, everything was open range and when the homesteaders started moving in, there was bound to be trouble. If you are heading up the South Loup Valley, be careful about going too far west. Course that's sandhill country anyway. Suitable for cattle raising and not much else. Most of the bottom lands are now homesteaded or bought and paid for by huge cattle ranchers. But you know there is a lot of good farm ground in the valleys between the South Loup, the Wood River, and the Platte Valley. Water used to be a problem, but with new well drilling rigs, everybody is putting in windmills. Some wells go as deep as 400 feet to find water.

Well, I got to be getting back to the office, so I'll wish you two gentlemen the best of luck and bid you adieu."

We thanked him for the information and for letting us join him for dinner. We spent the afternoon lining up a couple riding horses for tomorrow and buying a few provisions for our trip, then just walked around the city, learning a bit more about the area.

We arose early the following morning, retrieved our horses and provisions and rode to the northwest along the Kearney & Black Hills Stage route. It climbed a steep hill out of the Platte Valley and then after a couple of miles descended a gentle slope into the Wood River Valley. As we knew there was no land available in Buffalo County, we rode quickly through the area. We did see small settlements at Greendale and Stanley and marveled at the many homes built of sod cut from the prairie. Some had roofs built with framing lumber probably shipped from Kearney. Others used wood cut from trees along the river and often covered with layers of sod. There were next to no trees anywhere except along the river. There were occasionally thickets of plum brush or chokecherries started from seeds scattered by birds, but otherwise just mile after mile of prairie grasses and Buffalo grass.

Shortly after noon we came across another settlement on the north side of the Wood River called Armada. It was a little larger than those we had seen previously. It had a general store, a small hotel with a restaurant, a blacksmith shop, and a couple other small businesses, plus a combination church and school. We stopped there to rest our horses and let them get their fill of water. We entered the café and talked with the owner over a cup of coffee. He told us we were near to the Dawson County border a couple more miles west. He told us there was a stage stop a little further west called

Trappers Grove and then a few more miles to a settlement called Jewell. He didn't seem to think there was much good public land available to homestead until you got well past Jewell in the Wood River Valley, but there was quite a bit more if you went north toward the South Loup River Valley.

It was then that a couple cowboys came in for a cup of coffee. They sat down with the owner and us. They worked for Hammer & Wood and were on their way to Kearney for supplies when they had wagon trouble. They left the wagon for repair at the blacksmith while they grabbed a cup of coffee before going on. They told us that Hammer & Wood was a large cattle ranching operation with land along both sides of the South Loup then extending south clear to the Wood River. They thought it was probably eight to ten thousand acres altogether and ran primarily by brothers Josh and Perry Wood in partnership with their brother-in-law Louis Hammer from Council Bluffs, Iowa. Henry asked how many horses they had on the ranch, and they thought it had to be north of three hundred, with bunches of them not yet broke to ride. They said there were lots of wild horses in extreme northern Custer County years ago free to whoever could capture and break them and some of that stock was still kept at the ranch.

As they rose to leave, we did also, thanking the owner for his information and hospitality. We continued our ride to the northwest through Trappers Grove, and toward the end of the day, we finally reached Jewell. There was no hotel at Jewell, but a family there named Thomas welcomed us to stay the night with them. There were no beds to sleep on, but we had a warm corner on the dirt floor. They invited us to supper too and this was to be our first night sleeping in a sod house. The following morning before mounting up to head out, Mr. Thomas said he didn't think there was much point in going on west as he was sure all the land along the Wood River had already been claimed, at least for several more miles. He advised us to go north through the hills to the South Loup River Valley where our pickings might be better. He also said not to limit ourselves to river bottom land as some of the farmers in the hill country were raising crops just as good as those in the river valleys.

On that advice, we headed straight north in search of the South Loup River. We did see a few homesteads on our ride through the hills. However, it wasn't all just grass-covered hills. We saw some flat areas and bowls that appeared to be great areas for growing crops, and a couple of the homesteads we passed were doing just that. It was now fall so it was difficult to judge how good their crops had been, but they had turned some sod. It was nearing noon when we finally reached the South Loup River and what a beautiful river it was. While the Wood River had little flowing water and seemed to be little more than a creek bed with a muddy bottom this time of year; the Loup was maybe twenty or more yards wide with a healthy flow of water surrounded by giant cottonwoods and willows. From our high vantage point, off to the west on the south side of the river, we could see what looked like ranch buildings and corrals including a wood frame house. To our right and on the other side of the river were more ranch buildings or some kind of settlement. There was some kind of activity going on at the ranch buildings to the west, so we decided to head down and see what was happening.

As we approached the corrals, a man mounted his horse and rode right toward us, so we stopped to await his arrival. He pulled up alongside of us and asked, "Can I ask what you fellas are doing on our ranch?"

Henry answered. "We rode over from Jewell on Mr. Thomas' advice. We were looking for the South Loup River as we're kind of scouting for places to homestead. We did pass through a gate a ways back and we're sorry if we encroached on your land. We saw some activity down here so thought we would check it out"

"It's not my land. It belongs to Josh Wood. If you're looking for land to homestead, you just rode through it. All the land here by the river has already been claimed. My name is Brown and I'm the ranch foreman. We've had some cattle stolen in the past so when we spot strange riders we go and investigate. Come on up to the ranch and I'll introduce you to the owner."

Henry and I had both caught the name Josh Wood as being the same name we had heard from the two cowboys in Armada. After an exchange of names when Mr. Brown introduced us, we related that we had met a couple of his cowboys at Armada the day before. Mr. Wood responded, "Yeah, we still have to go clear to Kearney for some supplies, but since Broken Bow in Custer County has been settled and it's now the county seat and we have the Burlington & Missouri railroad up there, we get a lot of our supplies there. If we leave before daybreak, we get there and back in one day. Henry, are you planning on just being a sod buster or are you hoping to raise a few cattle too? Those hills you came through are pretty good for a little of both."

"Back in Illinois I mostly broke and trained horses, both saddle and draft horses. My hope is that I could maybe do some of that here, along with raising some crops."

"Well, I'll be damned! You certainly have come to the right place. We are constantly trying to break horses around here. With a place this size we do a lot of riding, and the horses start to break down earlier than you would think. We're just now getting ready for the fall round-up. We'll be out three weeks, nearly all of it up top, separating the breeding stock for winter quarters, moving weened calves to separate pasture, and then rounding up last year's calves or yearlings to sell. You looking to file papers this trip?

"No, we were mostly just scouting things out, but if you're saying you might push some horse breaking my way if we settle here, then I'm ready to say we'll be back in the spring to file papers."

"Sounds good to me. I'll notify my brother, Perry, whose ranch is a few miles east and if we got the time, we'll try to find a decent homestead for you."

"Would really appreciate that. Say, what's that place on the other side of the river, another ranch?"

"Yes and no! It's the H.W. George ranch but also Georgetown. He's got a small store there and that's where we get our mail. He also put in a small watermill by diverting a bit of the river for grinding grain into flour. Wheat flour, oat flour, cornmeal, he does it all."

"Well, we might head over that way on our way back to Kearney. Just to say hi and introduce ourselves. Is there a certain place where we should cross the river?"

"Yeah, you'll see where wagons have been crossing just west of Georgetown. Some bigger rocks were put across there, so it isn't all sand bottom. We have to redo it occasionally and hope to build a bridge there someday. You fellas are welcome to spend the night at the ranch and we can get to know each other a little better and I can fill you in on the history of Custer County."

"Thank-you! We accept and are looking forward to it. In the meantime, is there something we can do to help you around here?"

"Nah, don't worry about it. I've already given out today's assignments to the cowboys."

We then spent the afternoon and evening learning more about Custer County, (Josh was the first sheriff), the Wood families, the Hammer & Wood livestock operation, and homesteading in the county. The Hammer portion of Hammer & Wood referred to Louis Hammer, who was married to Josh and Perry's sister Rhoda. He was a lumber man from Council Bluffs, Iowa, and had made a lot of money selling railroad ties to the Union Pacific Railroad. He had invested the money in land and partnered with Josh and Perry to run the ranch operation. Josh, in turn, learned about Henry's experience with horses and a little of his life journey so far. It was also where we first learned that under a tree claim or a claim under the Timber Culture Act of 1873, you could file a claim without having to be living on the claim. This meant if we could find a suitable claim, we could file it before returning to Illinois, then return in the spring to begin fulfilling the requirements of the Act. Josh said he could show us some available land in the morning if we wished and we readily agreed.

We arose early the following morning and were fed a wonderful breakfast before departing for the hills we had ridden through just the day before. After viewing several options, Henry decided the NW1/4 of Section 32, T-13-N, R-19-W was the one for him. It had flat table land suitable for farming and ample pasture and hay ground, plus he liked the idea of planting 10 acres of trees along the North border as required by the Act in the hope it would remind him more of Ireland. Josh suggested we go to Grand

Island and file before going back to Illinois. He thought the filing fee was around ten dollars. We spent another night at the Josh Wood ranch with Henry and I trying to decide if we had enough money to both file a claim and secure our railroad tickets home. Also, we heard more about the wild days before it became a county with free range and settler disputes.

In the morning, we said our goodbyes until next year, mounted our horses and headed east. We crossed the Loup at the designated crossing and stopped briefly in Georgetown. We then followed the north riverbank in a southeasterly direction. It was a beautiful ride along a beautiful river. We did pass several homesteads with their requisite soddy. As evening approached, we stopped at the homestead of a German fellow and his wife and kids. His English wasn't real good but we understood his invitation to have supper with them. He said there was no room in the soddy, but we were welcome to sleep in the makeshift barn and to feed and water our horses. We took him up on his offer and managed to determine in the morning that if we went another mile there was a ferry across the South Loup and if we took that well-used trail south, we would end up in Kearney.

Back in Kearney, we returned our horses to the livery then went to the train depot to inquire about tickets home via Grand Island. It turned out to not be a big problem at all, though we were running low on money. We bought our return tickets with the additional stop in Grand Island and decided we would cut back on eating if necessary to stretch our money. It was too late in the day for any east bound trains, so we spent the night trying to sleep on benches in the depot. We arose at 5 am and boarded our east bound train at 5:48 am. We got off that train in Grand Island and inquired as to the location of the land office. We walked there and were at the door waiting for them to open by 9 am. We showed them the quarter section we wanted to file on under the Timber Culture Act, paid our filing fee plus a publication fee and were back at the train depot before noon. We boarded another train a little after 2 pm and continued our journey home to Virden, Illinois, arriving on the 30th of September just in time for the year's first hard freeze.

That concluded Tom's writing about their exciting trip to Nebraska but the big news at home was from our daughter, Frances. She had gotten engaged to be married to George (Doc) Orr while her dad and brother were gone and there was absolutely no way she was going to move to Nebraska. Frances was 17 and George 19. George's dad had died at a young age, so George often had to help his mother. They owned a recreation parlor in town and like us it was a struggle to make ends meet.

24

It was abundantly clear that Henry and Tom were leaving for Nebraska in the spring. It was equally clear that Frances had no intention of going with them. Throw in the fact that Tom couldn't wait to tell his girlfriend, Elizabeth Gatton, about his adventures and the wonders and beauty of the South Loup River Valley, nor could she wait to hear about them. Elizabeth had been raised by her father but lately the tables had turned due to his fondness for alcohol. It was now more of a case where she took care of him, and she had grown tired of it. Consequently, the whole family, including my mother Jane, had to find some way to compromise.

Mother, still having small children when dad died, had remarried a fellow named Thomas Lisle in the late 1860s and he was now in poor health. They lived on a farm six miles east of Virden. After much discussion and anguish, and Tom's announcement that he and Elizabeth intended to get married before yearend so she could go with them to Nebraska; it was finally decided Henry, Tom, and Sam, Tom's 14-year-old brother, along with Elizabeth, would all go to Nebraska in the spring taking whatever possessions the family wished to keep with them. I and the three girls, Frances and the two younger ones Annie and Nettie, would move in with Jane and her husband to help with his care. After Frances's marriage, scheduled for late in 1887, I and the other two girls would come to Nebraska by train. Frances agreed to continue looking after her grandmother and her sick husband if needed. In concert with the plan, Tom and Elizabeth Gatton were married on December 22nd, 1886, when both were 19 years old.

At the first sign of spring in 1887, Henry and the boys, Tom and Sam, started preparing our little place for sale and crating up the few possessions they would be taking with them. They were keeping a pair of Belgian draft horses and a young riding horse they felt they would need in Nebraska. By early April what could be sold had been and the girls and I were moved to the Lisle farm east of town. Henry, Tom, and Sam loaded their crates and horses onto a railcar, and along with Elizabeth rode by rail to St. Joseph, Missouri. There they bought a used freighter's wagon, harnessed up the Belgians and loaded the crates. Then, along with three other homesteader families that were too poor to afford to ship by rail, they made their way along old overland trails to near Nebraska City where they were ferried across the Missouri River. They followed the old Nebraska City to Fort Kearny Trail, now often bordered by railway tracks, and were often aided by homesteaders already firmly established along the route. Their biggest challenge and surprise was dealing with Elizabeth's morning sickness. Yes, she was pregnant, but stoically refused to let it interfere with their progress across the plains. After three weeks on the trail, they reached Kearney, where they separated from their fellow travelers. They made their way up the Wood River Valley to Armada. Along that final stretch, they passed crews preparing the railbed for the track of the Kearney & Black Hills Railroad.

They stopped in at the same café Henry and Tom had visited the year before and had coffee with the same owner, Mr. Graham, telling him they were on their way to their tree claim in Custer County. After relating that I and our two younger daughters would join them later, and hearing Elizabeth was with child, he volunteered the following information to Henry and his sons: "Boys, it's already the first of May and if you intend to plant trees you should be doing it right now. You can't take time to build a soddy or get a well drilled, which will be tough anyway with all the settlers wanting one, so I'll tell you what I'll do. As you probably saw, the railroad is going in on the south side of the Wood River. Consequently, it is missing Armada so us few businesses here are contemplating an attempt to move our buildings to the other side and form a townsite there when the railroad goes through. That's where you come in. I bought for a pittance from a broke land agent, a small two-room frame building behind my restaurant. You can store your stuff in there and live there if you'd like. While you fellas head on to the claim, why not leave Elizabeth here and she can help my wife in the kitchen a little in lieu of rent? All I ask is you keep the weeds down around it. That will keep your crated goods out of the weather and free you to go start planting trees and hauling water for them. You'll probably have to go to Broken Bow to pick up your seedlings and maybe a few tools like a moldboard plow to hitch behind that fine-looking team you have out there. What do you say? Do we have a deal?"

Henry looked at Tom and Tom looked at Henry, then they both nodded. "Yeah, yes, I think we can make that work. Much obliged, but we are willing to pay some rent."

With the deal made, they began unloading their crates from the wagon into the two-room shack. It did have a small cast iron stove where they could cook simple meals. They decided to leave Sam at the shack to set up some housekeeping as they could end up spending the winter there; while Henry and Tom would go on to the tree claim in the morning. They would attempt to check-in with Josh Wood then go on to Broken Bow for provisions. The café owner, now referred to as Mr. Graham, also gave them a couple of old wooden barrels to enable them to begin hauling water for their tree plantings. In the morning, Henry and Tom headed northwest with the team and wagon plus the riding horse, telling Sam and Elizabeth they could be gone for up to two weeks getting things squared away at the claim. Mr. Graham said he and his wife would keep an eye on them and see that they had what they needed.

The following morning, Sam began carefully uncrating some of the furniture, saving all the materials in case they needed to crate it up again. He assembled Henry and my wooden bed with the coil springs and mattress in the back room for Elizabeth, then moved the chest of drawers in there, along with the trunks of the girls' clothes. He set up the cast iron bed in the main room for himself, then reassembled the legs to the table and set it in the middle of the room, surrounded by six chairs. He moved the trunks with the men's clothes to a corner, then uncrated a few pots, pans, and dishes. The coffee pot and a few blankets had been unpacked the evening before when they had slept on the floor. Sam thought that was probably good enough until Elizabeth perhaps found there was something they needed to unpack. She had busied herself washing up the dishes and storing them atop one of the opened crates as well as arranging some of her clothes on the side of the bed.

Henry and Tom had harnessed up and headed along the north side of Wood River before daylight. Past Trapper's Grove they veered northwest away from the river, following a dry creek to its beginning. They crossed over a divide hill where all drainage was now toward the South Loup River rather than the Wood River. They could see a storm was moving in from the northwest but thought they could reach their claim before it hit. They had passed a few homesteads and dugouts before crossing the divide, but now saw nothing but hills and valleys covered with gently swaying tall grass no matter where they looked. They rode into a valley looking for Hackberry Creek which on their map looked like it began at their claim. They hoped to follow the creek all the way there.

They were wrong about the storm. A sudden wind shift and a blast of cold air was followed by a bright flash of lightening and a loud clap of thunder that spooked the Belgians off the trail in an attempt to break away. Henry managed to pull them under control and steered them into a side pocket of the canyon that afforded them some protection from the wind. Tom immediately hopped from the wagon and hobbled the riding horse to keep him from breaking away. The rain began with wind-whipped torrents followed by more bolts of lightning and thunder. Henry and Tom retreated under the wagon, though they weren't sure it was safe. The wind was whipping the canvas and wagon bows so hard they thought they might rip or break or the whole wagon might blow over on top of them. Thankfully, their full water barrel was strapped to the upwind side of the wagon and that may have kept it from blowing over. Both Henry and Tom had seen lots of thunderstorms, but neither remembered being caught out in one quite this fierce. Then just as quickly as it had begun, it was over except the run-off from the hills was now flooding the canyon floor where it looked to be flowing a foot deep or more. Henry, Tom, and everything with them was soaked through and through. They were wet and cold and there wasn't a dry scrap of wood anywhere to build a warming fire. Their only choice was to continue on, hoping they would dry off eventually. Toward evening the sun did break through the clouds casting shards of light across the hills and raising steam clouds above the drying prairie grass. They found what they assumed was Hackberry Creek and followed it northwest and reached their claim just at sunset. With no way to start a campfire, they satisfied their hunger with a can of beans. They draped some blankets over the wagon side in hope they would dry a little before they retired for the night, sleeping on the ground under the wagon and hoping another storm didn't blow through.

The morning brought a bright, sunny day with a clear, blue sky. Henry and Tom let the horses eat their fill of the fast-growing spring grass that surrounded them on all sides while they surveyed the lay of the land and formulated a plan for planting trees. The Timber Culture Act required at least two acres of trees be planted the year after the year of filing with 2,700 trees per acre. Tom computed that if they planted a tree about every 6 feet all along the north border of the property, then twelve rows would fulfill the 5,400-tree requirement. It sounded like a heck of a lot of trees and a lot of work. Henry said, "No time like the present to get started. Let's get the horses watered, harnessed up, and head to Josh Wood's ranch.

It was a couple of miles overland to the South Loup River and Josh Wood's ranch but when they arrived, Josh and his foreman were there to greet them. Josh said, "Well look who we have here! I gotta say, Henry, you have a powerful sense of timing. We just brought over four mares and three young geldings that are in need of being broke to ride. Maybe you could team-up a couple of them to work on a buckboard or hay wagon. You ready to go to work?"

"Pretty close, yeah. We spent the night on our claim and need to go to Broken Bow to pick up our trees, a plow, some barbed wire to fence in a horse pasture for our horses, and some other tools and supplies."

"Tell you what I'll do. We finished branding and working calves last week then moving all the cattle out to pasture. We've got a couple hands out mowing meadow hay, but it won't be ready to put up for a few days. You go ahead and make your trip to the Bow and when you get back stop here. I'll give you some posts for fencing that pasture as an advance against you breaking these horses. I'll even lend you a couple of cowhands to help Tom fence the pasture while you go to work here."

"I think that will mostly work. Only hang up I see is I got another boy, Sam, back in Armada with Tom's wife and we need to get him to the claim to help us plant trees."

"Let's have Tom set off where you want the pasture, and my cowhands can start setting posts while Tom takes an extra horse, goes to Armada, and picks up Sam and returns. Will that work?"

"I believe it will and thank you mightily! We'll head to Broken Bow and if all goes well, we'll be back tomorrow."

Josh gave them a few tips on where to shop and buy in Broken Bow and Henry and Tom were off. Night was falling when they got there, so they secured a hotel room then took their team and wagon to the livery. In the morning they discovered Broken Bow was a bustling place. Not near as big as Kearney but growing larger by the day. They had no trouble finding most of their supplies, but the tree plantings were a surprise. They came 500 to a bag with the merchant explaining the roots were wrapped in water soaked kraft paper also having nutrients, then all wrapped up in more soaked paper then packed in a double thick wax coated kraft paper bag. Both Henry and Tom surmised if there were 500 trees in that bag, they could be little more than twigs with roots. Having bought all their supplies, they were heading out of town when they noticed a well-drilling rig. They stopped to inquire if they could get a well drilled any time soon. The driller said he could add their name to the list, but the earliest he could get to them was now probably the summer of 1888 or over a year away. In addition, if they wanted a windmill, he handled a couple different brands, and if they came back in the fall and made a deposit, he could have it shipped in with his order for the following spring. They did add their name to his list but wanted to make it a point to ask Josh Wood about other drillers who may not be as busy or as far away.

On the way to Broken Bow, Henry and Tom had stayed on the well-worn obvious trail and had noticed the cedar tree-filled canyons to the west. They assumed that must be the canyons Josh Wood had spoken of where in the fall they took hayracks to fill with cut and trimmed young cedars to use as fence posts. With the influx of homesteaders, everyone was fencing their property with barbwire, and ranchers had discovered the cedar posts lasted much longer than cottonwood which tended to rot quickly underground but served moderately well as rails or lintels above ground.

As they continued, they couldn't help but notice all the soddys and dug-outs they were passing by. It did indeed seem like someone was homestead-ing on every quarter section. Filling in the checkerboard just as fast as the land could be claimed. Tom noticed a man watering trees off to their left, so they stopped to inquire how it was going on his obvious tree claim. He welcomed their questions, saying his name was Kelly and he and his fam-ily had settled here the previous year. He had planted the trees in the same manner as they were planning and probably about half of what he planted had lived, maybe a little less. But, as Mr. Kelly stated, the rules were to plant 2,700 per acre not that 2,700 had to live. Just a valid attempt be made to keep them alive. Mr. Kelly felt he had done that by trying to keep them watered, but when July and August arrived with their heat and little rain, he couldn't make it around to keep that many trees watered so a fair number died. He had replaced some this spring, but come July expected he would lose a lot of them again. Not a promising outlook for Henry and Tom as they thanked Mr. Kelly and headed the team to Georgetown where Tom mailed a letter home to Illinois saying they were all well, had made it to the claim, and Henry was going to work for Josh Wood breaking horses.

Tom dropped Henry off at the Wood ranch bunkhouse and then along with the two assigned ranch hands and their wagon load of posts, headed toward their claim and a night under the stars.

A lot of the ranch hands were curious as to how Henry was going to break the new horses. They were all of the bronco busting crowd where a bronco is squeezed into a chute, saddled, then released with a cowboy up top hoping he could stay there until the horse relented to his control—or not. Henry's method was different. He began with one of the mares in the corral with him and let her just circle around him as often as she wanted until her curiosity got her to stop and move closer just staring at him. Only then would Henry begin talking in a low soothing and friendly voice. When the mare was no longer in fear, Henry would reach out with a handful of oats. When the mare ate them, he would gently reach with the other hand and scratch her neck, building trust between horse and trainer. It varied between horses but eventually Henry could halter the horses while giving them a few oats. He then moved to letting the horse circle him, this time wearing a halter and at the end of a rope. Again, building trust with the horse learning no harm was being done and she might get some oats. Henry then moved to the saddle blanket on and off, on and off, then to the saddle on and off, on and off. Henry put in a long day working with all the mares the first day, giving each a few oats and a brush down after the workout. By the end of the second week, all seven horses could be saddled, bridled, and expected to receive oats and a brush down after their workout. The next step was left foot in the stirrup and then back down until the horses were comfortable with a rider on their back and knew no harm was coming to them. That was followed by reining and commands and if it was to be a saddle horse, work in the corral with one steer, cutting it left, cutting it right and then through a gate opening controlled by a cowboy. Getting horses to pull a wagon or farm implement is training the horse not to fear what is behind them. It takes a little more time, but it is again the horse learning to trust that they won't be harmed and will be rewarded.

After working with the horses, Henry called a meeting with Josh Wood and all the cowhands and said, "You've all watched me build trust between horse and rider. The horses have been taught that if they respond in a certain way, they can expect to be treated in a certain way. That means at the end of the day when they're unsaddled, they will be curry combed, brushed, and fed a few oats. If you break that trust, don't be surprised if they break it also."

They were all witness to the special connection Henry seemed to have with horses and had some doubts about their own ability to mimic it but agreed to give it a try. Henry had not been away from the Josh Wood ranch for over a month except for one brief Sunday visit to ensure Tom and Sam were getting the trees planted on the timber claim. Now, Perry Wood wanted him to come to his ranch and break some horses there, plus he was shorthanded and would like to hire Tom as a cowhand for Hammer & Wood. Henry said he needed to take a few days off to see how things were progressing on his homestead but would tell Tom of the job offer. An offer that Henry thought Tom would probably accept now that he was a married man with a baby on the way.

He arrived at the claim on a very hot, sunny day in early July to find Tom and Sam watering trees with buckets of water retrieved from barrels in the back of the wagon. The barrels had been filled at the Loup River some two miles away. Henry dismounted and asked how things were going as the boys just kept right on watering. Tom finally replied, "We have to pretty much keep up our watering rhythm or we'll never get around to all of them. Take a good look around and you can see we have been keeping busy."

With that Henry turned and walked east back down the line of trees, noticing that indeed most of the sticks were now sprouting leaves. He also saw the two-wire horse pasture the boys had built with help from a couple of Josh Wood cowhands. It ran inside the tree line to the west border then south to the flat table they intended to plow, then back east to the bottom of the canyon, then north to the point of beginning. It was those cowhands who also suggested plowing across a narrow in the small canyon and shoveling the dirt into an earthen dam to hold back rainwater for watering the horses, reducing the need to haul water for them every day. On the side of the hill on the west bank, the boys had taken the canvas and bows from the wagon, dug out a flat area and built themselves a dugout shelter for sleeping. In front of it was a firepit and beside it a pile of firewood they had hauled up from the Loup River. Walking back up the hill, Henry said, "Looks like you boys are doing a pretty good job. What else have you got going on? What you boys been eating?"

Tom answered, "Well, I've made a few trips back to Armada to check on Elizabeth. She is doing well and has met a couple other women about her age. She always cooks us up some food for me to bring back. Turns out Sam here is a pretty good shot with that old single shot 22 rifle and there seems to be plenty of jackrabbits here about. So other than Liz's cooking, rabbit and beans have been about it, though I did try my hand at making some sourdough bread with less than total success. I did go over and meet some of our new neighbors. We have Mr. George Smith to the east and the William Ritzow family on the southeast quarter. They go by here on their way to the river for water and gave us some chicken eggs on one trip. As far as what is going on, the Belgians can pull that plow through sod like a hot knife through butter. They act like they don't even know it's back there, so we plowed up a couple acres on the west side of the table and scattered oats over there. Hopefully, we can harvest enough to have feed for the horses this winter. I've been scythe cutting some prairie hay along that south slope and having Sam use a pitchfork to gather it into small stacks. Which brings me to a couple questions we have. We going to live here through the winter or are we going back to Armada? If we're going to be here, we need to be building us a sod house and also some kind of shelter for the horses and we don't know where you want them built?"

"Those are a couple of pretty good questions, but I think I can give you an answer you'll be glad to hear. We got a letter from Mom, and I had Josh Wood read it to me. Mom says she and Nettie and Annie are looking forward to coming to Nebraska this fall provided there is a school for the girls

in Armada. Also, because she is not about to miss the birth of her first grandchild. So, I think we should plan to spend the winter in Armada. She also said Mrs. Orr had taken ill so Frances and Doc Orr had put off their wedding until 1888 and Frances will stay with Grandpa and Grandma Lisle."

"Now for even better news, Josh and Perry Wood both said if it is an open winter, I am more than welcome to keep breaking and training their mustangs but better yet, Tom, Perry Wood said he could use you on his crew this winter to help feed cattle. You can earn some of your own money and he said you're welcome to stay in the bunkhouse with the other cowhands at times, if need be."

"I was thinking we could build a soddy on the flat below where you have a dugout, and we could shave off more of that clay bank across the way and use the bank as the north and west walls for a shed for the horses. Then we build a corral around it and a hay pen on the west. If our well-man ever shows up, we'll drill a well just to the south. But with the situation being what it is, we'll save all that for next year. You boys just keep watering those trees and maybe move that prairie hay into a fenced pen over there. We'll have a bunch more trees to plant next spring too."

Henry and Sam took the team and wagon to Kearney around the first of September and picked up me and the two younger girls from the train station and then returned to Armada with plans to stay there for the winter. Tom had taken the riding horse and had gone to work for Hammer and Wood and was staying in the bunkhouse at the Perry Wood Ranch during the week. Perry Wood also boarded the team of Belgians at the ranch in exchange for using them to haul hay sleds or wagons.

On the return trip from Kearney, Henry remarked on the Kearney Black Hills Railroad now being built, with tracks already being laid to the new town of Riverdale northwest of Kearney along the Wood River. Henry, Tom, and Sam's only return to the timber claim in the fall of 1887 was when they returned with a large load of cedar posts they had helped cut with the Hammer & Wood crews from the cedar canyons north of the South Loup River.

The winter of 1887-88 was not too eventful for Henry, Sam, and the girls, secure in their crowded little two-room shack in Armada, but for Tom it became a winter he would never forget. First, Elizabeth gave birth to a healthy baby boy on November 7th, 1887. In honor of his new boss and because both he and Elizabeth liked the name, he was given the first name of Perry, Perry Orrington Kearney.

Tom was still working at the ranch and he and the other hands had just finished feeding the cow herd on what seemed like a warm, January day. Then the wind shifted to the northwest and before they could make their way back to the ranch, they were caught in what came to be known as "The School Children Blizzard of 1888." It got that name for the country schoolteachers who literally risked life and limb to either get their pupils home or to protect them in place. Tom and the other cowhands took refuge in a calving shed in the canyon where they had just fed the cowherd, which also offered some protection to the cows. However, the mustangs in a pasture to the east and the yearling calves in a pasture to the west had far less protection. Both herds moved south with the raging snow and wind until coming up against fences. The ones to the rear kept pushing until those in front were either trampled or pushed on through the fence where they kept on moving. Most of the yearlings stayed together as a herd and eventually found some shelter in canyons around Black Creek. The horses, however, split into small groups and scattered for miles to the south, some all the way to the Wood River. The horses were branded, so Tom and the other cowhands spent every extra hour the rest of the winter searching for the ranch's horses. Most were eventually accounted for, but a few were never found and may have ended up as some homesteader's gift horse.

In the spring of 1888, Henry again began training horses and Tom took time off from the ranch to help Sam plant another 5400 trees while I and the girls plus Elizabeth and baby Perry stayed in Armada. It remained Sam's job to haul water to the trees, though this year either Henry or Tom would check in at the tree claim every few days. In June, Henry took some extra time and he and Sam got the frame up for their barn/shed next to the clay bank and hauled some cottonwood logs for the roof. Sam used some of their cedar posts and cottonwood rails to build a corral around the barn and more for a hay pen to the west.

Come July, though, things began to go wrong. It was hot and dry and there was no way Sam could haul water fast enough to keep the trees watered and many began to die. To make matters worse, grasshoppers, though not all that numerous compared to other years, seemed to favor the leaves and bark of the newly planted trees for their lunch, destroying even more. Henry returned to the claim to try and help Sam, but it was still a struggle. Then they received a card from me informing them that we all needed to move out of the shack in Armada before winter. The railroad right-of-way across the Wood River was being prepared for the laying of rails with tracks now laid nearly to the new town of Amherst. The residents of Armada had voted to move the wood frame buildings of their settlement across the river to the new townsite of Miller. The plan was to move existing buildings on skids across the river ice during the winter. A temporary dam was now being built in the river to bring the water level up to facilitate a nearly level bank to bank move when the ice was thick enough.

The railroads usually determined where towns were to be located along their tracks, usually every seven to ten miles, but the actual townsite was platted out by townsite companies. These townsite companies, often majority owned by railroad executives, bought the site from the railroad then resold the platted lots to waiting merchants and settlers. Before the first lot was ever sold, the townsite company often had a waiting list of merchants for a general store, bank, grain elevator, lumberyard, blacksmith, well driller, and others. Prime lots at town center and fronting wider streets at prominent intersections went to banks, general stores, grocers etc. Business area lots were only 25 feet wide, while residential lots were 50 feet in width. This sometimes necessitated the merchants to attempt to buy two adjoining lots, but sometimes they were turned down by the townsite company because they preferred to have two families with smaller stores rather than one large store. By the late 1880s most townsite companies had adopted the

T model for platting of townsites. This meant the railroad tracks were like the top of the T with the townsite totally laid out on one side or the other, though provision for a grain elevator, livestock loading pens, and perhaps a water tower were across the tracks. Earlier decades had seen a symmetrical layout with the railroad through the center and platted lots laid out on both sides. Lots for churches, schools, and perhaps government offices were often donated by the townsite companies.

To understand the scale of railroad building during this era one needs only to look at the total miles of track in the country at 8,500 in 1850 and nearing 200,000 by 1890. When you consider you had a homesteader on every quarter section, a townsite every eight miles or so starts to make sense. If you figure a town's trade area may extend a day's ride or so either side of the tracks, you have roughly a thousand families in the trade area, excluding those who actually live within the town. In addition, steam locomotives need to replenish their water every 24 to 30 miles, so would be stopping anyway. The railroads had a double objective, they wanted to be the first to lay tracks to haul settlers and all their needs, but also to be the settler's primary means of shipping their agricultural production back to the east.

With a deadline now in place for leaving Armada, Henry and the boys had to redouble their efforts. They still needed to haul water from the river to at least some trees every day. They also needed to finish the barn/shed for the horses and get started on building a sod house for the family. Plus, all homesteaders were now fencing in their land before subdividing it into fields and pastures. The Henry Kearney tree claim had been fenced on the north and west sides and George Smith, the homesteader on the northeast quarter, had erected a fence on the east, but the south, bordering the homestead of a family named Henning on the southwest quarter had nothing. In fact, none of the Kearneys had even met any of the Hennings yet. Tom took time off from Hammer & Wood to help Henry and Sam get everything done.

While Henry and Sam continued to haul water, Henry sent Tom with a Hammer & Wood borrowed team and wagon to Broken Bow to try and buy four windows and an entrance door and frame, as well as some hardwood wide boards to use as lintels above the windows and door, plus some pine 1 x 12s for that all important privy for the women folk. A task Sam was now familiar with as Mr. Graham had him dig a new pit and move the outhouse at the shack in Armada. On his way back out of town, successful in his quest, Tom stopped at the well driller's shop to see where they were on the list and was surprised to learn the driller was working east of their claim and hoped to be at their claim within a couple of weeks. He also had their windmill in stock and had just sent a letter wanting to know if he should also bring lumber for the tower? Tom told him yes, by all means bring the tower and even had enough money with him to pay for it. That pleased the driller, and he indicated he would be there before the first of September. Tom knew it would be a big relief to Henry to have water, and the driller told him they had been finding plenty of water at a depth of around 180 feet, so well casing and rods probably would not be needed as deep as they originally thought, saving a little bit of money.

Tom arrived at the claim just in time to meet Henry and Sam coming from the south and leading a cow. When they had finished watering trees, they had decided to go meet the Hennings to see if they could share costs for a fence along their joint border. They discovered Friedrich Henning along with his wife and four small children were in much the same predicament as the Kearneys—too much to do and not enough time to do it. They too were trying to get a home built, fences put up, and in addition, Friedrich was milking four cows morning and night. To make a long story short, Friedrich traded a milk cow to Henry, and he was sure she was bred to calf again in late March or early April, in exchange for him not helping to build the fence along the border though he would contribute a roll of barbed wire. The deal was made, though one of the Kearneys now had a chore to do every morning and every evening. On the plus side, they now had their own source of milk and butter.

Friedrich Henning had told them he didn't care if the border fence project waited until the following year, so Henry and the boys began work on their sod house, at least Henry and Sam's house. Tom figured he and Elizabeth would either file for their own homestead or buy one that had been relinquished once Tom turned twenty-one in January. Henry had paid attention when told how to build his soddy. He had seen those that had been put up too quickly and without attention to detail that were now falling down and having to be rebuilt. They leveled off a slight rise on the valley floor to their 16x24 foot exterior dimension leaving a 13x21 interior dimension. They carefully laid their first rows of sod ensuring things were level and square. When they reached the sill height of the windows, they covered their work with waterproof canvas or oilcloth with the intention of protecting it from rain, plus letting it settle for a week or two as the sod dried out. This gave them time to get the privy built, plus begin to dig into the bank behind the sod house for a sod-covered ice cave and a cellar.

Henry, Tom, and Sam had just finished adding another three feet to the soddy and had the windows and door placed when the well driller showed up. So, they once again covered their work so it could dry and settle for a week and switched to helping the well driller with his task, plus assembling the windmill and tower and gathering four strong cedar posts for attaching the tower at the corners. The driller hit water at 160 feet but went to 180 feet to give Henry a 20-foot column of water. The well man had two questions as they were completing their work. First, do you want a hand pump in case the wind doesn't blow and second, do you have a tank for the water or are you just going to fill barrels as needed? Henry decided they needed a livestock tank, so immediately sent Tom and Sam to Broken Bow with the wagon to buy one. He also thought the hand pump might be a good idea and had the well man install one.

It was mid-October before Henry, and the boys got the roof finished on the soddy and a stove installed so they could begin sleeping on the floor there. Henry still wanted to plaster the walls and install a wood floor before moving me and the girls in and hoped to get that accomplished by Christmas. It was now just Henry and Sam as Tom had returned to work at

Hammer & Wood. Tom needed to make and save money as he had learned Elizabeth was expecting again around the first of July of the coming year.

In November of 1888, Henry and I along with Annie and Nettie were driven by Sam to Broken Bow where we boarded the train to Virden, Illinois. Sam was to handle the home chores while the rest of us traveled back for Thanksgiving and the wedding of Frances to Doc Orr on November 29th. It was the first time Henry had seen his oldest daughter in nearly two years. It was also the first time both Henry and I felt assured that our homesteading venture to Nebraska was going to be successful and we would at last be landowners.

When Henry returned to the homestead, he and Sam got along well with the plastering, but it seemed word was getting around among the homesteaders of Henry's skill set. He not only had homesteaders stopping by to see if he could find time to break and train their horses, but somehow, they had heard he also knew how to tan leather and how to make animal glue from bones, horns and hooves not to mention shoe and boot repair, things he had learned years ago in Ireland but had never forgotten. They were suddenly in demand in the rapidly settling plains. Henry had learned he could order tanning supplies and chromium salts from a saddle shop in Broken Bow and buy the heavy thread for resoling boots and shoes from the same source.

Henry was not excited at all about tanning leather, though he had done some for Hammer & Wood when a horse had died with its hide yielding ample leather for making reins, halters, latigos, and rawhide strips for whatever use. He had made glue by grinding up bones and hooves and heating in a double boiler for repairing furniture and some boot and shoe repair. Fixing the heels of boots and resoling of boots and shoes had been confined to a few of the cowhands working on the ranches. Nevertheless, word had gotten around, and it seemed every day or so some homesteader was stopping to request a repair of something. Some even brought animal hides or a couple brought the whole dead animal which Henry cordially declined. He did accept some shoe repair just to be neighborly, but it seemed to always setback the completion date for their soddy.

It was finally finished in mid-January of 1889, and just in time because when they arrived in Armada to move me and the girls, buildings were already being moved across the river to the new town of Miller. Tom, Elizabeth, and little Perry had already moved into a small soddy on the Perry Wood ranch, but Tom would handle the chores at the homestead until we got moved. Henry and Sam crated up most of our belongings and loaded them on the wagon. They kept out some blankets and we slept on the floor the next night as Henry and Sam helped the Grahams ready their 2-story hotel and restaurant building for the move and indeed used their Belgian team to assist the move across the Wood River, now frozen with thick ice.

The Graham's building was 24 feet wide and 50 feet long, and Mr. Graham and others had looked long and hard to find two cottonwood trees tall and straight enough to fashion two 12x12 inch skids sixty feet in length. They had borrowed jacks and cables from the railroad to assist in the move. First, they jacked up the whole building after unbolting it from its foundation, trying to keep it level as they went up. Then they broke out the foundation in front and back and using cables and a team of horses pulled the skids into place. They installed separators between the skids to keep them equal distance apart and cross braces to avoid any twisting then lowered the building onto the skids. Several inches of snow had fallen to enhance the sliding of the skids all the way to the river. A track between the skids was cleared for the team of horses doing the pulling. Once everything was in place, Henry's Belgian team was harnessed to the skids and began pulling. A second team was required until the skids reached the snow, then it was like a sled on ice and pulled easily to the frozen river. There the team was unhooked from the skids and taken to the other side where, using cables, they were reattached to the skids. With what seemed like little effort they pulled the building to the opposite river edge, up a slightly ramped snow and ice bank and then to its new foundation. The whole moving operation took far less time than anticipated. They moved two more buildings that day with the Belgians, though a little smaller than the Graham's. The Grahams were deeply appreciative of the help provided by Henry, Sam, and their team of Belgian draft horses.

They offered to leave the little two room shack where we had been living as long as we wanted to stay there, but Henry said we would be leaving in the morning because he didn't want to get caught in a winter storm and he and Sam had chores to do at the tree claim.

The next morning was clear and very cold but with little wind, so we finished packing, had a pancake breakfast, and headed for our new home. I had been to the homestead a few times, but Annie and Nettie had never been there and were unsure what to expect. Henry had hinted that there was a late Christmas surprise waiting for me. Because of the shorter days, winter darkness was creeping in when we finally arrived. Tom was there waiting and had a fire going in the stove and a lantern lit in the house. He had finished milking the cow and had put some prairie hay in the manger for the horses. He had thought we might arrive the day before, but when hearing the story about moving the Graham building, he understood the delay. The only thing unpacked that night were some blankets, quilts, and bedding but upon entering the house, I was thrilled to see my late Christmas gift. Henry and Sam had gone to Broken Bow and bought a new kitchen cabinet, now sitting in the northeast corner of the house. It had two doors below with an interior shelf, two drawers below the work surface, and above that but shallower, were two more doors that opened to two additional shelves. The whole thing was made of oak and looked absolutely grand to me.

The move-in began the following morning even before breakfast as there was nothing to fix breakfast with until they unpacked it. Henry and my wooden bed was moved into the southeast corner, and Annie and Nettie's cast-iron bed to the southwest corner. Henry and Sam had built a thin wall below the center ridge beam which extended about 8 feet. They had fastened a wire to the cedar rafters on each side so curtains might be hung to separate the two bedrooms when desired. The chest of drawers was placed to the right of the window, against the separation wall. The girls' clothing trunk went to the foot of their bed and the same for Henry and my trunk and Sam's small trunk.

My sewing stand and supplies were next, then Henry's rocking chair next to the stove. The dining table was assembled and along with the six chairs, was placed between the front door and the stove which served as both a cook stove and our source of heat. A washstand with a door for chamber pot storage was placed behind the door next to the window. I busied myself finding the perfect place for dishes, linens, and pots and pans in my new cupboard. A flour box already half filled with flour was placed next to the new cabinet. Except for where to put some odds and ends, we were moved in. The girls were already saying they needed a hook here or a mirror hung there, etc., while I was already talking of hooking a rug to cut the noise from Sam walking on the new wood floor with his boots. It occurred to me as I turned and said, "Sam, where are you going to sleep?"

"Probably out under the stars in the summer, but Dad and I made a little cedar cot for me to pull out either in front of the door or between the bedrooms this time of year. It's out in the barn. I still have to nail a few leather straps on for the webbing between the rails, but it'll be ready by tonight. It folds flat so can be stored on end or under a bed out of the way during the day."

Henry and Sam still had work to do finishing the icehouse and cellar, plus Henry wanted to build a small sod milkhouse/chicken house combination next to the windmill, but for all intents and purposes the Henry Kearney family had moved into their home and was living on the Homestead by February 1st, 1889.

25

1889 was a good year on the prairie with ample rains and homesteaders raising good crops. Henry, with Sam's help, had raised a good crop of oats and corn on the table, plus put up enough prairie hay to last the horses and their milk cow all winter. They did a decent job of keeping the trees watered, which was much easier now that they had a well. Annie, Nettie, and I had planted a good-sized garden that Henry and Sam had enclosed with corn cribbing to keep out pests. It worked well, as I think we got more vegetables than the pests did. We had a good crop of potatoes and now have a cellar behind the house to store them in. The icehouse next to the cellar worked, but not as well as Henry had hoped.

Blocks of ice were sawed out of the Loup river during the winter by our neighbors and us, then our share was stored in an icehouse as long as possible. Icehouses were either a cave dug into the hill or a combination of cave and sod which is what Henry had tried. Ours was dug into the clay bank with three feet of sod around and on top of it. Straw was spread on the floor and between layers of ice blocks, giving homesteaders ice for the storage of meat, eggs, and dairy products often well into summer. Henry's icehouse didn't work that well because he hadn't insulated the entrance door enough. Summer heat entering through the door had melted our ice much quicker than he had hoped, even though it was in shadows behind the house late in the day.

Henry continued to break and train horses for Hammer & Wood, though not to the extent he had the prior two years and now he did it at his own corrals, usually for a few dollars but occasionally for barter like their bull servicing our milk cow or securing some cedar posts to finish our fencing. He also helped a few neighbors by training their horses, but said he was done tanning hides and mending shoes.

In May we heard the new town of Sumner was to be surveyed and platted next to the railroad just seven miles straight south, and the new town of Eddyville eight miles to the west, close to the Congdon settlement. The platting of both was completed in 1890 with the Kearney and Black Hills Railroad reaching the new town of Callaway thirty miles west by yearend. Merchants and residents were quick to move into both with enough population expected to incorporate as legal villages by 1893. Either one would be more convenient than traveling clear to Broken Bow. We soon adopted Sumner as our hometown because it was the closest and also the one chosen by most of our neighbors, and it had a good trail over the divide hill right into town.

In June of 1889, Henry and I got more good news. On the 30th our second grandchild was born right here in our new soddy. Perry now had a new little sister, Ethel Frances. She was the first of many grandchildren to be born in Henry and my little sod home. Apparently, I'm a pretty good midwife as, except for Frances Orr, all our children, or their spouses chose to give birth at our little sod house for at least some of their children.

There were enough homesteaders with children that country schools were opening every three or four miles in all directions to provide compulsory public education. District 184, named Hidden Hollow, was just a mile east of Henry and my homestead where all Sam's children would attend grade school. Lower Park Valley, District 36, 2 miles to the southwest in Dawson County was where Tom's children would attend school. Both would play prominent roles in the lives of Henry and me as well as our children. Country schools were much more than just schools for children. They also served as Sunday schools, churches, polling places, literary meeting halls, and pretty much anything requiring members of a community to assemble. They were the primary social gathering place for members of families to interact with their rural neighbors and to relieve some of the loneliness of living on the prairie.

The school year is divided into two sessions. Usually, October through March and May through August. Students are not assigned to grades by age but rather by their knowledge of the three Rs: readin, righten and rithmetic, with a little history and geography thrown in. Discipline was strict both at school and from parents for any sort of misbehavior. Boys were often excused for absences if they were needed to work, and many skipped the summer session altogether. There were county-wide tests to check the progress of the students and their promotion to the next grade. Students could be as young as three years old or as old as 18 or 19. School rooms were divided with girls on one side and boys on the other, and from youngest in front to oldest in back. Recesses and the lunch period provided great times for students to make new friends and build bonds that often lasted a lifetime. These bonds were not only between students, but often between the parents as well.

The success of the Kearney homestead along with many others was tested severely in 1890 and 1891. Both years were horrible for homesteaders and especially for those on tree claims. They were years of severe drouth with widespread crop failures and the loss of nearly all the trees on the tree claims. If not from lack of water, the trees were destroyed by the swarms of grasshoppers devouring every growing thing in sight. Hundreds if not thousands of homesteaders gave up and moved back east. That included many of our neighbors. I was reduced to tears when Henry told me the Ritzlows were leaving. Martha was my nearest and dearest friend on the prairie. She was the person I could go to for womanly conversation when the loneliness and fear of failure that embraced the prairie would start to overcome me.

We were fortunate that Henry was earning money by breaking horses for Hammer & Wood. Most of our neighbors, if they had no crops, had no income. Some were fortunate enough to sell their homestead, but others had no choice but to abandon their place and leave. The searing heat and desolation from the loss of neighbors made the prairie an even lonelier place. To add insult to injury, Congress repealed the Timber Culture Act in March of 1891 because of widespread fraud and because trees were simply not able to survive in the semi-arid great plains, leaving those with existing tree claims *in limbo as to what to do next. In April of 1892 Henry returned to the land office and refiled as a regular homestead. He paid the homestead filing fee again, now $14.00. Tom had gone with him and while they were there, he filed for a homestead forfeiture in the hills at the north end of Park Valley in Dawson County, some three miles west of Henry and my homestead. Tom, Elizabeth, and their two young children, Perry and Ethel, planned to move to the homestead, but Tom would continue to work for Perry Wood or Hammer & Wood on their winter hay feeding crew and work his homestead the rest of the year.*

1892 was another dry year, but not as bad as the prior two years. Henry and I managed to raise some crops and a good garden. We were also able to buy a used carriage, so the girls and I no longer had to ride in the old farm wagon and could ride in the carriage when going to town. Henry had begun buying wild horses, breaking and training them to sell to other homesteaders, while continuing the custom training of other homesteaders' horses. Sam, now 19 years old, was Henry's right-hand man. Annie and Nettie were to help me in the garden and did, but Annie, now 17 years old, had a mind of her own. Henry often said she was like her mother, strong-willed and stubborn.

Such was the situation when at a box social a handsome young man known as Doc Wellet happened to win the bid for Annie's decorated box. He was not a doctor but simply the son and helper of Amos Wellet, a well driller from Sumner. He was nearly ten years older than Annie and, ironically, I considered him too old for Annie. However, Annie, like her mother before her, gave her heart totally to her first love and they dated extensively all during 1892.

1893 was the beginning of a nationwide depression that lasted through 1897. Like many depressions, it began with a panic in the stock market. Some trace its beginning to the failure of Baring Bank, others claim it was due to an oversupply of silver, or the bankruptcy of the Philadelphia and Reading Railroad. At any rate, the prices for grain crashed, breaking many farmers and subsequently causing many rural banks in the west to fail. In addition, the boom time for building railroads came to an end with many branch lines going broke. That included the Kearney & Black Hills Railroad which was taken over by the Union Pacific and the name changed to the Kearney Branch. Henry and I managed to struggle through, but again many of our neighbors did not. They either sold out or went broke.

In early August of 1893 I returned to the soddy with a basket full of produce from the garden to find Annie lying on her bed crying her eyes out. I rushed to her side and asked what was wrong. Sitting up and still sobbing, Annie replied, "I'm pregnant and Doc Wellet has told me he is not going to get married."

I held her close. "He may have been shocked by the news. Maybe if we give him some time, he'll change his mind," I said, while thinking unkind thoughts toward Doc Wellet and wishing I had stepped in earlier to break them up.

Henry was not happy with the situation but told Annie, "We'll work it out some way. You are our daughter; we are family, and we love you, so we will be here for you." Remembering how horrible his parents had been treated back in Ireland decades earlier.

There was some discussion of having Annie go live with her sister Frances Orr back in Illinois, but Annie didn't want to do that. Especially after Doc Wellet appeared at the soddy door sometime later, professing his love for her but saying, "I'm nearly thirty years old and nothing more than a hired man for my dad. I have no means of supporting a family now nor any prospect of finding any. I will help support you and the baby all that I can, but don't think we should get married because I think you can do much better than me."

Apparently, that was it for Annie, she loved Doc and Doc loved her. So, much like her mother, there was to be but one man in her life. Sadly, in late March of 1894, the baby was born at rest. The unnamed baby was buried on the hillside above our soddy with wildflowers and flags, a kind of miniature Iris, planted around the grave by Annie and me. Annie was depressed for a while, but then found new inspiration in the women's suffrage movement. Amos Wellet gave his son a used well drilling rig, and Doc and Annie departed for Wyoming to start anew where women could vote. They were still not married and succeeded in giving me new things to worry about.

Through the depression years of 1895, 1896 and 1897, Henry and I, with our children Sam and Nettie, struggled to keep the homestead going. Crops were sparse and farm prices depressed. Thankfully, Henry's horse training reputation gave the family enough money to survive. The Belgian team of draft horses continued to give their all until the summer of 1896 when one was bitten on the jaw twice by a prairie rattlesnake. Her head and jaw swelled to unbelievable proportions and once the venom reached her blood stream she did not survive. There was no money to buy another Belgian draft horse even though Henry had been told a man at Mason City, Nebraska was now raising them. Fortunately, Henry and Sam had turned enough sod on the table land that our single Belgian could now pull the plow, or we could use a team of the wild horses Henry had broken and trained to pull implements.

Tom, Elizabeth, and their two children Perry and Ethel were struggling on their farm. Tom was still working in the winters for Hammer & Wood, which enabled them to keep going. Then, in April of 1897 Elizabeth became ill. Whether it was Ague or Grippe, as both were diagnosed, or something else we will never know, she passed away on May 24, 1897, leaving Tom with two young children ages 9 and 7. At least they were blessed to have their grandparents, Henry and I, a short distance away to help Tom when necessary. Elizabeth's death also became a unifying event for the Kearneys and all the homesteaders of Park Valley. Many were shocked by the death of the young mother and were quick to offer help of any kind. Tom as well as Henry and I were deeply grateful.

It was at a social event at the Park Valley School in the 1890s where Henry and I, with Sam and Nettie, were introduced to the William and Margaret Boyer family. The Boyers had homesteaded in upper Park Valley in the early 1880s coming from the Payne, Ohio area with their four children including Lizzie and George. It was around the time of the outpouring of support for the Kearney's loss of Elizabeth that George Boyer and Nettie took a serious interest in each other. So much so that they were married in Broken Bow on August 25 of 1897, so now just Henry and I plus Sam were living in the soddy.

It had been April of 1892 when Henry converted his tree claim to a regular homestead. It was now the fall of 1897, so Henry and I had put in our five years of living on and making improvements to our 160 acres. In other words, we had "proved up" and could now file for title to our homestead . . . except Henry had forgotten one of the requirements. Henry had filed his Declaration of Intention to become a citizen of the United States back in August of 1887, a full ten years earlier. However, Henry had never followed through, and now needed to become a citizen before he and I could get the patent letter to our homestead. We spent the next few months studying for the citizenship test and in December made the trip to Plum Creek, now Lexington, to take the test. After passing the test and swearing his allegiance to the United States of America, one Henry Charles Kearney became a naturalized citizen on December 18, 1897. We had now been living in Nebraska for ten years. We had survived blizzards, drouths, depressions, the death of loved ones, and the almost intolerable loneliness of the prairie. Henry had seen and lived through almost every human suffering and tragedy imaginable. Yet, we were now among the forty percent of the original homesteaders or "sodbusters" that proved up and could take ownership of their land.

With winter coming on and the hundreds of things required to be done for a homesteader to make it through a winter on the Great Plains, Henry waited to file until the spring of 1898 after he and his neighbors had planted their crops, because one of the final requirements was to have two witnesses swear that the applicant had met the requirements of the Homestead Act. It was early June when Henry, along with two neighbors, William Clouse and Nimrod Slack, made the trip to the Broken Bow Land Office and filed for Henry's patent letter or title to the northwest quarter of section thirty-two T13N R19W. An Affidavit of Publication was filed on June 4th, 1898. Henry's filing and the recording of his witnesses' testimony was on June 6th, 1898. However, because of the large number of filings in that year, it wasn't approved until July 28th, 1899, and was recorded at the Capital in Lincoln on August 16th, 1899.

Besides us finally getting title to our land in 1899, our younger son, Sam, was now dating Lizzie Boyer, George's sister. Plus, George and Nettie were expecting their first child in July. After the Independence Day celebration in Sumner, George brought Nettie to our little sod home because Nettie wanted to be with her mother for the birth of her first child. Little Neva was born on July 10th, 1899, while I again aided with the birth.

The new century brought deep sorrow. Our precious little Neva had struggled since birth and died on April 6th, 1900. It was a beautiful spring day under blue skies with the flags in full bloom and a meadowlark singing in the distance when we laid little Neva to rest on the hillside above our soddy, alongside Annie's stillborn baby.

In July, Sam got engaged to Elizabeth "Lizzie" Boyer and they were married on September 27th, 1900, in Lexington, Nebraska. The last of our children had married and moved out. Now, as we entered the autumn of our lives, we had our little soddy all to ourselves.

Sam and Lizzie bought the southeast quarter of section 32 for five hundred dollars so Sam could continue farming and breaking horses with Henry. George and Nettie had moved with the Boyers to Minnesota, so having Sam and Lizzie living close by gave us great comfort. Their choice to have all four of their children born in our little sod house with me assisting with their births is one of my greatest joys. Baby Lester Merle joined his three sisters on August 3rd, 1904.

26

I had finished reading MaryAnn's stories from the black metal box. She wrote no more after Merle was born. It was obvious Mary Ann was very proud to have delivered several grandchildren into the world at their little sod house. However, she also had indicated something troubling in the margins of the later journals. She had made several notations:

"Henry had another nightmare!"

"Henry didn't sleep well again and awoke in a cold sweat!"

"Henry awoke with a scream! I'm worried about his lack of sleep!"

She noted at the end of one journal that these recurring notations about Henry's headaches and horrifying nightmares he confessed to her were about dying and famine starvation in Ireland, or alternatively about men dying and getting blown to pieces in the Civil War. Sometimes even both ran together, seeing his father as a fellow soldier being blown to pieces or skin and bones soldier corpses thrown into the pit at Skibbereen. A theme, if there was one, was the open eyes always staring right at him. Eyes that would see no more like McKinney at the workhouse. At times it was his own eyes that could not see. In his dream, he could see himself dead with unseeing eyes but trying desperately to see through the blackness. It was always dying and death he was helpless to do anything about.

He initially told Mary Ann but confessed that he felt there was no one who could understand what he had been through or what he had seen. Originally, the nightmares were rare, but as the years progressed the nightmares occurred more and more often, sometimes literally crippling him with lack of sleep. In today's world it seems obvious Henry was suffering from severe PTSD or post-traumatic stress, but back then there was no diagnosis and no help.

On Thursday, October 20, 1904, just a couple of months after the birth of baby Merle, Sam and his family, along with Mary Ann, were going to visit the Freeze family and their new baby in Park Valley. Henry, who was staying at Sam's to handle the evening chores, asked if he could care for his new grandson while they were gone. He was told no; they were taking baby Merle with them so the neighbors could see their new baby as well. Alone at home and feeling old and useless as he sometimes said, it appeared he had sat in the rocking chair to take a nap, but perhaps had another horrific dream. Feeling he could take it no more; he grabbed a 12-gauge shotgun, one shell, and left the house. Behind a small outbuilding to the west, the life of Henry Kearney came to an end from a self-inflicted shotgun blast.

There was no investigation. No coroner's inquest. There was only a short telegram to the county sheriff in Broken Bow 30 miles away, followed by a notice in the Custer County Chief Newspaper: "Henry Kearney, a farmer and noted horseman from Loup Township, took his own life Thursday last, the 20th of October 1904."

EPILOGUE

Henry's suicide took place at his son, Sam Kearney's home in Custer County, Nebraska. Henry and Mary Ann still lived in their sod home, but on occasion stayed with Sam and Lizzie and their four small children. To this day you can still see where Henry and Mary Ann's soddy was built. As the sod walls collapsed, they formed ridges on the valley floor, now grass covered, but plainly visible.

Some years later Sam told his son, my father, that he sold that shotgun, but I have my doubts. At the time of Henry's suicide in 1904, that small outbuilding was supported by concrete blocks at the corners, but sometime later a concrete foundation and floor were installed. In the late 1970s or early 1980s, a rusted gun barrel shape began to appear on the southwest corner of that foundation. More recently, a crack has appeared, and you can clearly see the breech end of a shotgun. I believe that was the fate of Henry's shotgun, and that Sam buried it in the new foundation for the milkhouse outbuilding, near where Henry had committed suicide.

Mary Ann's journals had come to an end, and a regrettable and sad ending to Henry's life, but it was just the end of the first chapter for the Henry Kearney family in America. Either Henry or Sam had registered a cattle brand with the State of Nebraska with a reverse seven over the letter L. They referred to their joint horse and cattle ranch as the 7L ranch. The 7Ls referred to what they felt were the necessities to succeed as a rancher, and very well may have been conceived by Mary Ann. The first and most important was the **LORD**. Without him there is nothing. That was followed by **LIBERTY**. Without the freedom to make your own decisions, any success is not your own. Liberty is followed by **LOVE**. Without the love of your family and a love for the land, any success is hard to achieve. Love is followed by **LAND** and **LIVESTOCK**, the very definition of a ranching operation. The last two Ls are a needed part of every ranch operation everywhere: **LOANS** and **LUCK**.

I began to put MaryAnn's journals back in the black metal box for the final time when I noticed a small sheet of paper. It was creased and kind of stuck to the back and bottom of the box. I was able to remove it in one piece and could barely manage to read the faded ink written with a shaky hand.

> "Well Cora, I've torn down the old sod house, and as I pause a bit to rest My thoughts go wandering backwards to the early days in the west.
>
> Full twenty years and five have passed since I felled the giant tree that helped to build the sod cabin and make a home for you and me.
>
> Don't you remember, we were sweethearts then? Our paths were still untrod but many and many are the happy years we spent in that house of sod.
>
> Together we rocked the cradle upon its earthen floor. Together we fought the famine, when the wolf was at the door.
>
> And our children grew to man hood beneath the family tree and through many a storm and blizzard it sheltered you and me.
>
> But better than all the riches which for years we toiled to get and the greatest of all God's blessings is this, we are sweethearts yet."
>
> Levi Morgan

I recognized the name, Levi Morgan, as an early homesteader that lived north of Henry and Mary Ann, closer to Georgetown, across the South Loup River. Where and how Mary Ann had gotten the poem, we will never know but Mary Ann must have thought the poem fit her and Henry too and added it to her keepsakes.

I think to myself what a fabulous and valuable gift Mary Ann gave us with her stories and journals. Henry would be amazed. A poor, starving, Irish orphan who survived the famine and an Atlantic crossing aboard a coffin ship. Then being swindled, followed by being wounded in the Civil War and being a prisoner of that war. He lived through depression, blizzards, drouths, the deprivations and loneliness of the settlement of the Great Plains, to be one of the pioneers to actually "prove-up "and own a quarter section of land in Nebraska. A man whose progeny now stretches from coast to coast and from the Canadian border to Mexico. Perhaps a story not unlike the thousands of other Irish immigrant stories that were never able to be recorded because they could neither read nor write. The unwritten stories of the ones who managed to survive, despite those with eyes that do not see.

LIST OF REFERENCE BOOKS

The following list is not a bibliography in the normal sense. It is just a list of some of the books I read and some of you may be interested in reading to find out more about certain areas of the novel. I never intended the book to be any kind of scholarly endeavor with citations for every bit of history included in it. These books were simply helpful to me in writing a logical story for the life of Henry Charles Kearney.

History of Ireland: by Malachy McCourt—Running Press Publisher, Philadelphia, PA

The Famine Plot: by Pat Coogan—St. Martin's Griffins, New York, New York

Ireland: by Frank Delaney—Harper Collins Publishers, New York, New York

The Famine Ships: by Edward Laxton —Henry Holt and Company, New York, New York

The Book of Irish Americans: by William D Griffin—Random House, Inc., New York, NY

The Grand National: by Anne Holland—Orion Publishing Group, London, England

Time-Life Books The Civil War: Time-Life Books, Alexandria, Virginia

Railway Transportation History: by Frank L McVey PHD—Columbia Institute, Chicago, IL

Pioneer History of Custer County: by Solomon Butcher—Forgotten Press

APPENDIX

With

SHORT HISTORIES

ENGLAND vs IRELAND

THE POTATO FAMINE

STEEPLECHASE RACES

FAMINE SHIPS

THE CIVIL WAR

History of England vs Ireland

There was not a lot of involvement of England in Irish affairs up to the twelfth century, but that changed dramatically with the introduction of Dermot MacMurrough. He is perhaps the most reviled man in all Irish history. He was the deposed king of Leinster who went to England and swore allegiance to King Henry II. In return, he received permission to raise an army in any of Henry II's lands. He wasn't successful in England, but in Wales he found plenty of Normans looking for adventure including his most important recruit Richard de Clare, more commonly known as "Strongbow."

MacMurrough promised de Clare the hand of his daughter as well as the right to succession after his death if they were successful in regaining his kingship over Leinster. In 1170, Strongbow arrived with 2200 well-trained troops. The Anglo-Norman knights were armored and supplemented by expert archers with crossbows. The Irish had little but spears and battle-axes. They were armies from two separate times and the Irish were no match for the warfare of the Anglo-Normans.

MacMurrough died in May of 1171 and Strongbow was made king of Leinster. A mere five months later, Henry II of England landed in Waterford with upwards of 4000 men and the Pope's blessing because Irish Catholicism had strayed from the teachings of Rome and the Pope wanted them brought back in line. MacMurrough had invited these foreigners in, had welcomed them and set them up. Consequently, for nearly the next thousand years, the history of Ireland was profoundly influenced by the actions of the English monarchs.

For several centuries England was mostly concerned with Dublin and the surrounding area known as the Pale. They had little concern with what happened in the Gaelic world beyond the Pale. This changed in 1536 when the Irish Parliament (composed of mostly Anglo-Irish, defined as Englishmen owning Irish lands) confirmed Henry VIII as Supreme Head of the Church of Ireland—analogous to his title in the Church of England. This resulted in Henry VIII seizing all the land previously held by the Catholic monasteries and then granting it to supportive Anglo-Irish families (a practice continued by his daughter, Queen Elizabeth I). Destruction of many of the monasteries was soon to begin. This was followed in 1540 with Ireland being declared no longer a lordship but a kingship with Henry VIII as their king. In other words, Ireland was no longer a separate entity, but simply a part of the English monarchy. This was partially accomplished by Henry VIII's court by convincing the Irish chieftains to give up their lands to the king who would then grant the land back with an earldom to boot. In this way, large portions of Gaelic lands became subject to English law. This became but the first large taking of Irish soil and giving it to English subjects.

Through the years, there were attempts by the Irish to free themselves from England's yoke but with the "Flight of the Earls," Ireland was left with next to no Irish governing class. Owen O'Neill attempted to raise a rebellion in the 1640s and even brokered a deal with King Charles. But it was too late. King Charles was executed in January 1649. The British Crown was no longer an entity and into that vacuum came, as far as the Irish were concerned, the most despicable man in all of history—Oliver Cromwell. In August of 1649 he arrived in Ireland with an army of 20,000 well-trained soldiers and he was there to take Ireland for England once and for all. Cromwell was a man possessed with religious fervor, but also fiercely anti-Catholic and full of intolerance for the Irish. He and his soldiers killed Irish men, women, and children alike. He was determined to make Ireland into another

England and to do so by dispensing with legal niceties. His Act of Settlement confiscated another 11 million acres out of 20 million in total, and once again it was parceled out to English supporters. Any remaining Irish were forced to move to barren land in Connaught under Cromwell's decree: "To Hell or to Connaught where there's no trees to hang you, nor water to drown you, or enough soil to bury you."

The Irish did have one more attempt to attain freedom from England. It was when James II tried to regain the English throne. However, it was not to be as James II was defeated by William of Orange at the Battle of the Boyne in July of 1690. This was also the rip in the united Ireland cloth as the northern counties now inhabited and controlled by protestant Anglo-Irish sided with England rather than with their Catholic brethren to the south. Thousands of young, disillusioned Irishmen known as the Wild Geese then chose to leave the country rather than submit to English rule.

English aristocracy now owned and controlled nearly 90% of the available land but worse was yet to come. Ever since the Protestant Reformation, the English crown had been imposing laws on Ireland to segregate the Catholic population whether they be Irish or English Catholics. In 1695 what came to be known as "the Penal Laws" or the "Popery Code" was enacted. Its formal name was "The Laws in Ireland for the Suppression of Popery." Its purpose was to separate the Catholic majority from all political and economic power on the island.

To quote Professor Lecky, a British Protestant and ardent British sympathizer, the object of the Penal Laws were threefold: "To deprive Catholics of all civil life, to reduce them to a condition of extreme, brutal ignorance, and to disassociate them from the soil."

Among the provisions of the Penal Law were the following:

- The Catholic Church is forbidden to keep church registers.
- Irish Catholics are forbidden to exercise their religion.
- Catholics are forbidden to receive an education.

- Catholics are forbidden from entering a profession or holding a public office.
- Catholics are forbidden from engaging in trade or commerce.
- Forbidden to live in a corporate town or within five miles thereof.
- Forbidden to own a horse of greater value than five pounds.
- Forbidden to own land.
- Forbidden to lease land under a cash lease.
- Forbidden to vote.
- Forbidden to keep any arms for his protection.
- Forbidden to buy land from a Protestant.
- Forbidden to receive a gift of land from a Protestant.
- Forbidden to inherit land from a Protestant.
- Forbidden to rent on shares land worth more than 30 shillings a year.
- He could not himself educate his child.
- He could not send his child to a Catholic teacher.
- He could not send his child abroad for education.

The Penal laws were not universally enforced, and some were retracted during the eighteenth century. Most were no longer on the books after the 1820s, but by then the damage was done. Several generations of Irish Catholics had been reduced to peasantry with little or no education.

They raised what they could, usually potatoes, on the very limited amount of land they were allowed to till and then at harvest had to turn a portion over to their English landlord as rent. Plus, the tenants had little to no control over the amount of product the landlord could extract as rent. If it were a dry year and the crop was thin, the landlord could simply raise the rent to maintain his quantity.

Many of these English landlords were granted very large tracts of land. Some well in excess of 100,000 acres. These lords built huge mansions on their property in Ireland or remodeled old Norman Castles, and also built mansions in England. Even with all the proceeds from their rents, they still mortgaged their properties to support their lavish lifestyle of balls, fox hunts, expensive thoroughbred horses for steeplechase races, among other extravagances. Many spent most of the year in England, coming to Ireland only occasionally for business or pleasure. As you might guess, each of these huge estates supported hundreds of Irish Catholic tenant farmers with their meager existence. With the 1800 Act of Union, the Irish Parliament was dissolved, and Ireland was no longer a separate entity, but subsumed into the United Kingdom, along with Scotland and Wales.

The Potato Famine

Sure, I was aware of the Irish potato famine, but I knew little of the details about it. I just knew the potato crop had failed and a lot of Irish immigrated to America. So, I knew the what, but thought I should try to learn more about the who, when, where, and why, and how my great grandfather may have been impacted.

It has been said, at least in Ireland, "God caused the blight, but the British caused the famine." When I first saw that quote, I knew there was considerably more to the Irish famine then I had garnered from past readings. As I noted earlier, we knew the Irish Catholics had been reduced to a meager existence. Nearly all their land had been taken and they had been forced to live under the horrific Penal Laws, but the quote hinted at even more injustice.

The famine is usually considered to have begun in 1845 and to have run through 1851, so I decided to research more of what the ruling British politicians were doing during those years. The 1841 census of Ireland put the population at 8,175,124, but was probably higher because there were few roads and the peasantry especially in western Ireland was constantly moving around. Few lived in permanent homes, resulting in a likely undercount. By the time of the 1851 census, the tally was 6,552,365. A difference of 1,622,759. Now we know there was a continuous stream of Irish immigration. It had begun even before the famine and continued for a hundred years after it. The official estimate of deaths during the famine is put at 985,000, but there are numerous estimates that put that figure much higher, some as high as 1.9 million people dying in the years between 1846 and 1851. So, possibly up to 1,000 people per day.

As Mary Ann stated in her journal, the Peel government had expanded the workhouses, set up the Relief Commission, and started public works projects. But in the election in June of 1846, Peel and the Conservatives were ousted by Lord John Russell and the Whig party. Arriving with Lord John Russell was Sir Charles Wood as Chancellor of the Exchequer, and Sir Charles Trevelyan as assistant secretary of the Treasury. It was Trevelyan who had control of Irish famine expenditures and, to the Irish, came to be known as the modern-day Cromwell. In August of 1846, Russell ended the policy of distributing cheap Indian corn from America saying, "Whigs would not interfere with the regular operations of merchants for the supply of food to the country."

Not part of the politics, but as a humanitarian act because of awareness of what was happening in Ireland, in November of 1846 the Quakers of England began their relief operations by soliciting contributions from the Irish in America and setting up soup kitchens to feed the poor and starving. It should be noted also that the problem was with the politicians and not the people of England. On balance the people of England had great sympathy for the Irish and the horrors they were enduring.

Early in 1847, the Whigs gave up on their work requirement at the workhouses as the numbers requiring relief exceeded 700,000. They began phasing it out and replacing it with soup kitchens, (like the Quakers, but less nourishing.) However, in October, Trevelyan chose to close the soup kitchens for the winter and restricted relief to the workhouses and the Poor Law Unions. Poor Law Unions were areas of Ireland grouped together into a union for the administration of relief. In August of 1847, the Encumbered Estates Act was passed, which allowed for new owners to evict all tenants. As many landlords were absentee owners, they hired land agents to handle the evictions, often with military or law enforcement help. By September, over three million people were in need of assistance. The potato blight had been reduced, but because of a lack of seed potatoes the fall harvest was still only twenty-five percent of the normal volume. Ostensibly as an effort to force landlords to make contributions toward relief efforts, a type of land tax was introduced which caused the landlords to rid the estate of tenants to avoid the additional tax, thus exacerbating the problem rather than helping. Many of the landlords were already mortgaged to the hilt to support their lifestyle. Many were now unable to collect any rent so they could even pay the tax.

1848 was another year of blight with the harvest being only about one third of the normal volume and was accompanied by a cholera outbreak. The eviction rate soared as more and more estates were converted from potato raising to pasture ground for grazing cattle and sheep under the Encumbered Estates Act.

1849 was another year of blight, especially in the south and in the western counties. The Quakers, who had been so instrumental in providing relief, were defeated by the sheer size of the famine and announced the cessation of their operations. By August, when Queen Victoria made a very managed visit, there were 800,000 on outdoor relief and another 250,000 living in the workhouses. 220,000 emigrated in that year alone and another 210,000 in the following year when more than 20,000 families were evicted.

In 1851 and 1852, again nearly a quarter of a million people emigrated in each year, though eviction numbers begin to decrease by 1852. Through all this misery it should be noted that Ireland had no shortage of food. The problem was the Irish peasantry had no means to purchase it. They had been deprived of acquiring any assets and received only the most basic education for generations. Between 1846 and 1849, the mostly Protestant Anglo-Irish farmers of Ireland produced over 700,000 pigs and 700,000 head of cattle, over a million sheep and large quantities of wheat and oats. Under Russell's government the prevailing thought was let the market decide the price, causing much of the production to be shipped to England and the continent rather than retained to feed the native population. Trevelyan and his cohorts felt the Irish famine was likely God's will and would right itself in time, when enough of the Irish were no longer on the land, then it could be converted to more productive uses like livestock raising. It seemed that whether the Irish immigrated or starved, it made little difference to Trevelyan as long as the land could be better utilized.

I cannot finish this section without mentioning the diseases that accompanied the famine. A lot of the deaths were not from starvation but from related diseases. The most common was what was referred to as the fever or putrid fever. Although some deaths were caused by more common ailments like influenza and the common cold, others were caused by tuberculosis, typhus, dysentery, scurvy, pellagra, and even smallpox. Pellagra is a disease caused by a lack of niacin with symptoms including inflamed skin, sores in the mouth, diarrhea, and dementia. Dysentery is caused by bad food and poor hygiene. The workhouses were ideal places for the spreading of these diseases with their filth and severe overcrowding. For example, the workhouse at Skibbereen in county Cork was built to hold 800 but during the famine held as many as 2400*.

Steeplechase Races

Both Michael and Henry/Hank were talking about Aintree and steeplechase horse races. I had never heard of Aintree and knew very little about horse racing, and of steeplechase, I knew even less. So, once again it was back to the history books to see what I could learn. Aintree was easy. I quickly learned Aintree is what we would now call a suburb of Liverpool. It was in that small town in 1829 that one William Lynn, a racing syndicate head and proprietor of the Waterloo Hotel in Liverpool, leased land from William Molyneux, 2nd Earl of Sefton for the purpose of building a racecourse complete with grandstand. Lord Sefton laid the corner stone on February 7th, 1829. The first large Hunt race (I learned the terms steeplechase and hunt race were interchangeable and informally, steeplechase and hurdle races are both called "jumps.") was run on February 29th, 1836, and won by The Duke. He won again in 1837 while Sir William won in 1838. I also learned that steeplechase horses were older, the riders larger, and the course longer and having up to 30 jumps or more. The first official Grand National Steeplechase at Aintree was in 1839. Except for the war years, the Grand National has been run at Aintree every year since. It is now billed as the largest hunt race in the world with a total purse exceeding 1,000,000 pounds.

By the 1840s, Edward Topham, a respected handicapper, turned the race into a handicap event, and he took over the lease in 1848 from William Lynn who was suffering from ill health. The Topham family bought the course outright a century later.

As an interesting side bar, Tipperary Tim went off outside of 100 to 1 in the 1928 Grand National against 41 other starters. He won the race as the only horse not to fall and one of only two horses that finished the race.

In reading about steeplechase or hunt racing I discovered several other interesting facts. For one, in the 19th century, flat racing (no jumps) was much better organized and controlled. The Jockey Club, which had been formed in the 1750s by owners, breeders, and gentlemen jockeys (in other words, land owning aristocrats), began issuing regulations to not only standardize practices, but to help insure a "clean" race. Large sums of money were bet on the races by not only the elite but also the merchant or working class. By the 1870s, the Jockey Club began to control flat racing by issuing rules about all aspects of racing including registering owners, jockeys, and trainers and issuing rules on weights, stabling, and betting by participants. The Jockey Club themselves would not be involved in any disputes concerning betting.

National hunt racing on the other hand had no over-arching ruling organization and had been turned down by the Jockey Club in the 1860s as improper horseracing. Consequently, steeplechase races were much more of a free-for-all that attracted a bad crowd involved in drinking, brawling, thievery, and with blood sports as additional attractions. Part of this was due to the fact that flat racing had a "longer card," several races on the same day. Hunt races, though over a longer course, usually just consisted of the main event, perhaps with a novice race preceding it. However, there were some established rules. One big one being that a thrown rider could remount and continue racing. In 1866, the Grand National Steeplechase Committee was formed and began issuing regulations for hunt races and hurdle races. Eventually, they issued regulations on course inspection and stricter regulations concerning amateur jockeys.

This was the rule that more than likely caused Henry/Hank's name never to show up in any list of jockeys. You needed to belong to one of a select list of clubs, be an officer or a magistrate in order to qualify. Technically one could be balloted in, but you still needed to be nominated by a club member. Consequently, Henry was destined to always be an amateur jockey. As such he could ride in training sessions and even in warm-up sessions at the various tracks but was never listed as a horse's jockey for a sanctioned race.

Whereas several large landowners and aristocrats had their own stables and training tracks, other thoroughbred owners used independent stables to train their horses. These stables were often started by successful jockeys and/or trainers and often failed if they didn't produce winners. The monetary output to open a stable was sizable. You not only needed the correct type of land to build a training track and stable, but needed to hire stable hands, grooms, jockeys, trainers, and often a farrier and a cook besides. A highly speculative gamble if you failed to produce winners.

The racehorse trainer's job was not an easy one. He not only had to determine the right amount of exercise and diet for each horse, but he was often faced with conflicting views from jockeys or grooms. Then he had to judge what it was the owner was trying to achieve--riches, prestige, or honor, any and all of which could change from day to day. Generally, horses were exercised twice per day with workouts varying between speed and endurance, with each stall being cleaned and swept while the horse was absent and fresh bedding put in place in the evening. Diet was also day to day depending on what stable hands reported about the horse's condition. The steeplechase or hunt race season ran year around, with the major races falling mostly between March and June. Consequently, the trainer's job was a seven-days a week job all year and usually started at 4:00am and ended around 9:00 pm. Some did manage to have a few hours off on Sundays for church services. If those were the hours for the trainer, they were pretty much the hours for all other employees too.

Famine Ships

The history of the famine ships (or as I learned, sometimes called coffin ships) and how they played into the mass migration of Irish immigrants to America or to British North America as Canada was known at the time:

There were thousands of ships of every size imaginable involved in the transport of Irish peasants across the Atlantic, but the vast majority made but one trip. There was a multitude of reasons, including the treacherous crossing, crews abandoning ship, the poor condition of the ships, and stricter American Maritime Passenger Act requirements. The ships sailed from numerous ports around Ireland. However, during the famine years, nearly seventy-five percent departed from Liverpool. Destination ports in the United States were Philadelphia, Boston, Baltimore, New Orleans, and New York, with the vast majority landing in New York.

The Liverpool port had been heavily involved in the slave trade and consequently was home to a large number of slave ships. Prior to England banning English ships from hauling slaves to the Americas in the 1830s, Liverpool ships had a great business hauling iron and finished goods to north Africa, then slaves to the Americas, followed by sugar, cotton, and lumber back to England. When they could no longer haul slaves, Irish immigrants filled the void nicely. They also provided the incentive of paying up front and the ability to haul a larger load. Slaves were a commodity with a value. The ship's owner had a vested interest in keeping slaves fed and healthy in order to sell them for more money in America. No such value was there for Irish immigrants. The ship's owner was paid up front and it mattered little to him how many safely disembarked on the American shore.

During the early famine years, British ships were to provide each passenger each week a total of only 7lbs of food, consisting of bread, flour, oatmeal, potatoes, or rice. A mere sixteen ounces of food a day, little more than starvation amounts. Passengers themselves were responsible for anything else needed. The Passenger Acts were amended in 1849, decreeing tea, sugar, and molasses be issued twice per week and requiring more space for each passenger on board. Each bunk was to be 2 feet by 6 feet. The bunks were built in the ships hold, four tiers high and two wide between narrow aisles, not that the provisions of the act were strictly enforced. The sheer number of immigrants and ships as opposed to inspectors was simply too great. This was years before the implementation of the Plimsoll line on ships to indicate the maximum weight the ship is allowed to carry so they were routinely overloaded. However, the provisions on board were often in-line with the required amount for the ships stated tonnage, thus not nearly enough for the actual number of passengers being transported. It's interesting that the requirements for British ships transporting prisoners or slaves were much more rigorous than for ships transporting Irish immigrants.

There were numerous disasters at sea, including reports of ship owners insuring ships they knew were incapable of making the voyage in order to collect the insurance money (coffin ships). But the biggest obstacle besides sinking at sea was starvation and disease. The voyage on a good run could take two months. With storms or simply no wind to fill the sails, the trek could take much longer, depleting all food and water on board. Trips in winter could include blizzards and ice flows to boot. There are several instances of survivors being rescued from icebergs.

Death from disease, though, was the biggest threat to those on board. The ship's hold became a cesspool of filth after weeks at sea. The cramped quarters, lousy food, and seasickness all contributed to the rapid spread of disease. Disease became a complication for the ship's captain because the United States imposed fines on captains unloading diseased or destitute passengers. It was to his advantage to stay at sea and let the sick die and be buried at sea before docking in America (more coffin ships). Thousands upon thousands died at sea during their crossing from the same diseases inflicted on them at the workhouses.

The Civil War

Like my knowledge of Irish history, my Civil War knowledge consisted of what I had learned in school plus what I had read in articles or books about that period of American history. But did I really *know* about the Civil War? What had the soldier at the front gone through, how had they fought and died? What was their medical care like? What did they do in their free time? What if they were captured? I think my generation, at least, was taught the big picture and the names of principals involved. I'm not at all sure today's students even get that much. But even my generation was not taught the nitty-gritty.

Fortunately for me, my father-in-law had acquired a whole series of books on Civil War history where I could read details I had never heard before. I'm including some of those details here to impart a better comprehension of what those soldiers, both North and South, went through during that God awful war.

To begin, roughly 650,000 men died from all causes during the four years of the war, or about 500 per day. Countless others were maimed for life. Two thirds of those deaths were from disease rather than battle wounds. More died from bayonets and the sword than from gun fire. At the beginning of the war, both sides were using Napoleonic war tactics where troops marched shoulder to shoulder with another line of soldiers a mere two feet behind, and they marched straight into musket fire. The cap and ball musket being the most familiar and common long gun in the beginning. The development of rifles and rifled cannons called for drastic changes in tactics. Rifles were much more accurate, and bullets could be fired at much greater distances. Sharp-shooters with rifles could fire from 800 yards and rifled cannon balls carried over two miles.

Neither side had much of a standing army before the war started. The South had none and the North fewer than 30,000 soldiers. Most states had militia units as a carryover from the war for independence and the public's general distrust of a standing army. The state militia unit's high posts were filled with political appointments by governors as rewards for backing them, and as a result were severely lacking in military qualifications. Still, it was these voluntary militia units that formed the bulk of the armed forces for both the Union and the Confederacy. These militia units were combined into regiments consisting of ten companies of approximately 100 men each. Senior officers were often appointed by the governor, or they simply confirmed those elected by the soldiers. Many of these units began informal training months before the actual start of the war because after the southern states seceded, they felt war was inevitable. Thousands of men rushed to join these militia units and new ones were formed on both sides. It was the general consensus that the war would be over quickly, in the North because they thought the smaller population in the South would be easily crushed, and in the South, because they thought the North would soon capitulate to the formation of the Confederacy. Consequently, men rushed to sign up for their one chance at glory before it was all over.

Leadership for both armies soon fell to the officers from West Point because of the lack of any military training within the militia units. Roughly thirty percent of the West Point officer corps sided with the South and the rest with the North. However, this meant both armies were effectively operating from the same book. All had been West Point trained, so army formation, training, and tactics were nearly identical.

Because both armies were primarily made up of farmers and small merchants, intensive training was sorely needed to instill military discipline and precision. However, because of time constraints and the demand for more troops, training often suffered. Though, from the soldier's perspective, the constant drills and training seemed an arduous chore.

For all their perceived differences, the soldiers for both North and South had much in common. The majority were white, native-born, single, Protestant and young. The minimum age to join either side was 18, but many were younger. Often because recruiters simply ignored the age requirement and there was no age requirement for anyone claiming to be a musician or a drummer boy. Though most may have been native-born, there were very sizable contingents of immigrants on both sides. Especially the Irish famine refugees and Europeans that had fled the revolutionary upheavals of the 1840s. So, were these armies either fighting to end slavery or to preserve slavery? Maybe in the press and in the halls of Congress, but to the average soldier, not so much. There were very few Southern soldiers who ever owned or even hoped to own a slave. Among the Northern soldiers, most were indifferent. It is somewhat telling that the Northern soldiers did not want black soldiers in their companies. They were perceived as lazy and of an inferior race even though some black units did distinguish themselves later in the war. To most of the Northern soldiers, the war was about the preservation of the republic. The grand experiment where the government served the people, and it shouldn't be undone by a group of rebellious states. For the Southern soldier, it was about his freedom to choose. Many had escaped tyranny in Europe where a fickle and often cruel ruling class had made all the decisions. Now they had built a new life in America and, once again, a political elite in the North was telling them what they could or could not do.

Once the new soldier was mustered in, he was given a cursory physical, issued a uniform and accessories, issued a gun and accessories, and then assigned to a company unit in a camp. His first few days were spent learning military procedures and requirements. Then the training began. Hour after hour of marching in formation. Hour after hour of training on the specific procedure for loading and firing your cap and ball musket. Hour after hour learning to clean your gun and clean and polish your uniform and accoutrements to pass inspection by the Inspector General. He was no longer a civilian but learning to become a soldier. He would learn discipline, army organization, and chain of command. He would learn how to pitch and strike a tent, how to kindle a fire, and how to stand guard in total darkness. He would build camaraderie with his fellow soldiers. All this was in an effort to make them into a smooth-running fighting machine. Fine in theory but seldom attained in the heat of battle. It worked when breaking camp and marching for hours, then setting up camp again, but when the bullets started flying, it often broke down. The really large battles were relatively few, so the constant drilling and marching grew tedious and boring. Free time was spent reading, writing letters, playing cards, or gambling. Snowball fights were popular in the winter. Prostitution and drinking could become big problems, especially if the camp was near the cities. Officers were allowed a certain amount of whiskey, but enlisted men faced rather severe penalties if caught with it. Leaves to go home were rarely given but one- or two-day passes were often spent in brothels close to camp. Some brothels even followed the soldiers from camp to camp. Like the hated sutlers who sold goods at inflated prices, the prostitutes would show up around payday.

Venereal disease was a serious problem for both the North and South. During the war, roughly 8% of Union soldiers were treated for venereal disease and a great many cases went unreported. While figures for the South are sketchier, they were probably similar.

Gambling was the universal time killer and popular for soldiers both North and South. Dice and various card games were the most popular, but betting on races, boxing matches, and cockfights also occurred. Even betting on lice races happened, where a louse pulled from one's bedding or hair was raced against another's louse after all bets were down.

Foraging for food was another activity during downtime. Soldiers were encouraged to be self-reliant so would hunt for berries or trap small game to supplement their often-meager meals. Sometimes, the line between foraging and stealing was hard to discern. Farmers close to encampments often complained of their garden being raided or missing a chicken or two, not to mention missing eggs.

For those so inclined, there was a chaplain assigned to every regiment, and he provided services every Sunday. Like the officers in both armies, the quality of the chaplain varied greatly. Some provided many services besides the Sunday sermon, supplying comfort or counseling to whomever wanted or needed it. They also would often write letters home for troops who didn't know how to write. Although church services were often poorly attended, attendance would swell to overflowing before going into battle. Soldiers on both sides wanted to be right with the Lord in case their time on Earth was about to end.

The treatment for battlefield injuries and the sickness endured by both armies behind the lines is almost unimaginable. 60,000 men died of battlefield injuries received during the war. As many as 360,000 died of disease contracted from the filth of their camps or at the hands of the very doctor who was treating them. Doctor education and training was haphazard, medical knowledge was scant, and sterilization of equipment unheard of. Infection and pus were considered part of the healing process. First there was the problem of unfit troops being accepted into the army with all their pre-existing maladies, followed by the congregation of large numbers of rural inhabitants who had never been exposed to common viruses like measles, chicken pox, or whooping cough.

Eventually, as the men developed immunity to these common infectious diseases, instances greatly diminished, but they were followed by far more serious diseases spawned from the filth of their camps. Fleas, flies, and lice swarmed all over the camps, spreading disease as they went. Epidemics of dysentery and typhoid fever followed. Bowel disorders were the most common complaint. Nothing the doctor might prescribe did any good and occasionally made matters worse. The actual death toll from dysentery remained fairly low, especially when compared to deaths from typhoid fever or "camp fever" as it was commonly called. Nearly 25% of all non-combat deaths were due to typhoid fever. Scurvy and malaria would also claim soldier's lives, though quinine helped keep the actual number of deaths low from malaria. At the time, malaria was thought to be caused by poisonous vapors arising from swamps, not the real cause of millions of mosquitoes filling the air.

The quality of food served to the troops in both armies was also problematic. Though mostly sufficient in quantity, quality was severely lacking. Meat was often rancid and often so tough the men complained to headquarters to quit throwing in the hooves and horns. No matter what either side did, eventually the meat was filled with worms or maggots. As was the hardtack, a mixture of flour and water, referred to as "sheet-iron crackers" or alternatively "worm castles." As the war dragged on though, the soldiers began to refer to it as their only source of fresh meat. There was never much in the soldier's diet to help ensure good health, so whatever the contributing factors, disease among the troops took an awful toll.

The soldier's greatest fear may have been falling to a bullet or sword in battle, but his chance of dying was much greater if he was wounded in battle and then carried to the surgeon's tent, usually a couple of miles behind the battlefront. Both North and South tried to get the wounded to medical treatment within forty-eight hours. After that time, the shock would wear off and infection would set in as would the pain and agony. Both North and South treated the wounded with respect whether they be a "Yank" or a "Reb." At the rear they were separated into three categories: the mortally wounded, the slightly wounded, and those requiring surgery. The mortally wounded were made as comfortable as possible and left to the chaplain. The slightly wounded were treated and sent back to their units. Those needing surgery were placed outside the surgery tent or whatever was being used as the surgery center, which was often an abandoned building with a ripped off door to be used as a surgery table. If they were available, the wounded were laid on blankets or straw mats, but the sheer number of wounded often necessitated laying them on the bare ground soaked with their own blood and in full view of the ever- growing pile of amputated limbs.

In the interest of speed, when one patient was removed from the operating table, another was immediately brought in. No effort was made to sanitize the table or instruments. The surgeon often just wiped his hands on his apron and proceeded to the next patient. Anesthesia was given before surgery, usually chloroform, but wasn't considered necessary as the surgeon probed the wound with his fingers, trying to remove bullets, or bits of cloth or shrapnel in the wound. Of the operations performed during the war, a full three-quarters were amputations. If the amputation was performed in the first forty-eight hours, the patient had a decent chance at survival. After that time, infection had usually set in and the chance of survival dropped to less than a third. By then, gangrene, blood poisoning, or bone infection had usually already become established.

If you were not killed or wounded in battle, nor counted among those who survived, then you were captured and in the hands of the enemy. Neither the Union nor the Confederacy had made any provision for prisoners-of-war. Initially they were simply placed in holding pens until a prisoner exchange agreement was reached in 1862. However, the agreement disintegrated in less than a year with charges of bad faith from both sides. Eventually more than 150 locations were used as prisons. The Union adapted public buildings and the Confederacy converted tobacco warehouses. At any rate, all tended to be awful. Not so much by intent but because of the demands of war. The South fed prisoners the same as they were feeding their own troops but was often short of food to feed either. The North was little better. Restricting food because they thought the South was starving their prisoners. In the end, prisoners were poorly fed by both sides and the food they did receive was atrocious. Prisoners turned to trapping rats for their meat supply, comparing it favorably with fried squirrel.

Water supplies also tended to be tainted, partially because of all the filth that built up both inside and outside the walls. Vermin was so thick they were reported to be performing regimental drills. Lice infected garments were never discarded because no clothing other than what you wore upon arrival was provided. The living seized the garments of the dead, even knowing they were rife with insects.

Like the rest of the military, prison commandants ran from unfit ("the greatest scoundrel that ever went unhung!") to deep compassion for the suffering of the prisoners. Likewise with the prison guards; some were incompetent and others, especially veterans, sympathetic to the prisoner's plight. Of all the prisons, three stood out as the most infamous: Camp Douglas in Chicago and Elmira, New York for the Confederate prisoners, and Andersonville in Georgia for the Union prisoners.

Lastly, if you were not with your unit, you were not dead or wounded, and you were not captured by the enemy, you were a deserter. A crime, if you were caught, punishable by hanging or death by firing squad, though many escaped with much lighter sentences. There weren't a lot of executions, but there were some. Later in the war when additional troops were hard to find, leniency was granted to any who were willing to return to military service. Especially in the South, desertions increased dramatically late in the war as men left out of concern for their families in front of the advancing Union forces.

This completes a brief history of the actual men who did the fighting during the Civil War. They sometimes spent weeks marching before the day of battle. The incredible fortitude it must have taken for these men to march shoulder to shoulder into a hailstorm of enemy gunfire is unimaginable. An enemy whose line of guns and bayonets they could plainly see. As artillery bombardment began, it is easy to understand why some would try to break and run only to be forced back by a file closer (a man charged with keeping a tight formation). These were followed by the officers trying to make sense of it all through the black powder smoke of cannon and musket fire and the flying debris and fallen men.

* * *

During the winter of 1861, the Union army under General George McClellan devised a plan for the taking of Richmond and destroying the Confederacy. The plan was known as the Peninsula campaign and was designed to move up the Virginia peninsula and capture Richmond. McClellan thought the Confederate army was massed around Richmond to protect the capital of the Confederacy. He also reasoned correctly that the Union Navy was vastly superior and could be used to ferry soldiers and supplies up the James River rather than having to move overland by wagon or rail. He also thought the Union Navy could shell Confederate positions by sailing up the James River.

The campaign began in March of 1862 when the Union army landed at Fort Monroe and moved northwest up the Virginia peninsula in early April. Confederate General John B. Magruder surprised McClellan's army along the Warwick River where the rebels had built strong defenses along the Warwick line. McClellan's plan for a surprise and quick advance now foiled, he ordered his army to prepare for a siege of Yorktown. Before those preparations were completed, the Confederate army withdrew toward Richmond. On May 5th there was heavy fighting at the Battle of Williamsburg, followed by the Battle of Drewry's Bluff on May 15th. That battle turned back an attempt by the United States Navy to reach Richmond by way of the James River.

The Union army continued toward Richmond, meeting little resistance until May 31 when the rebel army under Joseph E. Johnston in a surprise attack engaged the Union army at the Battle of Seven Pines. Over two days, heavy casualties were suffered by both sides in an inconclusive battle. 5,031 casualties for the Union and 6,134 for the Confederacy, but beyond the casualties the battle had lasting effects on both sides. After the Battle of Seven Pines, the wounded confederate commander, General Joseph Johnston, was replaced by General Robert E. Lee. Lee did much to strengthen his newly named Army of Northern Virginia. He strengthened discipline, ordered new armaments and uniforms, and replaced incompetent officers with ones proven in battle. The battle also served to further convince McClellan the Confederate forces were much larger than they actually were and to give up his assault and retreat back down the peninsula to Fort Monroe or Harrison's Landing against the strong opposition of some of his generals. McClellan's delay at the front, ostensibly for dry weather and dry roads, gave Lee nearly a month to prepare his army of Northern Virginia.

General Lee devised an offensive strategy at a meeting on June 23 to attack the retreating Union army. However, McClellan had received word that Lee was preparing to attack and that General "Stonewall" Jackson and his troops arrival from the Shenandoah Valley was imminent. He decided he would start an offensive before Lee could. The battles over the next week became known as the Seven Days Battles. The final battle at Malvern Hill on July 1st involved over 50,000 troops on each side. Lee attempted a frontal assault on the Union's strong defensive position atop the hill, fortified with infantry and a strong artillery position. This was the first heavy action that Henry's company was involved in, and they suffered heavy casualties with 182 soldiers either wounded or killed.

ACKNOWLEDGMENTS

I'm grateful to and especially want to acknowledge my immediate family for their assistance in innumerable ways. My wife, Denise, my two daughters, Kimberly and Shawn, and my granddaughter, Kiara.

I extend grateful acknowledgment to my editor, Jennifer Cerruto, for her valued suggestions and having to endure my serious lack of word-processing skills and my forgotten proper English writing skills.

To Lois Hoffman and her entire team at The Happy Self Publisher. Without their help this book would never have been completed.

To Steve Kearney, Ron Kearney, Bob Reier and Steve Turner. readers of early drafts who encouraged me to keep writing.

Kent Kearney Biography

Kent Kearney is retired and decided to explore his creative side by taking up watercolor painting and now writing. He lives with his wife, Denise, in Colorado Springs, Colorado. They have two daughters and one granddaughter. He was born in Kearney, Nebraska in 1946 and grew up on a cattle ranch in Custer County, Nebraska which still includes his great grandfather's original homestead. *Eyes That Do Not See* is his first novel about the life of his great grandfather, an orphan, Irish immigrant and confederate Civil War veteran.

In 2017, Kent and his youngest daughter took a trip to Ireland in an attempt to find more information about his great grandfather, Henry Kearney, but were largely unsuccessful. They found little about him but learned a great deal about the history of Ireland. Kent decided to write his first novel using what little information he had about his great grandfather, but also using the history of the times he lived in.

Kent is a graduate of the University of Nebraska in Lincoln with a degree in Business Administration. After graduation he worked in public accounting and became a Certified Public Accountant. He went into private business in the 1970s and in the early nineties he went to work as the Chief Financial Officer for a manufacturing firm in Kansas before retiring in 2008.

Printed in Great Britain
by Amazon

38415840R00148